THE FATE OF ETERNITY

KC KEAN

To everyone here for Kryll's monster dick. You're a filthy hoe, and I love you!

"I would rather fail trying than not try at all."

ONE
ADRIANNA

The thundering of my pulse feels out of control. Not like my heart is racing twice as fast, but as if there are two; side by side, pounding out of time, each in tandem with the rage and terror warring within me. It's exhilarating and all-consuming at the same time.

Every breath ricochets in my chest as I remain rooted to the spot. I blink between Kenner, in the doorway of the public bathroom, and Cassian, who stands between us.

In one split second, my life has changed forever.

I was certain it would solve everything, and I'm pretty sure Cassian was too, but as I look at Kenner now, I know it was all for nothing. Maybe not nothing, per se, but we've willingly fallen into his trap. There's no time to acknowledge I have a fated mate or that it was Cassian all along, never mind the fact that I'm standing in a fucking public bathroom draped in fur in the form of a wolf.

Not just any wolf.

My wolf.

The pain that echoed through my limbs as I shifted quickly morphed into euphoria, but it was swiftly laced with dread the moment Kenner opened his fucking mouth.

"You did the job I wanted of you without even trying, son. And you, Adrianna, I knew you would seek out your wolf the moment you were told not to, just as I planned."

Those words linger in the air around us, the tight space growing thicker and thicker with tension as the sneer spreads across his lips, growing wider with every passing breath.

Fuck. Fuck. Fuck.

I can make mistakes, I can even fucking live with them, but when it's been orchestrated by Kenner? Fuck, I can't stand it.

He has to pay. He has to pay right the fuck now.

Anger vibrates through my bones, and even though I'm standing on wobbly paws, I still can't fight the urge to charge at him. I make it all of two steps before a flash of fur darts in front of me, beating me to the chase.

Cassian.

Just as he gets within an inch of his father, the

man in question darts through the door and out into the hallway. I inch backward, tail brushing against the wall behind me as I count my breaths, willing myself to remain calm, despite the new senses now battering me from every angle.

Cassian's tormented gaze finds mine a beat later as we find our way back toward one another, sorrow and anger blurring his stare.

"Addi," he murmurs directly into my thoughts, a new skill I'm completely unprepared for, especially when the solemn tone of his one word matches the torment in his eyes.

He thinks he's at fault, his father's words solidifying it, but I know with raw certainty that whatever his bullshit of a father is hinting at, Cassian had no clue what he had planned.

Our stare-off is interrupted when the door swings open behind Cassian, sending a jolt of adrenaline through my body, but the panic subsides when I realize it's Brody. His eyes widen with surprise as he steps into the room, the door opening further behind him as Kryll and Raiden come into view.

"Holy fuck," Brody breathes, gaping between Cassian and me, and my vulnerability seems to shoot even higher.

A whimper parts my lips and I back up another step, my tail curling behind me as I lean into the wall. Cassian watches my every move, taking a tentative step toward me, attempting to come across as gentle as possible. Or that's what I'm hoping, based on the way his face lowers to the ground and his tail dips between his legs.

"It's okay, Addi. I've got you."

His words infiltrate my thoughts once again before he takes a step back and effortlessly shifts into his human form. I blink at him as a new sense of awe washes over me when he cracks his neck and appears dressed in his suit like nothing has happened.

I want to say it's magical, but the lingering effects from Kenner's presence sours the moment.

"It's okay, Alpha. Take a deep breath, settle your heart and allow your instincts to guide you," Cassian states, crouching beside me when he gets close. I frown at him, no longer sensing his thoughts in my head as I try to understand what he's explaining. He knows what I need when I can't even process the thought, nevermind the words, but that doesn't mean it makes it any easier for me. "You've got this, Alpha," he repeats, extending his hand to run his fingers over my white fur, and I lean into the touch.

He nods, just once, and I let my eyelids fall closed.

I can sense the others watching me, but I will sink under the pressure if I focus on that too much, a feeling I'm not familiar with, and despite this new addition to my magical being, I'm not about to start sinking now.

Paying close attention to myself, I take a long, deep breath, exhaling slowly as my heart rate starts to settle. Nothing happens for a beat, then two, but just as I'm about to blink my eyelids back open, my mind settles with a calmness I can't explain.

Serenity envelops me in it's sweet hold, where it almost feels like I'm floating, before pain burns through my bones. My legs give out at the same time as the back of my eyelids brighten from the excruciating pain before my world falls still.

"Adrianna?" Raiden's rasp vibrates through my chest, forcing me to pry my eyes open. It takes a few blinks before my gaze settles and I can properly take him in, but when I do, he blankets me with another sense of peace.

He reaches his hand out toward me and I nervously do the same, wiggling my outstretched fingers when my eyes settle on them.

I'm me again.

That doesn't sound right.

I was always me.

Wolf or human or fae.

Fuck. I don't know what I am.

My thoughts are paused as he pulls me to my feet, wrapping his arms around me and pinning me to his chest. I bask in his embrace, letting him ground me in the moment until a chest presses against my back, sending heat surging through me.

Kryll.

"What did Kenner want?" Brody asks, his voice muffled in my ears from the two men encasing me between them.

"You guys saw him and didn't stop him?" Cassian snarls, his tone a complete contrast to the one he used with me moments ago.

"He was taking off down the opposite end of the hall. What's going on?" Kryll asks, his chest vibrating against my back.

Cassian sighs. It's harsh and deep, a rumble of angst amid the uncertainty that we aren't prepared for going forward.

"I don't know, but he made it clear that it was his plan to have Addi find her wolf and shift," he admits, and I don't need to look to know his face is dipped, his chin pressed against his chest as a sense of defeat takes hold of him. I can feel it along my skin, deep in my bones, and in the air around me.

I've always had a good read on them, for the most part, but this feels different.

"Fuck," Raiden grimaces, pressing his lips to my temple.

"What do we do?" Brody asks, his question lingering in the space around us for a beat as I take a deep breath and step out of the warm embrace between Kryll and Raiden.

Four sets of eyes trail my movements as I run my hands over my black dress, standing tall as I stiffen my spine and try to rid the tension from my limbs. The words dance across my tongue, ready to lay claim to our path and solidify who we are and who we have always been.

As individuals and together.

Despite the unknown possibilities of our future, the clarity in our unity gives me a new-found strength that I didn't believe could be possible. But I know it is. It has to be.

Sweeping my gaze over each of them once more, I take a deep breath.

"We do what we always do. We fight."

I can talk a big game, promising a fight, but I need a few minutes to gather myself first. I don't have the luxury of slinking off to my room where I can hide behind the safety of my carefully built walls and allow myself to crumble beneath the weight of my emotions. Instead, I've got about twenty seconds to acknowledge the new layer of bullshit that surrounds me before I must compartmentalize and get on with it.

My main concern is wasting the whole twenty seconds on figuring out where the fuck to begin tackling all the obstacles we face.

Gripping the marble vanity, I stare at my reflection, noting nothing different, which finds a way to piss me off. I feel different; I should look different, too.

I sigh. The corner of my mouth tilts up as I acknowledge the fact that maybe nothing looks different because I haven't changed at all. I've simply released a piece of myself that was dormant and there's no hiding it anymore. Whether I like it or not.

"I am a fae princess."

"I am a wolf."

"I'm the fucking dragon princess."

The words taste humorous on my tongue as I speak, the reality of them not truly sinking in, but I know with all certainty that my soul is connected to Kryll and Cassian in ways I can't describe.

I'm not ready to either.

I am a wolf, though. I let Cassian claim me, breaking the suppression I didn't even know was in place until the moment it was lifted. Despite the pain, shifting felt raw, real, and... special. A moment I'm sure I'll replay again and again, but the way it felt in that moment will never be erased.

Kenner's words rear their ugly head in my brain, tainting the moment as they cloud my thoughts.

"And you, Adrianna, I knew you would seek out your wolf the moment you were told not to, just as I planned."

What the fuck does that even mean? I don't have the answers, and a part of me doesn't want them if they circle back to him, but I get the feeling I'm going to find out eventually. We need to get this mess over with, then I can have a real conversation with Cassian that results in him understanding that I really don't hold him accountable for his father's actions. That man is a horrible specimen all on his own, and he definitely doesn't reflect on his estranged son.

But what is this lingering mess? What the fuck is Bozzelli doing with this spontaneous trial? Who is it benefiting? My knuckles whiten as my grip tightens, and I shake my head. Bozzelli already gave me the explanation for that: The Council.

It seems they're hell-bent on forcing me to be fated mates with the men I'm already in deep with. It's an idea that's almost appealing if it doesn't leave us vulnerable to their cause. Does me being a wolf still play into their plan? Or is that Kenner pulling a surprise move on everyone?

Fuck if I know. I'm not going to get the answers standing here, but I don't care all that much for going out there to get them, either.

A knock sounds from the door to my right, pulling me from my thoughts, and I turn to find Flora peeking through the small gap. I gulp at the sight of her, completely lost for words, but the shimmering glaze of pity in her eyes tells me she already knows what I'm up to. I've never been more grateful for someone taking control and explaining to my friend the hell I'm living so I don't have to find the words myself.

"You look good, Addi," she breathes, a soft smile gracing her lips as she steps inside and shuts the door behind her. I smile back, rolling my shoulders as I stand tall, meticulously putting my metaphorical armor in place. "Are you ready?" she asks when I exhale a long breath.

"Am I allowed to say no?" I muse, making her smile spread, but it doesn't meet her eyes.

"Sure, I just don't think you really have a choice," she admits, the truth grazing my skin like barbed wire, cutting deeper than necessary, but I don't let it threaten the structure of my mental walls, which are preparing for battle.

"True."

Silence descends over the room until Flora clears her throat, running her hands over her pretty dress as she peers at me. "I can tell them you need a few more minutes—"

"No, I'm good," I interject, nodding as I head toward the door. She opens it wide for me with a flourish to reveal Kryll, Cassian, Raiden, Brody, and Arlo on the other side.

My chest tightens at the sight of my Kryptos as Arlo wraps an arm around Flora's shoulders. They're each dressed to the nines in their suits, just like earlier, but now a tension ripples through them. It ripples through all of us, holding us all prisoner as I join them in the hallway. My dress is sweet and whimsical, hiding the truth beneath the fabric.

No words are exchanged as we fall into step. Brody is on my left, fingers ghosting over mine as Raiden takes my right, his fingers splayed across the small of my back.

The ballroom consumes my senses a moment later, the chatter mingling with the harp playing in the corner of the room as the food is brought out to the tables. Weaving our way through the madness, Brody points out a large table with most of the seats vacant. Flora and Arlo take off first, their parents occupying two seats to the left, and Raiden presses a kiss to my temple before heading off toward the man seated opposite them.

My steps falter as I approach, unsure where to sit, but my stress is quickly alleviated when I spy the name cards in front of each seat. Brody pulls my seat out for me, and as I murmur my thanks, I scan the room, eager to spot the assholes wreaking havoc on my life, but I come up empty.

No Bozzelli. No Kenner. No Professor Halloway. No Councilman Orenda. No one.

I can't enjoy the sentiment of *out of sight, out of mind.* Their lack of presence only causes me greater concern.

"Ah, this must be the delightful Adrianna

Reagan. It's a pleasure." I blink at the man seated three chairs to my right, Raiden at his side, and it's instantly clear that this is his father. His tone is... questionable, his attire is flamboyant, and his smile is almost fueled by insanity.

A maroon velvet suit frames his figure, with a crisp white shirt underneath. A cigar occupies his right hand, although it isn't lit, while his chin is tilted in my direction, exposing his perceived superiority.

"And you are?" I reply, cocking a brow at him. His lips spread into a ridiculously wide smile as Raiden covers his mouth with his hand.

"You're as fiery as my son promised."

"I'm shocked that he didn't choose to downplay my lowly fae abilities," I muse, teasing my vampire over the shit he called me when we first met. He grimaces, but his father lets out a laugh sent straight from his gut.

"I liked your father."

I tilt my head at him. "The verdict is still out on the reciprocation," I state, earning a wink from the older man as he nods.

"I definitely like her, Son." He turns his attention to Raiden, who rolls his eyes at his father.

"I'd rather you didn't," he mutters, pulling out the seat beside him. He settles in with Cassian next to him and Kryll nestled between the two of us.

Brody plants his hand on my thigh from the left,

injecting me with another layer of confidence as plates of food are placed in front of us. Layers of potatoes are accompanied by steamed vegetables and thin slices of beef. It smells delicious, but I'm too worked up to even consider lifting the fork to my mouth.

My desire to eat quickly went out the window on the wings of the catastrophe that this evening has already been. Looking around the table, I find only the adults digging in, the appeal of eating lost to the rest of us as we await the unknown.

The music dies down when someone taps on a microphone, saving me from the misery of the plate before me, and I look up to find Bozzelli center stage. Her fake smile is plastered across her face, hair styled in tight curls, and eccentric makeup coating her eyelids. If that wasn't enough, her bright purple dress acts as a beacon in the dimly lit room.

Anticipation lodges my next breath in my throat, her lips parting only tightening the knot. "Good evening, ladies and gentlemen. I want to thank you all for attending such a phenomenal evening tonight, one I feel has been much needed to increase morale among students after some witnessed the severity of the frenzied vampire attacks." Murmurs ripple throughout the room, whispering their agreements, and it only serves to irritate me more. "I want to thank you all for going through the extra security measures in place this evening to visit us on campus. After another unwelcome visit on-site, we feel it's necessary to proceed with caution and restrict access on both ends."

I scoff, unable to hold it in. Her ban is pointless. Cassian managed to get off campus easily enough the other night, and she invited the very man who attacked me to begin with. None of it makes sense. If anything, it feels like another failed attempt at control on her end.

"I can't believe a single person is capable of spewing so much bullshit in so few sentences," Brody whispers under his breath, making me grin as I hum in agreement.

"With that in mind, leading a kingdom is no easy feat, and we must be prepared for any situation," Bozzelli continues, and my stomach twists, knowing her next words before she speaks them since we heard her plan to Kenner earlier. "Tonight feels like the perfect opportunity for a trial." She throws her hands out wide with glee, earning a few cheers from some members of the crowd, but surprise and concern is what mostly fills the room. "Before we roll into the excitement of what the trial will entail, I think it's also an excellent time for our students to work on speeches. Addressing the public is another key role in being the heir of the Floodborn Kingdom, and what better way to gather ourselves than in the company of our loved ones?" Grunts of agitation circle the room, making Bozzelli smile manically as she finishes her own speech. "I apologize for the lack of preparation, of course, but we must be honest and realistic, and one thing is for certain: war waits for no one."

Speeches? Fucking *speeches*? They're not really giving us much to prepare for with this. Let's not forget the fact that I really hate this shit. There's enough going on in my life right now that I don't need to add this to the list.

Exhaling, I try to shake my frustrations and focus on one thing at a time. It doesn't help that I can't think straight with all the people muttering quietly in the small room we're cooped up in. Agitation lays heavy on my chest, making it impossible for me to even think about making a damn speech. Not when I know Kenner and most of The Council will be waiting for us the second the trial is over.

"Are you okay?"

I blink up at Kryll, a tight smile gracing my lips as I take another deep breath. I can't muster the words to deny the fact that I'm hanging on by a thread. Thankfully, the knowing look in his eyes confirms that he's understanding as best he can.

His fingers lace with mine, providing me with an anchor and grounding me in the madness. I lean into him, letting him feed me with the strength that I desperately need.

Gazing around the room, my eyes settle on the giant notice on the wall.

<u>Speech Requirements</u>
Address the people
Express your beliefs
Promise of victory
Recommendation: Speeches should be made as if entering an unavoidable battle.

I huff at every single expectation. There is such little guidance, and yet they want us to excel. I don't know why I'm lingering on this fact. I think it's because this is all out of my control. I've got Kryll's hand in mine to keep me grounded, but otherwise, it feels like I'm floating.

"Are you thinking up a badass speech in that pretty little head of yours, Dagger?" Brody asks, appearing at my other side. His hand instantly finds the small of my back.

"I'm coming up blank," I admit with a muttered

breath. "The lack of preparation is making me spiral," I add, and he shakes his head.

"No, Addi. The impending carnage that awaits us is what's wreaking havoc on you; the speech is nothing. Besides, if this was a real-life event, you would address the kingdom on a whim, using mainly your instinct, and you'd have them all eating out of the palm of your hand," he says with a wink, extracting the last of the air from my lungs.

He's right.

I think I hate that he's right.

Damn mage with his pretty eyes.

Taking a deep breath again, it seems to take root this time, and the tension bunching my muscles together eases just an inch.

"You have the gift of the gab," I reply, a real smile tilting the corner of my mouth. "I thought you would be all over this like a pro."

Brody smirks at me, the knowing glint in his eyes like always. "Please, of course I am. It's grumpy assholes one and two over there who should be concerned," he states, pointing at Cassian and Raiden.

Cassian glares back at Brody from his spot a few steps ahead of us, while Raiden turns to give him his full attention.

"I'm a vampire. I know how to lead a crowd." He

stands taller, fixing the sleeves of his suit jacket even though there's nothing wrong with them.

"Sure you do," Brody retorts with too much humor for my vampire, who rolls his eyes in response.

Their bickering should be a distraction, but among the chaos, it feels more comfortable, calming my breaths and easing my racing heart.

A moment later, the door opens in the far corner of the room and Professor Fairbourne fills the space. He doesn't cast his gaze in my direction. Instead, he reads out a list of names, causing a slight panic among the students. My breath stutters when the final name he calls is Kryll.

My fingers tighten around his as he offers me a soft and reassuring smile. Wordlessly, he leans closer, staring deep into my eyes before he eliminates the distance between us and crushes his lips to mine. It's too short but oh-so-sweet, and then he's gone.

I press the pads of my fingertips to my mouth, eager to recall his touch, but the remnants of his lips against mine are dimmed when the door closes behind the named students.

"Well, this just got real," Flora muses, filling the empty spot where Kryll had stood a moment ago, and I nod. "What are you going to say?" she asks, and I stare at her, trying to find the right answer, but I still come up empty.

"I don't know," I admit again. I'm trying, I'm really fucking trying, but it's not easy. My brain is processing words, but none of them are sticking.

"Are you okay?" she asks, concern crinkling the corners of her eyes.

"I'm good."

"You can say if you're not, you know," she murmurs, squeezing my arm in comfort, and I try to smile at her.

"I know."

I also know that the possibility others may overhear my vulnerability exists in this room of diverse origins, and I'd rather not reveal that if I can help it.

A shadow casts over me, drawing my attention forward, where I find Cassian looming over me. Brody's hand draws circles on the small of my back while Raiden watches from a step away, and the attention from all of them threatens to leave me breathless.

"Cassian?" I question when he doesn't initially speak.

He stares at me, like really stares, slipping deep into my eyes and searching my damn soul. For what, I don't know, but it's consuming nonetheless. Inching closer, he presses his lips against my ear, his words barely more than a whisper.

"You are hands down the most stunning wolf I have ever seen in my life." I shiver against him, his words heating my veins, and I'm almost certain I can feel my wolf inside of me. I can't explain it. It's euphoric and amazing, leaving goosebumps along my skin. "You're also my mate, Alpha. My. Mate. I won't let anything happen to you." He leans back, his gaze still consuming mine as I gape at him in wonder.

"I didn't think you would," I muse, tingles running through me, and he nods.

"Yeah, now the impulse is worse." His jaw ticks as he strokes his thumb over my cheek.

Before another word can be spoken between us, the door opens again, Fairbourne stepping back into the room as he starts calling out names. Panic clings to me once again when Cassian, Brody, and Arlo are called out.

Fuck. Fuck. Fuck.

Cassian's grip on my chin tightens a fraction before his lips capture mine in a searing touch that reignites the ghost of Kryll's kiss earlier. I pout the moment he takes a step back, tearing his lips from mine as Brody shifts his hand from my back to my waist and pulls me in close. Smothering my pout, it wanes under the swipe of his tongue as he delves into my mouth like a starved man.

Just as quickly as he obliterates me, he takes an unwanted step back before following the others through the door.

"Girl, you are so done for," Flora says with a

snicker, pulling me from my longing thoughts as I turn to face her with a raised eyebrow.

"What?"

She matches my stance, cocking her brow at me as she nods toward the closed door. I sense Raiden move toward my right, his presence sending tingles down my spine as I try to focus on my friend.

The staredown she gives me is enough to challenge the mightiest of warriors, and as much as I try to prevent it, I relent under her intensity.

"You're right," I mutter with a sigh of defeat. Admitting the truth usually tastes sour on my tongue, but in this instance, I rather like it.

"I know I am. Any guesses what the trial may be?" she asks, moving on to the impending topic like I didn't just reveal a vulnerability to her in the form of my Kryptos.

"No, but the thought of them using it as a tactic to..." My words trail off, unable to express the reality of overhearing what Bozzelli and Kenner were whispering about earlier.

"It's fucked up, Adrianna," Raiden murmurs from my side, running his fingers over my neck. "Very fucked up," he adds, driving the fact home, and all I can do is nod in agreement.

"I'm more confused about why Kenner—" I stop myself before I start running my mouth and someone hears me. Raiden senses the shift and squeezes my shoulder.

"I know."

Flora steps around me so she's facing us both, shaking her head in disbelief. "If I thought this place was fucked up before..."

Once again, words fail to describe the circumstances. It doesn't matter because in the next moment, Fairbourne is back at the door, calling the remaining students to follow him, and the three of our names are obviously in the mix.

My heart races, and my pulse thunders in my ears as we follow him down the hallway and back toward the ballroom. I find Brody, Kryll, and Cassian first, their presence, along with Raiden's, helping to calm me, but just behind them, I spy the flashing cameras of the media.

The lights are blinding, distracting me so much that I almost don't hear Bozzelli call out my name. Raiden squeezes my hand, but I don't pull my stare from the woman in question. I manage the smallest clench back before I head toward where she waits at the top of the podium.

With every step I take, clarity settles over me, taking root in my bones and calming the storm that's been brewing inside of me. Bozzelli addresses the crowd, but I don't hear it; with my mindset, I'm completely focused.

I don't know what anyone has said before me, and it doesn't matter either way, but I have an audience, an audience that derives from more than just the academy and the council. I didn't offer the media a single word earlier, but I won't make that mistake twice.

She takes a step aside, waving toward the microphone with a smug grin on her face, one I return before I turn to face the audience.

I don't clear my throat, I don't try to wet my dry lips, and I don't let a single ounce of uncertainty show. Instead, I stand tall, prideful, and ready.

"Good evening, people of Floodborn Kingdom. It is with great sadness that I address the terror in our land. It has rooted its way into our core and wreaked havoc for long enough. We must now take action. Threats have gone unheard, wicked promises whispered in the shadow of night, and as a united kingdom, we won't stand for it anymore. We've been under attack from their poisonous actions for long enough."

Perfect pause.

"Now, The Council must pay."

Murmurs dance in the air from the crowd and media as their cameras continue to go off. I'm on a roll now, and there's no turning back.

"Powerful gems that were once banished from our kingdom are now being used to control some of our own citizens. I'm sure the flash of amethyst on my neck at the last ball didn't go unnoticed. Above all of that, they are taking matters into their own hands to orchestrate the bonding of fated mates."

Gasps ring in the air and I can feel Bozzelli's gaze burning into my skin from beside me, but I keep going.

"Against the will of those involved and against the true foundation of freedom that our kingdom yearns for. The time for The Council has passed, along with their ability to make selfless decisions for our people."

What did the noticeboard say?

Address the people.

Express your beliefs.

And Promise for victory.

Steeling my spine, I believe in every word, cementing them into my heart as I breathe them out loud. "With all that I am, I will not stop fighting for my people. Not just fae, but wolves, vampires, shifters, humans, and mages alike. We are one. We will find strength in uniting together, and we will fight as one to right the wrongs of the past."

"Get her off that stage. Now."

The ragged order is a snarl I'm familiar with. Bozzelli's rage is becoming something I'm almost accustomed to, and even though she's keeping her voice low enough to go unheard over the media chatter, it still rings in my ears like a warning.

Smiling politely, I take a step back from the microphone, my gaze set ahead as I make sure to look directly into the lens of each camera aimed my way. Bozzelli appears in front of me a split second later, eyes ablaze with unspoken anger as she straightens her outfit and turns to address the gathered crowd.

I take a moment to saunter off the podium, finding my insane vampire grinning from ear to ear, but before he can mutter a single word in my direction, Bozzelli's voice echoes around the room.

"I want to take this opportunity to thank each

and every one of you for being here today," she starts, earning my attention. Just as I turn in her direction, her stare lasers in on me.

She looks—*really* looks—almost as deeply as Cassian did earlier, but unlike with him, I bolster my walls in place, refusing to let her reach the pits of my soul and see my weaknesses.

Her head tilts, her assessment continuing for what feels like an eternity before she turns to face the audience once again. She clears her throat, running her palms down her waist as she beams at the crowd.

"I also want to acknowledge the powerful speech from Miss Reagan. I'm sure we can all agree that she fulfilled the expectations we were looking for today. So much so that no more will take place this evening. I can say with true certainty that full marks will be honored for such a strong and victorious address to the nation. What a great imagination you have."

Her eyes find me again, her last words bouncing off my unfazed façade as she presses her lips together and twists her fingers nervously.

What is going on?

Bozzelli doesn't know how to be anything but a cut-throat bitch. It's almost as if she's second-guessing herself, but for what? I don't know. A single nod, more to herself than anyone else, and she's back facing the media.

Another throat clearing, a swipe of her tongue over her bottom lip, and a slight adjustment to the sleeves of her suit. Her body language screams nervous, but if anyone else notices it, they remain as silent as I do.

"It's with great surprise that I reveal to the students that there is not, in fact, an additional trial this evening." Murmurs erupt throughout the space, mingling with a straight-up "what the fuck" from Raiden beside me. I frown, perplexed by what the fuck is even happening right now, when she continues to speak. "Tonight was about finding the appropriate words to address your kingdom before a life-threatening event. I'm sure you'll be relieved that tonight is not a life-threatening time to be concerned with." She purses her lips before fixing her smile. "And with that revelation, I bid everyone a fair evening and a wondrous future as we continue the search for the heir to the Floorborn Kingdom."

"Who the fuck is this woman, and where is the real Bozzelli?" Flora whispers, and I huff in agreement, unable to take my eyes off the woman in question.

Her gaze is fixated on me as she steps down from the podium, and it only drifts off when she comes to a stop at my side.

"You. My office. Now."

I rear to the side, not appreciating her close prox-
imity. "But—"

"Now, Miss Reagan," she growls, struggling to
keep her voice down as she takes a step, expecting
me to follow.

"She's not going anywhere with you alone,"
Raiden retorts, earning himself an eye roll from the
devil that is our dean.

"I don't imagine she will."

Blinking at her, I can't help but gape as she
continues toward the door behind us.

"Is she actually agreeing to me being present?"
Raiden asks, his brows gathered in confusion as he
turns his attention my way.

I shrug, my lips parting to speak when Cassian
beats me to it. "Fuck that. We're all going," he grumbles, throwing his arm over my shoulder as he guides
me toward the exit.

"I'll stay here with Arlo and make sure there's
nothing else at play," Flora states, disappearing into
the crowd before I can say a single word.

Exhaling with relief, I fall into step between my
vampire and my wolf, with Brody and Kryll right
behind us. The walk is swift and silent, drenched in
uncertainty that I can't truly place.

Entering her office is like stepping into the lion's
den, but when Bozzelli takes her seat on the other
side of her desk, it is clear she's rattled. Her gaze

travels across the five of us, and back again, repeating the motion five times before she finally says anything.

"So, the five of you."

"The five of us," Brody states, shrugging like he knows what she's hinting at while I blink like a fool.

"Take a seat."

I scoff, shaking my head. "The last time I did that, you had me frozen in place to insert the kiss of death into my skin."

She sighs, irritation swirling with desperation as she laces her hands together. "I didn't know then what I still don't seem to know now." I frown, completely confused by what she's trying to say. She must sense that we're not following what she means because she sighs again, heavier this time. "Somebody better explain to me and explain to me now."

"About what?" Kryll asks, folding his arms over his chest as he glares down at her.

"About what Miss Reagan just said," she barks back, unwavering beneath his looming presence.

"Which part?" Raiden adds, rising to my defense.

"Don't play dumb. The Council," she snarls, slapping her palms against her desk.

With the way she's acting, you would think... does she *not* know?

"I don't know what else you need to know. They

are a plague on this kingdom," Brody states all matter-of-fact, like his own father isn't a member.

She rolls her eyes. "There's always a plague somewhere, Mr. Orenda. I mean the fated mates. How do you know that to be true?" she pushes, throwing her arms out in frustration as her eyes swirl wildly, as if she's trying to navigate the stormy seas without any form of life raft.

I can sense it. Deep in my bones, and despite my better judgment, I let my mind magic flutter over my skin. I'm instantly met with panic, betrayal, and uncertainty.

She doesn't know.

She doesn't fucking know.

"Because they've tried it before," I blurt. I'm not entirely sure I'm making the right decision to share that information with her, but it feels like I've got nothing to lose.

"When?" She stills, frozen in place at my admission, and it only serves to confirm my thoughts. I can sense the guys looking at me, unsure if I'm doing the right thing, but none of them try to interject.

"After the last trial. When Brody took me off campus to heal from the poisoned vampire bite Vallie gave me."

Her eyes widen, the surprise undeniable as she blinks at me. "The night her father went missing.

You killed him." To my surprise, there's no anger in her tone.

"Yes." I breathe the truth, watching with bated breath to see what her reaction will be.

She leans back in her seat, assessing me with new eyes. "I thought she was lying."

"On this one occasion, she wasn't," I say with a shrug, still waiting for her to go bat shit crazy on me for my actions, but it doesn't come. Instead, she clears her throat, assessing the five of us once again before tapping her desktop in thought.

"What do they expect to achieve by forcing the five of you to be fated mates?"

"That's the question I'd love to know the answer to," Cassian grunts, swiping a hand through his hair as Brody takes a step forward. His eyes find mine, considering me for a moment before he turns back around, planting his hand on her desk as he speaks.

"I'm assuming it's to control us in our weakened state in order to maintain control of the kingdom. Make us beacons of hope to our people, name us the heirs, and control us like puppets."

Her lips curl, almost giving the sense that she's not happy, but that can't be true. Not if—

"I will not allow it," she snarls, anger flowing from her in waves.

"Huh?" Brody stands, confusion crinkling his

nose as Bozzelli follows suit, fixing her jacket as she stands tall.

"I will *not* allow it," she repeats before pressing a button on her desk. "I want everyone off campus now, and I want the containment placed back on the academy immediately. Nobody in, nobody out." It takes me a second to realize it must be an intercom or something as she ends the call and settles her stare on Cassian. "And that includes you too, Mr. Kenner." The five of us gape at her in surprise. "He expected you to leave, he made sure I exempted you from the powers last time, but I won't do it again," she explains, and Cassian nods.

"Understood."

Wait... is she... she's not... she can't be on our side... can she?

"What now?" Raiden asks, and she scoffs, a sense of delirium lightening the dismay.

"Now? I don't know. I need to think about the madness that wreaks havoc on my academy. The havoc that always seems to circulate around you, Miss Reagan." I open my mouth to point out the fact that it's not my fault—well, not *always* my fault, at least—but she's waving her hand dismissively before I can even consider defending myself. "Go. Sleep. None of this is over. Far from it. We must prepare now. For what, I can't be entirely sure, but the fact that I have put tonight's full trial on pause will only put us all in the line of fire."

The bedroom door clicks shut behind me as we all filter into Raiden's room. As much as relief floods my system from the privacy we're now finally offered after a chaotic evening, it still doesn't settle the uncertainty in my chest.

We're wading our way through uncharted waters, murky with the sins of others, leaving us at their mercy. The fact that Bozzelli wasn't aware of The Council's true plans shouldn't surprise me, but her now knowing, and what she may or may not do with that information, only serves to fuel my distress further.

"What do we do now?" Brody asks, pulling Addi into his side, and my gaze falls to her face.

"We sleep," I grunt, earning a look of surprise from each of them, Addi included.

"Sleep?" Raiden snaps.

"We can't just sleep," Kryll adds, and I shrug.

"Maybe you can't, but she needs to," I state, pointing at my fucking alpha. She's dead on her feet, exhaustion clinging to every inch of her. I don't need to look at my brothers to know they see it too.

In true Addi style, she waves me off. "I'm good," she breathes, stifling a yawn.

"If that's what good looks like, I don't want it," Brody muses, pressing a kiss to her forehead before she peers up at him with a deathly glare.

"Hey," she warns, and he boops her nose.

"Please, I'm teasing and you love it."

"It's questionable," she mutters, covering her mouth to hide the next yawn.

I nod at Brody, who takes the hint, tightening his hold around Addi's shoulders and leading her toward the bedroom in Raiden's ridiculously huge room.

"Come on, Dagger. I've got you," he murmurs, and she follows after him. Just as they reach the doorway, she peers back over her shoulder.

"We're all sleeping here?"

"Yes. Is that okay?" Raiden offers, tilting his head at her, which earns him a pointed look.

"Are you actually asking?" she retorts, and he snickers.

"No." The smile on his face is unbearable.

"I didn't think so," she states, waving us off as she looks up at Brody.

"I need to get out of this dress."

"That's what I'm here for," Brody says, wagging his eyebrows before they both disappear from view.

Addi snickers, the noise sweet as it dances through the air. "For a player, you have some pretty cheesy lines."

"That's because my player days are over, Addi. I told you that." The fucker ushers back to the door, kicking it closed without a single glance in our direction, keeping our girl all to himself for a moment.

Swiping a hand down my face, I take the few steps over to the sofa and collapse back with a sigh. I'm consumed with exhaustion and the tendrils of wonder that cling to my bones. A feeling I've never even come close to experiencing before.

"Did you ever think a public bathroom would play such a magical part in your story?" Kryll asks, dropping down on the sofa beside me.

I shake my head, bewildered now that I finally have a moment to think about it all.

"What actually happened in the bathroom?" Raiden adds, taking a seat on the sofa across from us. "Why do you look all whimsical and shit when we bring it up?" he pushes, and I quickly try to smother the smile touching the corner of my lips.

He knows. I already know he knows, and for

once in his selfish vampire life, he's being selfless. Even if it's just for a moment. Letting the question sink in, I allow my whimsical smile to return as my eyelids fall to half-mast.

"I found my mate." The words are warm on my tongue, igniting a pull in my bones, eager for me to get my alpha in my sights again, but I fight against it.

She needs to rest and recuperate. She shifted for the first time, and that's going to be a lot on anyone. Including her.

"She shifted," Kryll breathes, understanding in his tone as he looks up at the ceiling, and I nod.

"Yeah, she shifted for me."

Happiness is the only word I can think of that remotely describes what I'm feeling, but I know it doesn't truly represent my core emotions right now. Content, aware, and filled with a sense of purpose, I feel like a new man.

A new wolf.

A claimed wolf.

"I can't decide if you look happy or mad about it," Raiden states, interrupting my thoughts, and I scowl at him.

"I've never felt calmer in my whole entire life. But the need to protect her, to defend what's mine, it's overwhelming." The truth slipping from my lips melts the tension from my limbs as Raiden gapes at me.

"More than before?"

"More than before," I repeat, acutely aware that it shouldn't be possible.

"I'm jealous," he grumbles, making me frown.

"Of what?" Kryll interjects, his expression matching my own.

"Of her not being a vampire like me too."

"Of course you are," I say with a sigh, certain Raiden's vampire selfishness is firmly back in place, but to my surprise he leans forward in his seat, bracing his elbows on his knees.

"So, to recap the hell out of our night, Addi is now a wolf, as well as a fae princess. Kenner wanted her to do it, to shift I mean, and Bozzelli called off the trial because she was in shock over the information Addi gave to the entire kingdom in her speech." He looks between Kryll and me, waiting for confirmation, and I nod.

"That about sums it up."

"She's a dragon princess too," Kryll states, further relaxing into the cushions behind him as a smug grin curls his lips.

"A dragon princess too. Thanks for that," Raiden grumbles with a huff, shaking his head with irritation. "And what are we supposed to do with all of this now?"

"I'm going to do what every grown shifter does,"

Kryll states, rising from the sofa and pulling his cell phone out of his pocket.

"What?" I ask, intrigued by whatever plan he's got, but the bashful smile that takes over his face catches me off-guard.

"Call my mom."

Reality clings to my skin, working hard to pull me from my deep sleep, and try as I might, I can't seem to prevent it. My eyelids are heavy, grogginess weighing on my limbs as I sigh, but confusion quickly floods my thoughts as I struggle to stretch out.

Maybe it's not the grogginess weighing down on me but the limbs of others smothering me beneath the bed sheets. Blinking, I fight off the exhaustion that still claims me to find Brody sprawled over me from the left and Raiden pressed along the length of my right side.

It's definitely a sight to wake up to, but the heat they're generating is on the verge of suffocating. Shifting between them, I spy Kryll lying on the other side of Brody while Cassian fills the chair in the corner of the room. His chin rests against his chest and his eyelashes lay softly against his cheeks.

I take a moment to soak it in. Four men, *my* four crazy men, who can be sharp, cutthroat, and deadly, yet they look so angelic when they sleep.

It's another layer of them, one I want to claim for my own. I want to blame the thought on my connection with my wolf, but if I'm being honest, it's been there all along, growing stronger with every passing day until I can no longer avoid the truth.

I muttered the words to Kryll back in his home, but now I feel them through my entire body.

They're mine. And I am theirs.

A shiver runs down my spine, and I don't know how, but I do know that acknowledging the fact makes my wolf happy. *Very* happy. It's a weird sensation, feeling something so strongly, but it's something I'm going to need to get used to.

Brody shifts beside me, offering a minuscule opening between us, and I take it. Shuffling between the two hot furnaces, I manage to reach the foot of the bed before the sound of a deep, raspy voice makes me freeze.

"Where are you going?"

I cock a brow at the wolf still filling the chair in the corner. His eyes are open, but otherwise, he hasn't moved an inch. "Out of the depths of Hell. It's fucking hot in here," I answer, pointing over my shoulder, and he smirks. *Fucking* smirks. Who knew Cassian Kenner was capable of such a thing?

Without a word, he rises to his feet, sauntering toward me with his usual cocky stance. My mouth dries, betraying the calm and collected vibe I'm trying and failing to exude as he falls to his knees before me.

He skims his palms over my thighs, leaving goosebumps in his wake as I shiver.

"Are you okay?" he asks, earning nothing more than a nod as my breath lodges in my throat. "Are *we* okay?" he adds, uncertainty flickering in his eyes for a beat before it disappears, and I nod again.

He searches my eyes for answers I can't seem to verbalize, and whatever he finds must be what he's looking for because in the next moment, his palms lift, taking the oversized t-shirt I stole from Raiden's closet with it, until his skin is flat against my stomach. With a little pressure, I silently follow his guidance, lying back on the bed as he remains above me.

Looking down the length of my body and seeing him nestled between my thighs is enough to unravel me, and it only intensifies when he grabs my thighs, dragging me closer before spreading me wide. Only then do I lose his eye contact. His gaze shifts to my core as he places my feet flat on the bed, offering himself the perfect view of my pussy, leaving me completely exposed.

He stares, and stares, and... stares, for what feels like a lifetime. I try to clench my thighs together, but his grip denies me the opportunity as he holds me in place. His fingertips press into my flesh, causing my breaths to release in shallow puffs, and I can't take it anymore.

"Cassian," I breathe, pushing up on my elbows to get a better view of him.

The motion pulls him from his thoughts as his eyes latch on to mine. "You're mine, Addi. Mine. Not just because I brought you to the brink of an orgasm and made you say it last night, but because you are my mate. My Alpha."

My body vibrates at his words, my brain short-circuiting as I peer down at him, unable to offer anything more than a nod. Not that he seems to need words from me, because his focus is gone from my face again with his next breath, which coasts over my exposed pussy, making me shiver.

"Ca—oh fuck," I gasp as he eliminates the whisper between us, swiping his tongue through my folds. My fists clench, bunching the sheets at my sides as my head falls back.

"Eyes on me, Alpha," he rasps, his lips brushing against my sensitive skin with every word. I shiver again, a ball of coiled nerves, needy for more.

It takes everything in me to tilt my head back in his direction, even more so to open my eyelids, but the second I do, I'm rewarded with him feasting on me again.

One swipe, two swipes, three. His tongue lashes at my pink center before swirling around my clit. I buck up off the bed, desperate for friction, as another moan parts my lips. "Cassian, please." I don't know what the fuck I'm begging for, but I need it, and I need it now.

He rakes his teeth over my tight nub, continuing to hold my thighs apart as I seek more, but he thankfully puts me out of my misery a moment later when he thrusts his tongue into my core. I melt into the bed beneath me, my subconscious aware that the others are sleeping, but the desire coursing through my veins makes it impossible for me to worry about waking them.

His fingertips press into my thighs so harshly I know there will be bruises once he's done. The thought only strengthens the tingles that zip down my spine, racing me toward my climax. I'm a jumble of gasps and groans as he works my body with only his tongue. Every time my hips lift off the bed, he sinks his teeth into my clit, leaving me feral and pushing me beyond the point of no return.

"Cassian." His name on my lips is the only warning he gets before I'm thrust over the edge of ecstasy, writhing beneath him as wave after wave washes over me, rendering me helpless as I succumb to his touch.

I fall flat on the bed, gasping for breath as he slowly trails kisses over my thighs, likely tracing the bruises he's left behind. I'm still nothing more than a ragged breath when I hear a sigh, but it's not from Cassian... it comes from behind me.

"I could wake up to that every morning." Brody's voice dances with amusement and satisfaction as I sink deeper into the mattress.

"Same," Kryll and Raiden add, confirming the audience I didn't know we had.

"Let's—" Raiden's next words are cut off by the distant sound of a knock. He grumbles under his breath as he storms out of bed. I watch his ass as he goes, but my view is quickly consumed by Brody's face as he leans over me. He strokes a finger down my cheek, his lips parted, but before he can get a word out, Raiden is stomping back into the room with purpose. "Well, it seems this morning you're being summoned by some fae chick to go to Fairbourne's office," he states with a huff as I rush to sit up. But Kryll speaks before I can even process what's going on.

"Fairbourne? He's been about as useful as a chocolate teapot. What the fuck could he want?"

"Don't you think it's a bit late for Fairbourne to be requesting a meeting?" Brody asks, scrubbing a hand over his chin as he glances at the four of us. The early morning sun does little to offer us any peace, despite the storm last night, but it does give us the opportunity for a fresh start and a clearer mind. It doesn't, however, allow for any answers to surface, which means there's still a chance we're going to be blindsided.

Again.

"It was more like a demand," Raiden grunts, his jaw tight despite the rest of him appearing unfazed. I'm not sure whether he's just not a morning person or if he was keen to dip his dick in the honey jar, but either way, he's in a bad mood.

Eager to keep everyone focused, I take a step

ahead. "I don't know what Fairbourne wants, but showing up works in our favor."

"How do you figure?" Cassian asks, just as irked as Raiden.

"If we stay hidden, we won't know what he wants, and *not* knowing what he wants only hinders us. If we're going to figure any of this out then we're going to need all the information we can get our hands on."

"Figure what out?" Kryll asks, and I scoff. If that isn't the million-dollar question, then I don't know what is.

"Fuck if I know, but this shit all has to end, right?" I shrug. It's more of an attempt to shake off the uncertainty that clings to me, but if the guys notice, no one says anything.

"That's right, Dagger. The five of us together," Brody sings, throwing his hands out to gesture at everyone as we cut across campus. He earns an eye roll or two from the others, but it makes my chest warm and a smile creeps across my face.

It's strange to think I don't have to face the mountain that is life alone anymore, but I can't deny how much I like it. They may just be simple words, but there's no denying that they instill a strength in me like I've never felt before.

All too quickly, we're taking the hallways

through the main academy building, beelining for Fairbourne's office. I've turned it over in my mind a million times since the knock came at Raiden's door, but for the life of me I can't figure out what Fairbourne may want.

He's aware of everything that's happened, and my father said I can trust him with my life, but his actions have yet to prove that. Before a miraculous answer comes to mind, Fairbourne's office door looms just ahead of us. My steps slow, but Raiden's quicken, hand poised against the wood, ready to knock as he peers back at me.

"Ready?"

"Yeah," I answer, not entirely sure, but standing here without any answers won't get me anywhere.

He nods in response, but before he knocks, he turns his attention to Cassian. "No shit from you." Cassian's eyes narrow as Raiden raps his knuckles against the door.

"Shit from me? For what?"

"You're hotheaded," he retorts with a shrug, and I huff a laugh. It's so amusing to me that *he's* the one saying that of all people.

"And—" Cassian's response is cut short as the door swings open, revealing Professor Fairbourne on the other side.

He looks from Raiden to Cassian, to Brody, then

Kryll, before he settles on me, his eyes narrowing with every pass.

Clearing his throat, he adjusts his suit jacket. "Adrianna, I expected you to come alone."

"You expected wrong," Cassian snarls, hands balling into fists immediately, and Raiden whirls around to him without missing a beat.

"We haven't even gotten in there and you've already started," he barks, a pointed look etched into his features. Brody tries to hide his amusement behind his hand but fails miserably when his chuckle rings through the air.

All I can do is gape at them in a mixture of surprise and amusement, leaving Kryll to jump in and handle the situation.

"Professor Fairbourne, I'm sure you can understand after last night, we don't believe it's safe for Addi to travel alone. Not with the attack from Kenner being so recent too," he explains in an attempt to smooth over the shitshow that's already unraveling.

Fairbourne drops his gaze for a split second, nodding in understanding as he clears his throat once again. "Of course, of course. But as the head of the fae origins on campus, I can assure you Miss Reagan will be safe in my office. You're more than welcome to wait—"

"If you think we're waiting anywhere but at her side, you're in for a shock," Cassian gripes, taking a step in Fairbourne's direction.

Desperate for this to not become another scene, I reach for Cassian's arm, squeezing in what I hope is comfort, but could most definitely be anger. "Cass—"

"Ah, Miss Reagan, there you are."

I spin around in frustration, irritated with another interruption instead of being any closer to getting answers. But when I find Professor Tora, Kryll's brother, marching toward us, my frustration dissolves, curiosity replacing it instantly.

"Here I am?" I ramble, tilting my head as I stare him down, and a second later, Kryll's hand is wrapped around mine.

"Beau?" The question in his brother's name confirms he's not entirely sure what's going on either.

"That's Professor Tora to you," he retorts, pursing his lips at his brother, who shakes his head dismissively.

"You're my brother, and we're not in class."

Tora takes a step toward his brother, ready to continue arguing his point, when Fairbourne reminds us of his presence.

"Can I help you, Professor Tora?"

Kryll's brother plasters a fake smile across his lips as he takes in the leader of the fae origin. "No, not now that I've found who I'm looking for." His answer is clipped, but if Fairbourne notices, he lets it go right over his head.

"Oh, it may have to wait, Professor. We were about to have a meeting."

Beau shakes his head. "I'm afraid it's going to have to wait."

"It can't," Fairbourne states, a tic fluttering in his jaw as his eyes narrow.

"Unfortunately, Professor Fairbourne, my mother waits for no one," Tora offers, his words slow and deliberate, like he's talking to a child, and Fairbourne blusters under his tone.

"The academy is on lockdown," he insists, and Professor Tora simply shrugs, unfazed.

"The ethereal queen is summoning someone; lockdown be damned. Besides, Bozzelli is aware," he adds for good measure, and Fairbourne takes a reluctant step back, his head hanging in defeat for a brief moment before he nods in understanding.

"My misunderstanding. We will meet soon." His eyes are narrowed on mine, waiting for confirmation, which I willingly offer him.

"Sure." There's clearly something going on with him and I'd like to know what that is, but for now, it seems Kryll's mother awaits us. For what? I'm not sure, but once again, waiting here won't get me the answers I'm seeking.

Looking at Kryll, he nods for us to follow his

brother, who is already near the far end of the corridor. The door clicks shut behind Fairbourne as we take off after Tora when Raiden steps up to Kryll's side, nudging his arm.

"It appears your call to Mommy worked."

"I never doubted it would," he replies with a shrug that matches his brother's nonchalance.

"Clue me in," I blurt, looking between the four of them, but no one utters a word until we make it outside. Professor Tora waits in the middle of the pathway, but Raiden doesn't seem to mind when he steps up to my side, arm slung around my shoulders as he whispers against my ear.

"He called Mommy for help, so now the Queen of Dragons is answering."

Turning to Kryll, I'm surprised to find his gaze downcast as he scrubs nervously at the back of his neck. I slip out of Raiden's hold as I make my way toward my dragon. It's only when I'm right in front of him that he looks up, worry swirling in his eyes.

"I—"

I press my lips to his, effectively cutting off whatever excuse was going to fall from his mouth. It takes a second for him to catch up, but when he does, his lips are firm against mine, making it even harder for me to pull back. The moment I do, he leans forward, bracing his forehead against mine as I peer into his eyes.

"As long as I get to see Nora and my father, I don't care."

"You don't?"

"No. They'll make me feel whole, and after last night, I need them more than ever."

"Addi!"

There's no time to brace for impact. Even with my name being yelled in advance, I still can't prepare for it.

A single breath and I'm knocked to the floor, the air gone from my lungs as Nora lands on top of me, squealing with delight.

If I thought the breath being knocked from me was the end of my time, the deathly grip she has on me proves me wrong. Either way, death by sister is what my tombstone will say if she doesn't relent.

My face heats, the strangled breaths doing nothing for me until Nora finally releases her hold on me just enough to plant her hands on either side of my face, looming over me with a monstrous smile.

One breath, two breaths, three.

I exhale, relief flooding my body as I glare up at

my sister, but it falls flat when I see just how happy she is.

Carefree. Joyous. A fucking delight.

The complete opposite of me, and I love it. She deserves it.

"So this is what it's really like for you to have those legs working, huh?" I panic my amusement might hurt her feelings, but thankfully, she throws her head back with a laugh.

"Please, I was made purely to bring you disaster and delight. You're welcome," she sings, pushing up to her feet and offering me her hand, but before I can lace my fingers with hers, another body looms over me.

"She really was."

My smile spreads across my face, my heart racing with happiness instead of despair, which is exactly the shift I need. Taking his hand, I stand and quickly wrap my arms around his middle.

"Hi, Dad."

"Addi," he breathes into my hair, warming my bones from head to toe as he squeezes me tight.

"Was there a reason you two were rolling around on the floor?" he asks, pressing a kiss to my temple before he slackens his hold.

"I'm being disastered and delighted, apparently," I explain, using Nora's words, which makes her giggle, filling my heart with joy at the beautiful sound.

"Kryll." A woman's voice cuts through the air, pulling me from my father's embrace.

"Mother," he replies, cutting the distance between him and the ethereal queen, who stands with her arms out wide, ready to embrace her son. It's amusing watching the bulk of a guy soften in his mother's arms, but it's a feeling I experience with my father, and I know all too well how it's grounding and not weakening like I once thought.

"Oh, you brought the handful," the queen muses, releasing her son to glance at the others.

"Which one is that?" I blurt, completely intrigued, and I get my answer before she can even open her mouth.

"What? You love me more than your own sons. Don't play me like that, Mamma E," Brody says with a pout.

"I've never known a mage to be so sure of themselves when it doesn't relate to wisdom," she muses, rolling her eyes at the *handful*.

"I'm one of a kind. You're welcome," he retorts with a wink, strolling toward her with his arms out wide, and she hugs him just as tightly as she did Kryll.

"You're something," she mutters, the amusement

clear between them, but the moment she lets him go, the jokes are gone, and our problems linger in the air.

I clear my throat, feeling acutely aware that I'm pretty much the reason we're here. No one says it, and I'm sure no one will, but I feel it nonetheless.

"Shall we discuss what's going on?" my father offers, reaching for my arm with a comforting touch.

"We should," the queen declares with a nod, eyes glancing over the five of us. "Have you eaten?"

"Not yet," Cassian answers, speaking up for the first time, and she nods in understanding.

"Then let's eat and talk," she insists, waving for us to follow after her without a backward glance.

With my father on my left and Nora on my right, I let my walls down for a split second, allowing myself a moment to bask in the true warmth of their presence. It doesn't last long, but it's enough for me to feel settled, especially after last night. A fact I must explain to my father too.

I gulp, the panic threatening to work its way up my throat, but I quickly tamp it down. I'm half-wolf. I'm not ashamed or embarrassed, and I know my father won't make me feel anything but pride, either. I just need to find the words.

The queen leads us out to the patio where I first met her, only the table is bigger, offering enough space for all of us. I settle between my father and sister, much to Raiden's disappointment. He sits directly across from me, his jaw tense and his gaze narrowed on me, but to my surprise, he keeps his mouth shut.

I make a mental note to thank him later. It's clear he's taking a rare moment to be selfless, even with something as small as me sitting with my family, and he deserves a pat on the back, at least for being a good little vampire.

I bite back a smile that curls at my own thoughts, schooling my face before anyone asks. Instead, I take in the spread of food laid out around us, watching as everyone serves themselves.

Everyone but me.

Everything Nora puts on her plate, she insists on putting on mine, explaining how delicious and amazing it all is until there's not a single inch of space left.

"You're awesome, Mamma E. Thank you," Brody declares, followed by everyone else mumbling their thanks before a comfortable silence drifts over us.

The food is as delicious as Nora promised. From fresh chocolate croissants to strawberry compote french toast. By the time I'm done eating, I'm certain I won't be able to move for at least an hour. Possibly more.

"So, what happened for you to reach out, Son?" the queen asks once everyone has placed their utensils down, and a server approaches with a carafe of coffee.

I hold my mug to my chest, the freshly brewed cup of Heaven warming my hands as I listen to Kryll explain last night's events. Despite the emotions I felt when it was all happening, I manage to detach myself from them today, which is a huge leap of progress.

"I'm so sorry you had to deal with that, Addi," my father murmurs once Kryll gets to the part where Bozzelli sent us to rest. A fact I still can't quite get over. I'm still expecting another surprise move from her. Obviously, it hasn't come yet, but it's better to be prepared than caught off guard.

"It's not your fault, Dad," I insist. He may have trained me, but it was my idea to attend the academy when the announcement was initially made years ago.

The soft smile he offers doesn't quite meet his eyes, confirming the fact that he takes the blame despite my insistence. But I'm also aware that the only person who can change his perspective is himself.

"Is there anything else?" he asks a moment later, as if my soul is burning in my eyes, revealing the last fact that Kryll breezed over.

I nod, my throat drying, and remember my

earlier thoughts, steeling my spine with confidence when I meet my father's eyes.

"I unleashed my wolf." The words hang in the air, expanding between us as my father's eyes widen in surprise before his chair drags back and he drops to his knees beside me.

"Oh, Addi," he breathes, unshed tears swimming in his eyes as Nora grips my arm tight. I can't look at her, though; I don't know how much she knows. "I'm so proud of you for embracing every piece of yourself," my father adds, cutting my thoughts short as I gape at him.

I expected pride from him, but the relief that floods my veins at his acceptance leaves me speechless.

"How do you feel?" Nora asks, her voice raspy as I blink, slowly turning to face her.

"I'm not sure, but I'm not sad about it," I admit, my voice as croaky as hers as she nods, a watery smile consuming her features.

"Does Bozzelli know?" the queen asks, reminding me we're not alone, and I shake my head. "Good. Keep it that way," she states, confirming my thoughts.

A foot nudges against mine under the table, and I know without looking that it's Cassian. A tugging sensation forms in my chest, and I know it's my wolf reaching for him. I don't know how, but it's the truth.

"What do we do now?" Raiden asks, his gaze flicking across everyone at the table.

"You head back and play the game," Nora blurts, her hold on my arm tightening as she nods, a fierceness washing over her as her nostrils flare with anger. "They don't get to win. Not now, not ever." Her stony stare settles on me. "You can't let this go on. It has to end. Someone set the idea of this academy in motion because we needed a change. I don't care how hard those assholes try to hold on to the little control they have left, but you fight, Addi. You fight with everything that you are and take what's rightfully yours."

I gape at my sister as my heart thunders in my chest. I should scold her for cursing, but damn, if that wasn't the speech I needed, I don't know what is. The fire she pumps into my mind is undeniable.

"Well said, Nora," the queen agrees, making my eyes bug out of my head. There's so much in such a simple statement, and I don't want to read into it more than I should, but it's too late. I know I'm where I'm meant to be. I know the fate of eternity for our kingdom is hanging in the balance, and I know I have a role to play. I'm the heir. I want it. I *need* it. And her agreement with my sister feels like a degree of approval. "I think the five of you deserve a little reprieve before you succumb to the madness that is the Floodborn Kingdom," the queen offers, a soft smile on her face as she places her hand on top of her son's. "Spend the day here. Bozzelli and the academy can wait until tomorrow," she adds, and I nod instantly.

Sometimes, to find your fire, your purpose, you have to take a moment to soak in the embrace of calmness and serenity. It's a fact my father has told me time and time again, but maybe now I truly know what he means.

To be calm and collected, I can't just reach for those emotions, that state of mind, in a moment of crisis. I need to find it in the peace too.

"Thank you," I breathe, a sense of contentment fluttering through my chest. Looking between my father and Nora, emotions rise to the surface, threatening to pour out of me. For once, I consider letting my feelings show, but a thought comes to mind when I spy the smallest scar on my father's neck from where the gem was embedded into his skin.

"If you're all Aeternus dragons, why did my father say you were extinct?" It's probably a rude question to ask, but it's passed my lips before I can think better of it.

"Oh, only Kryll is blessed to be an Aeternus dragon, Adrianna." I blink at the queen, startled by the fact that she isn't the same as her son.

"How?" The word is a whisper on my lips as I

look at my dragon, a smirk on his lips as he takes me in.

"Because that's what the fates chose for him," the queen offers, so matter of factly, and Brody snickers.

"Let's go," Kryll states, rising from his seat, and the others rise with him.

I smile at the queen before embracing my father and sister, squeezing tighter than usual before I fall into the safety net that is my men. Kryll leads us toward the staircase as Brody takes two steps ahead, turns, and starts to walk backward.

"So you're all special, huh?" he says with a wag of his eyebrows, and Kryll snorts.

"You already knew that, but I can show you just how special if you like," he retorts, cocking his head from side to side, and I giggle, basking in the playfulness we so rarely get to embrace.

"With your monster dick?" I blurt, quirking a brow at my dragon, whose cheeks turn pink at my words while Brody waves his hand, making everyone stop in their tracks.

"His monster *what*?"

"I don't think I'll ever tire of this view." A sigh falls from my lips, cementing the truth as I stare out at the dragons swooping through the air in the distance. Kryll's balcony offers a snippet of Heaven, and I'm quickly getting addicted.

"Me either," my dragon muses, and just like last time, when I turn to peer at him, his sights are set on me and not the view I'm admiring.

Rolling my eyes at him, I turn back to watch the City of Dragons. "Don't smart talk me," I grumble, unable to keep the lilt out of my voice and the smile from my lips.

"Me? Never." I feel him inch closer, and the second he drapes his arm around my shoulders, I lean into his touch. "What are you thinking about?"

"That obvious, huh?" I glance up at him, and the smile on his face confirms I've been quiet for a while.

"Just a little."

"I don't even know how long I've been standing here," I admit, resting my head on his chest as I continue to stare at the floating city below.

"Long enough. Now, what's running through your pretty head?"

I exhale as a small shrug tugs at my shoulders. "Just about how everything here feels different. Untainted, not drenched in carnage, and somewhat peaceful."

"I can agree with that."

I look at him again, noting the crinkle at the corner of his eyes, and something about it grounds me. Back in Floodborn, deep in the City of Harrows, there's a lot going on. It's more than just Kenner's vendetta against me, or whatever the fuck it is, and more than the damn academy. It's the scheming from the entire council and the frenzied vampires wreaking havoc on our people.

Here, it's just... tranquil.

I purse my lips, irritated at myself. I'm supposed to be enjoying the tranquility I speak of before I face the mess that awaits us, but instead, I can't help but worry about it, constantly seeking a solution that's just out of reach.

"Where are the others?" I ask, eager to distract myself, and Kryll scoffs.

"Off threatened by my monster dick somewhere," he states, a cock-sure grin spreading across his face, and I shake my head, patting the back of my hand on his chest.

"Stop," I warn, but it doesn't seem to register because a moment later, he drops his lips to my neck, skimming them against my skin as he leaves goose-bumps in his wake.

"You don't need to be thinking about anyone else but you right now. Not your men, not your family, not the other students at the academy, not the people of Floodborn Kingdom, and definitely not the members of The Council. You just have to think about you," he explains, his lips dancing over my collarbone before he retreats, lathering the same attention to my other side as I sigh, leaning into him more.

It's on the tip of my tongue that him listing out all of my responsibilities only brings them to the fore-front of my mind, but just as my lips part, he nips his teeth along my flesh, making me shudder. The world is forgotten as I feel his fingers in my hair, my jaw falling slack as he undoes my braid, one sweep at a time.

I'm frozen in place, feeling each strand of hair fall around my face until he's laced his fingers through the entire thing. With his hands pressed against my shoulders, he turns me on the spot so we're facing, and I melt under his intense gaze.

"You're beautiful, Addi. So fucking beautiful." His words are almost swept away into the wind, making me strain to hear them as I ball my fingers into his t-shirt, clinging on for dear life. "And I know, one day, you're going to look even prettier without the weight of the world on your shoulders and a sparkly crown on your head."

I can barely breathe, let alone summon a response, as his words threaten to lift me off my feet and cast me over the balcony. He surprises me, time and time again, and all he gets in response is me staring up at him in awe.

"K—"

He presses his finger against my lips, hushing his name from parting my them after I worked so hard to remember how to talk, but any argument on my part dissolves at his next words. "So, for today, I'm going to give you a slice of what that looks like."

I gulp. "And what does that involve?" I rasp, his finger still firmly planted against my lips as his eyes darken and his gaze fixates on my mouth.

"Whatever you want."

I gulp again, but it does nothing to aid my dry throat or parched lips, yet the words find their way to my tongue nonetheless.

"I want to sink into nothingness." I don't know what it means, but the twinkle in his eyes tells me he does.

"I can help you with that, Princess." He cups my cheek, switching his finger to his thumb against my lips as a ridiculously sexy grin spreads across his cheeks. "Maybe this time I'll do it out here where anyone could see, just like I wanted to last time."

Fuck.

The shiver that spirals down my spine leaves my knees weak, only serving to make his grin spread wider.

"You like that."

"Maybe," I rasp, my knuckles burning, my grip on him is so tight.

"Definitely, maybe," he retorts, leaning closer until his lips are only a breath away from mine. Only his thumb stands in the way, but he seems to like teasing me and holds it as a barrier between us as he speaks. "Especially since Cassian got you started this morning."

I hum in agreement, my thighs tightening at the reminder of the wolf between them. It feels like a lifetime ago, but I guess that's the case when drama continues to drown me. As much as I'm thankful to be here, I can't even walk to a professor's office without something else popping up.

It seems my side quests in life are in full movement, and all I can do is succumb to it.

Before my mind can wander any further, Kryll presses his lips to my cheek in a ghost of a kiss as he lets my cloak gather at my feet. His hands move to the hem of my t-shirt, and I reluctantly release my hold on him to raise my hands over my head, aiding the removal of the fabric.

"Do not even think about fucking her in the open."

We both freeze at the bark before I peer around Kryll's frame to find Cassian, Raiden, and Brody standing at the drapes that separate the balcony from Kryll's room.

"What?" Kryll's gruff question echoes my own thoughts as I narrow my gaze on the wolf who not-so-politely interrupted us.

"You've had me in more compromising positions," I point out, but that doesn't seem to matter to him.

"Right now, you're just for our eyes only," Raiden states, backing up his friend as I feel my cheeks heat.

"Oh, she likes that," Brody says with a snicker as he rubs his hands together. "Say it again."

I part my lips to argue back, but my grumble turns into a squeak when Kryll sweeps me off my feet. It only takes a few steps before the lighting changes, and the noise from outside drifts into nothing, confirming we're in the confines of his room.

"Looks like you've got yourself a fully participating audience right here, Princess," Kryll breathes against my ear as he lowers me to my feet. He turns me on the spot to face the three new arrivals, and I have to sink my teeth into my bottom lip to hold back the groan threatening to unleash itself.

"We're no fucking audience, Troublemaker. You've got yourself four fully-pledged volunteers. What are you going to do about it?" Raiden's eyes are deadly, rendering me speechless as my body tingles with excitement.

Four participants. *Four?*

Can I handle that? I don't know, but my body is screaming for me to try.

"I think someone needs a moment to stop dominating the kingdom and relish in what it feels like to submit to their body's desires." Brody's words make my eyes widen as I gape at him. My chest clenches with a sense of truth in his words. Thankfully, instead of needing to find a response, Brody takes an answer from my silence. "Just nod once if you want to feel, Dagger. Just one little nod, and we'll do all of the thinking."

Can I do that? Give up control, offer no restraint, and just... feel?

"Trust us, Adrianna. Trust us to take care of you."

I blink at Raiden, his eyes practically black as they rake over me again and again. An encouraging nod from Cassian, combined with Kryll's hands on my waist, and I do something I never thought I would.

I trust.

One nod.

One blink.

One inhale.

And they all bounce into action.

Kryll lifts me off my feet, dangling me in the air as Brody steps up and strips me bare. Every trace of his fingers against my skin is another mark on my heart, surging my desire to the surface before I'm placed on the bed.

Four sets of eyes stare down at me, taking in my naked body as I struggle to catch my breath. Anticipation clings to my limbs, holding me captive as I wait for their next move.

Raiden is the first to cut the distance between us, shedding his clothes in record time as he kneels on the bed before me. He reaches for my ankle, pressing a delicate kiss to the inside of my leg before he trails his lips up to my knee. He repeats the process on the other side, only this time, he makes it right to the apex of my thighs. Teasingly, he stops just a breath away before returning to the other knee and starting the process again.

I'm a smitten mess by the time he's back at my core, watching with bated breath for him to touch me exactly where I want him, but the second his gaze collides with mine, I know he's up to something.

Just as his tongue flicks over my clit, his hands grab my hips and spin me. I grunt as I land on my front while he works my waist into position so my ass is in the air. The feel of him raking his elongated teeth over the globe of my ass makes me shiver, but his words that follow completely eviscerate me.

"This ass is mine."

"It is?" Brody questions, a hint of excitement in his words, but I can't see him to be sure.

"It is," Raiden repeats as he thrusts two fingers into my pussy. "It definitely is; she's already fucking dripping, aren't you, Trouble?"

All I can do is gasp, ecstasy and exhilaration coursing through my bones as he fucks me with his fingers.

"If her ass is yours, then her pussy is mine," the mage snaps back, and I feel the bed dip further a moment later.

Just as Raiden did, Brody appears by my side, naked, as he maneuvers me how he wants me, all while keeping my ass in the air for Raiden. Once he's settled, I find him nestled beneath me, every inch of his body pressing against mine as he peers up at me with a sultry grin.

"Hey, Dagger," he breathes, stroking his thumb

down my cheek as another groan bursts from my chest.

"Hey," I croak before slamming my mouth shut in case I drool all over him. My nipples pebble against his chest as he coasts his other hand down my side, settling at my waist just above Raiden's grip.

It reminds me of the night I was curled up in his bed and Raiden showed up. They both touched me then too, but this... this is different.

"You're going nowhere near her pussy until my fingers are dripping with her release, asshole," Raiden barks from behind me, but his order doesn't seem to make Brody falter. If anything, he likes it more than me, and it's my climax we're talking about.

"Come for him, Addi. Start marking us all as yours, right now," he breathes, encouraging his friend's efforts.

My palms dig deeper into the sheets as I struggle to hold my position. Raiden's fingers plunge and twist, taking me to the brink with precision until I'm nothing more than a trembling mess.

"Something is holding her back," Cassian states, and when I try to turn toward the sound of his voice, Brody stops me, capturing my lips with his as he consumes me.

Every brush of his mouth makes my brain short circuit, my mind and body acutely aware that his lips are on mine and Raiden's fingers are deep inside of me.

Fuck.

"Give it up, Princess," Kryll whispers, heating my skin, and at his command, I shatter.

My body becomes a million pieces, floating through the air as Brody swallows each of my cries, which slowly morph into whimpers.

No sooner does my pussy finally stop spasming, does the mage in question replace the vampire's fingers in my core with his cock. This time, he releases my lips, eager to hear my moans as he fills me to the brim.

"Holy shit," I rasp, adjusting to Brody inside of me while, at the same time, I feel Raiden teasing my other hole. My body tenses initially, but there are hands everywhere, touching every part of my body in soothing strokes, and it makes my limbs relax.

I trust them, that's what I offered with that one single nod, and I'm sticking by it.

"That's it, Addi, rock back on him. We've got you," Brody murmurs, whispering his lips over mine before he tilts my head to the right. "Now be a good little alpha for your wolf and suck his cock," he adds as Cassian appears stripped bare with his cock aimed in my direction.

"Fuck." One grunted word from the wolf in question as I let my jaw fall slack, inviting him closer.

The weight of his cock on my tongue distracts from the foreign tingles that race down my spine as Raiden slips a finger into my ass. He twists, the touch so explosive that the cry from my lips burns in my chest.

Brody starts to move, his hips flexing in tandem with Cassian's as they set my body alight. Raiden's intrusion is now two fingers, scissoring me wider as perspiration clings to every inch of me.

"So fucking beautiful, Addi," Kryll states, his praise washing over me in the heated moment like a safety blanket, promising me their intentions.

"It's time, Adrianna. Tell me you're ready," Raiden rasps, but Cassian doesn't attempt to relent with his cock in my mouth for me to form a single word. Instead, they're a garbled mess around his length, and when I glare up at him, he only fucks my mouth harder. "I guess just a nod will do," Raiden grumbles, and I manage to spy him out of the corner of my eye.

I nod, nervous but desperate, as he takes my signal and lines his cock with my back entrance. I panic at the initial intrusion, struggling to breathe, when Kryll sweeps a hand through my hair, brushing the loose locks off my face.

"Push back on him again, Princess. Make him yours," he encourages as Brody's thrusts relent enough for Raiden to continue his exploration.

My breath stutters at the back of my throat, lodged in place by Cassian's cock, as Raiden finds himself fully seated in my ass. My body is on fire, my mind obliterated, and my soul is the most content it's ever felt.

It's too much and not enough all at once.

I need more.

Now.

Retreating from him, my toes curl at the sensation before I push back once again, hinting that I want him to move, and it seems to do the trick because his grip on my waist tightens in the next breath as he does just that.

He works in tandem with Brody. As one enters, the other retreats, making it impossible for me to do anything other than feel. Cassian's cock hits the back of my throat on repeat, the occasional gag reflex kicking into action as I try my best to relax my throat.

"That's it, Dagger, take us. Fucking take us," Brody chokes, his hold on my waist growing tighter as he peppers kisses along my chest or whatever inch of my skin he can get his lips on.

"She needs a hand for Kryll. We can't come without him," Cassian grunts, twisting his fingers into my hair as he nudges my head back, fucking my throat.

I sense movement, but I can't be sure; the only confirmation I have is Kryll appearing beside

Cassian a moment later with his hard cock on display, and my heart lurches in my chest.

Taking all four of them seems impossible now, but I *need* to feel all of them at once. The tingles of my orgasm firing across my skin confirms it.

"What in the monster dick is that?" Brody snaps, earning a chuckle from Kryll, who winks down at me, but my vision blurs with watery eyes at the unrelenting force of Cassian's cock.

Blindly reaching out a hand, I almost lose my balance, but Brody keeps me in place as my fingers wrap around Kryll's cock.

My heart settles, feeling all four of them at once. Thankfully, Kryll takes control, as promised, fucking my hand as I all but float between them.

"That's it, Adrianna. Come for us. The second you do, we're all going to tumble after you," Raiden breathes against my ear as he leans forward, plastering himself along my back as he continues to thrust into my ass. "You're so perfect, Troublemaker. So damn perfect, I swear," he adds, raking his teeth over my shoulder blade.

The combination of the four of them together takes it out of my hands as I combust. The ripple starts in my toes, racing up my legs and dancing through my fingertips before I shatter over Brody's cock.

Wave after wave crashes over me. I'm on the

verge of passing the fuck out. It feels so damn good, but through the sex-induced haze, I can feel Brody's thrusts stutter before he finds his release in my core. Raiden is a step behind him, his roar of ecstasy ringing in my ears as he continues to whisper sweet-nothings in my ear.

I'm prepared for the salty taste of cum on my tongue from Cassian as his thrusts become short and his moans dark and edgy, but at the last second, he pulls out, coating my exposed skin with his release.

"Paint her with me, Kryll," Cassian snarls, breathless, before I feel Kryll's cock tense beneath my touch. His release merges with Cassian's as my body goes limp, unable to withstand anything more.

I'm spent.

I'm worn.

I'm content.

"You look truly fucked."

I pry my eyes open to find Nora grinning down at me, mischief written all over her face. It takes me a second to process where I am and what she just said, but once I do, I hurry to pull the sheets tighter.

"Nora," I gasp, pushing my hair back off my face as I stare at her with wide eyes.

"What? You do," she retorts with a shrug. I'm definitely not having this conversation right now.

"That's because she is."

My jaw falls slack as my eyes widen, watching as Brody saunters into the room without a care in the world.

"Brody!" I yell, ready for the ground to open up and take me now, while all he does is smile down at me with innocent eyes.

"What?"

"Stop. Oh my—"

Laughter echoes through the room and the three of us turn to the source to find Raiden leaning against the door frame. His hair is spiked in every direction, his composure is relaxed, and he almost seems... carefree.

"Oh my days, is Fangs laughing? I didn't think he could do that," Nora states, pointing a finger at him as she grins in amusement.

I steel my spine, ready for him to be irritated with my sister's nickname for him, but to my surprise, he pays it no mind as his gaze settles on me.

"Hey." The smug look on his face should piss me off, but apparently, I'm incapable of negative emotion at the moment.

Nora takes a seat on the bed, making me inch the sheets even higher as Raiden strolls closer.

"Stop acting like you're her favorite," Brody grumbles, sticking his middle finger up at the vampire.

"But I am," he retorts, planting his hands on his hips as he gives Nora a pointed look, eager for her to correct the mage.

"He's not," Nora states, making Raiden gape in surprise.

"I'm not?" He seems genuinely shocked, while I'm genuinely confused as to why this conversation is happening right now. I'm thoroughly fucked, lying in bed after napping for who knows how long, and I need a minute to pull myself together.

"Are you forgetting the part where I used to have dead legs? *He's* my favorite," she explains, pointing over to the doorway where Kryll is standing with Cassian at his side.

"I mean, that's a little unfair. We can't all be fancy dragons with healing abilities. I'm doing the best I can with what I've got. Besides, you nicknamed me. That *has* to mean I'm the favorite," Raiden insists, fighting a point with my sister despite this being about her thoughts and opinions.

Nora stands, rolling her eyes at Raiden as she points at him. "Fangs." Her finger shifts to Brody. "Wizzy." Cassian. "Howler." Kryll. "Favorite." With far more sass than I could ever muster, she turns back to Raiden. "Does that spell it out for you?"

Raiden, for once in his life, is speechless, and it's not at my hands for a change. My sister is far too pleased with herself as she sashays out of the room without a backward glance. Only when the door clicks shut behind her does Raiden exhale. "Whatever. She's confused right now. She will change her mind," he grumbles, and I can't decide if it's aimed at us or at himself.

"I have no idea what that was, but is everyone ready to eat?" Kryll asks, clapping his hands from where he remains by the door, sensing an air of hostility from the grumpy vampire.

My stomach grumbles at that very moment, answering for me, and the five of us wordlessly get ready. Back in my fitted combat pants and tee, with my black cloak over my shoulders, I use my magic to braid my hair into a crown against my head again before I join the others.

No one speaks. No one has to. It's perfect.

The queen's laughter greets us first as we round the corner, the patio setup coming into view. Nora hurries toward me like a raging loon, blustering past Brody and Raiden unapologetically as she links her arm through mine.

"That's her," she whispers, nodding toward the table like I'm supposed to know what she's talking about.

"Who?"

"Dad's lady friend," she explains, and I accidentally draw to a stop as I take her in. Brown hair falls in a short bob, framing her face and matching eyes. She laughs along with whatever story he's telling.

I start to move but freeze once again. This time, my eyes shift to Cassian.

"What's wrong?"

"I'm..."

I'm what?

Fuck.

Shaking my head, my vision blurs as noise tingles in my ears.

"Alpha?"

I shiver at his nickname for me as I try to piece together what feels different. Something does, I just can't process it.

Swiping a hand over my face when shaking my head doesn't work, I manage to focus on the present, but I'm still left empty-handed about what I'm feeling. Cassian takes a step toward me, but I wave him off, opting to fixate on the woman seated beside my father again.

As I watch them together, I try to remember a time when my father smiled so wide or laughed so naturally, but I fall flat. Whatever my father says has the woman giggling once more, only this time she looks our way and I catch a shift in her eyes. It's only for a split second, but it was there.

"She's a dragon," I breathe, familiar with the movement in her eyes, having seen it in Kryll's before.

"She's beautiful," Nora adds, and I nod in agreement.

"It seems the rest of our guests have arrived. Come on now, I'm famished," the queen orders and we all shuffle toward the table with the same hunger vibrating through us, too.

"I'll move," the woman murmurs as we approach.

Nora takes the seat on the other side of my father, and when the woman smiles nervously at me, I know she's moving for my benefit.

"Oh, no, please, stay where you are. I'm good over here," I insist, pausing her before she stands completely. A wide smile blossoms across her face as she murmurs her appreciation while my father's megawatt smile turns my way.

Joining my guys on the other side of the table, Kryll sits the farthest away, closest to his mother, and Brody takes the spot beside him. Raiden leaves a spot, pulling the seat out and waving for me to take it as Cassian grumbles from his spot at the end.

I'm just about to mutter my thanks when my legs give out and I fall to the ground. Agony echoes in the cry that parts my lips as pain takes over my body. Every bone, every muscle, it's all throbbing with an unbearable ache.

"What's going on?" My father shouts from across the table, panic in his voice as the sound of chairs dragging across the floor echoes around me. I should be embarrassed, but the pain makes it impossible for me to worry about anything else but the torment rippling through my body.

"I don't know, I—" My words cut off as another groan bursts from my lungs. My head dips, my chin pressing against my chest as my teeth grind together. Attempting to try to breathe through it does nothing, but after a few moments, it feels as though the pain is subsiding.

"Did we break her?" Brody whisper-shouts, earning a scoff from my left, but I can't be sure if it's Cassian or Raiden.

"Don't be dumb, asshole," Raiden bites when the woman's voice cuts through the air.

"Could it be her wolf?"

My wolf? How does she know about my wolf?

Biting through the remnant ache that latches onto me like a second skin, I manage to maneuver myself so my arms are braced on my seat as I remain on my knees. I lift my head in time to see a look passing between Cassian and my father before the latter curses under his breath.

"Shit. The blood moon." He swipes a hand through his hair, frustration pouring from him as a cold cloth is suddenly placed on my neck.

I startle when I look up to see my father's 'lady friend' is the one pressing it against me. "Hi, I'm Julietta. I just want to... I don't know what I'm doing. Helping, I think, but if I'm overstepping, just—"

I shake my head, cutting her rambling off as I take a deep breath. "Hi, Julietta. Thank you," I breathe, wincing as pain floods my bones again. "I'm sorry to be rude. I'm sure there's a good conversation waiting for us, I just... what about the blood moon?" I ask, offering Julietta a tight smile before turning to look at Cassian.

"You've heard of a—"

"Of course, I've heard of a blood moon," I interrupt, irritated with my own tone and lack of composure in front of the queen, but hot damn, everything hurts. "But what does that have to do with me?"

Cassian drops to his knees, a half smile shifting on his face. "You're a wolf, remember?"

I groan again, breathing through clenched teeth as I try to suffer through it until it once again subsides enough for me to speak. "Why does it hurt?"

"The blood moon forces wolves to shift. It reminds those who don't always believe in their inner wolf that there's no escaping it."

"Are these warning pains as if I'm about to shift?" I rasp, one step away from pleading with fuck knows who to end me now and put me out of my misery.

"Basically," Julietta murmurs, a pinched smile on her lips as I sigh.

"Great."

"Are you okay?" Raiden asks, a helpless look on his face as I nod.

"I'm good."

"Are you sure?" he pushes, scrubbing the back of his neck with uncertainty as I bite back a pained sob.

"No."

"Let's get you back to the academy," Cassian declares, making me frown as I stare up at him.

"What difference is that going to make? If anything, it's going to leave me vulnerable."

"I don't know, but being here won't help. Besides, you have the four of us to protect you. No vulnerability here," he insists, a worried crinkle marking between his eyes.

"Why won't being here help?" I ask, boycotting the rest of his statement.

"The blood moon doesn't touch these lands, and these warning pains are a beacon, telling you to come home."

"Why aren't *you* getting them then? And if you say you are and I'm just overreacting to this hot mess, then you can fuck all the way off," I grumble, help- lessly aware of the mess I'm in. Again.

Now I can't even walk to the dinner table without an issue arising.

I'm a literal walking catastrophe.

"It always starts with the women, Alpha. I'll likely feel it in a few days, but never like this. Maybe heading back will help ease the pains."

"Maybe being a wolf isn't for me," I whisper, recoiling at the ache that clings to me, and he grips my chin, forcing me to meet his eyes.

"You were always meant to be a wolf, Addi. It's a

lot, you're going through more than most could even imagine, but you're right where you're supposed to be, and we're going to be right here with you every step of the way," he insists, waiting for me to nod in agreement before he turns his attention to Kryll.

"Reach out to Beau. It's time to leave."

I'm fucking up.

Majorly fucking up.

I can barely keep my leg from bouncing with agitation as I stare at the blonde curls that have slipped free from Addi's braid as they dance in the gentle breeze. Waiting for Beau is worse than waiting for my father to realize the error of his ways. Only, the latter is never going to happen.

That's not a thought for now, though. I need to be focused on Addi. She needs me now more than ever and I'm letting her down. She's barely been connected to her wolf for twenty-four hours and I'm not aiding with the transition. Not enough to make a difference. That fact is clear as she braces her elbows on her knees, failing to bite back another wince of pain as she folds in on herself.

My jaw tics, irritation clawing its way through

me as I shake my head. We really don't have time to wait for Beau. Brody could use his mage abilities and transport us anywhere in the Floodborn Kingdom, but my damn Alpha insists on waiting him out.

I get why it makes sense, but that doesn't mean I have to like it. Not when the corners of her eyes crinkle with discomfort. It's *my* fault for not considering the blood moon. It's *my* fault for not putting her wolf first. It's *my* fault for being swept up in the moment and not considering the adjustment this actually means for her.

Nobody considered my needs when I shifted for the first time, and I'm letting history repeat itself with her. Thinking back to my first time shifting, my gut twists. It wasn't in a damn public bathroom with some asshole's cum inside me and the weight of the kingdom hanging in the balance.

Yet, it still felt tainted.

Pain weighs heavy on my chest. Panic rings in my ears. A whimper bursts from my lips as I fight like hell not to drop to my knees. My vision blurs with unshed tears as I stumble down the stairs, tripping over myself at the last step, but with some grace of a miracle, I manage to catch myself before I face plant on the floor.

My teeth chatter as if I'm cold to the bone, but there's a burning inferno creeping up my spine, threatening to take hold of me.

I need air, and I need it now.

Determined, and fighting against the pain, I manage to make it to the front door, yanking it open with a groan that takes root deep in my gut. The second the cool night air surrounds me, I hope it will calm the rage inside of me, but it does little to appease the anguish tormenting me.

I stagger beneath the dark night sky and my jaw slacks as I gape up at the moon that shimmers from the other side of the tree line. Heat continues to curl through my veins, my breaths falling harsher and shallower with every pass, when the pain ricocheting through my bones reaches new heights.

The fall is inevitable. It happens so fast, I don't know whether the ground rushes up to my palms or I race to it, but regardless, the sharp pain against my hands is short-lived when the sound of bones cracking thunders in my ears.

A roar heats my chest as excruciating pain claims me, and all I can do is pray that death greets me sooner rather than later.

Unfortunately, it seems death isn't ready for me yet.

It feels like forever, my throat hoarse with broken sobs until the pain that echoes through my limbs finally begins to subside. When I dare to blink my eyes open, it's to find myself curled up in a ball. But the fetal position isn't made up of a tangle of arms and legs. No. It's made up of paws and fur and... holy crap.

I'm a wolf.

My heart races as the thunder sings in my ears and I stare at myself.

I've been waiting for this day since the first time I saw someone shift right before my very eyes, and now it's finally here.

On nervous legs, I rise, feeling the mud beneath my paws as I take my first true breath as a wolf.

"Cassian? Is that you?" My head moves so fast I'm shocked I don't snap my own neck as I turn to find Janie a few steps away. A soft smile tips the corner of her lips up as she assesses me before dropping to her knees. "It's okay, Cass. I'm right here."

Her soothing words calm the nerves that tingle from head to toe, fueling the excitement and hope that simmers in my gut instead.

I take a step toward her, then another, and another, until she's close enough to reach for me. The first brush of her fingers in my coat makes me shiver, and her smile grows as she watches me.

"I know it's going to be a lot right now, Cass, but it's okay. Everything is absolutely okay, and anything that may feel weird or strange is highly likely to be okay too. You're beautiful, by the way," she adds, booping me on the nose, and I shake my head, which only makes her snicker at me. "Do you want to—"

"Cassian." The bark from my father's lips cuts off whatever she was about to offer. Her shoulders slump and her eyebrows pinch. Thankfully, her back is to my father, who looms a few feet away, so he doesn't see her reaction to his arrival. My father's judgemental gaze sweeps over me before he nods. "It's about time, Son. Now, come."

"What are you little shitheads doing?"

I startle at the sound of Beau's voice, instinct lurching me to my feet, but the quick realization that we're not in danger calms me as I swipe a hand down my face.

Fuck.

Shaking my head, I sense eyes on me, but I fight past it as I try to clear my thoughts. A trip down memory lane is not what I'm looking for, nor will it ever be. Thankfully, Beau interrupted my thoughts before they could get any worse.

I shifted alone, but the lack of care from my father's end and the things he put me through afterward will forever torture my soul. Memories of those times are meant to be buried deep.

Everyone starts moving around me, shuffling to leave and speaking softly as Beau hugs his mother, but I can't settle on anything. My brain is too wired.

"Are you ready?" Beau asks the group, earning a round of yeses from everyone as I immediately shake my head. My shoulders stiffen, the muscles bunching in pain as Adrianna clocks my discomfort first.

"We can't go back to campus, not yet," I blurt, eyes boring into hers as she frowns.

"What do you mean? This was your idea to head back," Raiden grunts, folding his arms in irritation as he glares at me.

"Fuck, I know that, but..." Fuck. If I'm going to even attempt to explain, then I need to piece it together for myself first, but that doesn't seem possible right now. "I mean, Addi needs a minute to learn her wolf, on Floodborn ground, but not at the academy," I state, hoping like hell that it makes sense.

Even if it does, Beau shakes his head at me. "You've been gone long enough."

"She needs a little more time," I bite, anger rearing its ugly head as my hands ball into fists at my sides.

"What's going on, Cassian?" Addi murmurs, inching closer to me despite the pain I know she's in, and I feel like a total ass, but I just need to appeal to her and she'll understand.

Gulping, I attempt the best deep breath I can muster before I reach for her hand. "I need to take you to Janie."

"To Janie?" she repeats in confusion, and I nod. She raises her eyebrows in question, but when nothing immediately comes out, she pushes for more.

"I can't figure out why unless you explain it to me." Her words are soft despite her pain, and I take a little strength from that as I turn to Beau.

"Are you Beau, Kryll's older brother, right now, or are you Professor Tora?"

He frowns but stands taller. "Beau, always Beau first," he insists, and I peer at Kryll, needing a nod from him before I go any further. I get it instantly, and the flicker in Kryll's eyes tells me he has a sense of where I'm going with this.

Clearing my throat, my hand tightens on Addi's. "I was never given the chance to connect with my wolf after my first shift, but you have that chance."

Addi blinks up at me, but it's Beau who speaks. "Wolf? You lifted the spell?"

Ignoring his need for confirmation, I look deeper into Addi's eyes. "You're not going to get a moment on campus, and the head of the wolf origin isn't going to be of any use either," I insist, the need to get her to Janie only growing stronger with every passing second.

"So you want to take her to Janie?" Brody asks, his head tilted as he stares at me, and I nod.

"I don't want to. We *have* to."

"Don't make me regret this." A handful of words, but Beau's threat is clear. Even if it's not aimed at me, I sense it. I'm trying my best not to freak the fuck out over the fact that I can hear him clearly, despite him standing a good few yards away whispering with Kryll.

Since everything has started to spiral and pain aches throughout my body, I know this is all part of being a wolf. It's overwhelming but euphoric all at once, and I'm slightly obsessed.

Should I be listening in? Probably not, but it's not my fault. It's new magic and I don't know what I'm doing. That's my excuse, at least.

"We won't," Kryll promises, which makes Professor Tora snicker.

"Why do I get the feeling you will?" I can even

picture his raised eyebrow as he stares his brother down, but I can't see it for sure from here.

"Because you're an ass," Kryll grumbles, shoving at him like the situation is more casual than it actually is, but I'm not getting involved. If Cassian's gut is telling him I need to see Janie, then I trust him on it. He was lost in his head before Beau showed up, his face scrunched in distaste, so now I'm here for the ride.

I expect them to trod back over to us, but something makes Kryll pause, reaching for his brother's arm before he can take a single step. "You knew about the spell?"

I freeze, the question catching me off guard when I realize it's about me but not aimed at me.

"Honestly, I assumed. Her mother is a wolf, of course," Beau answers calmly, but there's something beneath the surface that I can't quite decipher with the aches still trembling through my bones.

"That's all?"

"That's all. Have I ever given you reason not to trust me before, brother?"

Ah, there it is. Beau's not used to Kryll questioning him, it seems.

"No, but I've also never had someone like her to protect," Kryll states, all matter-of-factly, as I hide my face in my hands, willing the heat from my cheeks to disappear.

A beat passes between them and I pry my fingers open to peer through the slits at them. I find them both in a stare off. "Something tells me she's set on protecting you too," Beau finally says, squeezing his brother's shoulder in comfort before he marches toward the rest of us with purpose.

The queen has gone, my father, sister, and Julietta along with her. The goodbyes were quick this time, my pain and discomfort causing a new level of urgency that smothered the idea of long, lingering farewells.

"Let's go," Beau orders, snapping his fingers at Brody, who rushes into action.

My stomach tightens, and we're moving. I'm not sure if my insides have been left where I was sitting a moment ago or if they're going to spill out at my feet any time now, but one thing is for sure: the aching in my bones dwindles to nothing more than a cramp.

"Holy shit," I breathe, keeling over with relief as I plant my hands on my knees and take a few deep breaths. I never thought I'd feel that tingling in my chest again.

"Are you okay?" Raiden asks, his polished shoes coming into view first, before I slowly tilt my head back to stare at him.

"Is it too soon to confirm I feel like a new woman?" I ask, attempting a smile, but it falls flat.

Pain still weighs heavy on my limbs, despite the immediate throbbing dissipating.

"Technically, you are a new woman, Trouble-maker. A new animal and species, if we're being accurate," he rattles off, earning a pointed look as I shake my head at him. Amusement dances in his eyes, but it's a relieved sigh that falls from his lips as he strokes a hand down my back. "Truthfully, you already look better. The color in your cheeks is back and your eyes have their usual sparkle," he offers, winking at me as I stand tall again.

"Oh, he's got sweet-talking going for him now; who knew?" Brody muses, wagging a finger at Raiden, who offers him a two-finger salute in response. Kryll snickers in amusement as Cassian grunts, rolling his eyes in irritation.

"Wait here," the wolf grumbles before disappearing through the tree line, and I quickly realize we're at Janie's restaurant.

I rub my lips together nervously as I stare at the space that sits between me and the building, the same one that seems to have changed my life forever. It's exactly where I was standing the first time I was called out and challenged to a duel. A duel I wanted nothing to do with. A *wolf* I wanted even less to do with and a stupid bitch calling for my head, all for what?

At the time, it felt like a huge inconvenience, but

now? Now I know it was a pinnacle moment, one we haven't turned back from since.

Before I can ponder any more on the matter, Cassian comes rushing out of the building in a blur with another figure at his side. When they halt in front of us, I smile at the appearance of Janie.

Her brown hair is swept back in a low ponytail and her black and red plaid shirt is unbuttoned, revealing a white tank top underneath.

"Hey, Warrior."

"Warrior?" I repeat, the question clear as she grins at me, but her eyes meet Cassian's.

"Sorry, inside joke."

"Amusing," I breathe, unsure how I feel about it, but the fact that there's no hostility lingering in the air sets me at ease.

"He is, isn't he," she retorts, turning back to me with a shit-eating grin that I match with one of my own. Cassian grumbles under his breath, but she ignores him as she takes a step toward me. "I hear my expertise is needed."

"I didn't say expertise," Cassian barks, rolling his eyes at her dramatics, and she shrugs.

"You didn't have to." The power play between them is hilarious and completely reminds me of Nora. Just like Janie, she's the one with all of the power. "Why don't you guys head inside? Jake will feed you all," Janie offers, waving for them all to head toward the restaurant, but Raiden scoffs, wrapping his arm around my shoulders as he levels Janie with a stare.

"I'm not leaving you alone with her."

"Why?" The perplexed look on Janie's face makes it clear she has no idea what his issue is.

"*He* could show up."

One generic word, two letters, and my spine stiffens. It's clear who *he* is. No further introductions are necessary.

"I understand your concern, but he hasn't shown his face in days. Not since the trial that was supposed to be aired to the kingdom was abruptly canceled. Nice speech, by the way," she adds, grinning at me, and I blush.

"Thanks," I murmur, caught by surprise that the trial was public to the outside world, only a surprise to us, and more shocked by the fact that Bozzelli still pulled it.

Damn.

"You can fuck off now, Cassian. Take these assholes with you," she states, offering a sterner look this time.

To my surprise, Raiden presses his lips to my temple before taking a step toward the others. The four of them sulk off without a single word, which is more amusing than anything, but Brody pauses as he reaches the door, eyebrows drawn tight as he looks me over.

"I'm good. Save me a steak," I say, and he winks, the tension easing from his frame.

"That's my girl."

"She's *our* girl," Kryll retorts, glaring at the mage in question, who doesn't relent.

"But she's *my* Dagger," he insists, earning a shove from Raiden.

"Shut up, Brody," the vampire snaps before they all disappear inside.

I stare at the empty space, certain one of them is going to come barreling out at any moment, but nothing happens.

"So, a fae wolf, huh?" Janie murmurs, cutting through my thoughts, and I nod.

"Apparently."

"How is that going for you?" she asks, eyebrow cocked as I shrug.

"Not so good." It's the truth. I don't know whether she deserves it, but if Cassian trusts her, then I have to as well.

"Cassian mentioned something about pains from being away from the blood moon?"

I rub my lips together nervously as I nod again. "Apparently."

"Hurt like a bitch?" she questions, and I scoff.

The little tension clinging to my stance that I hadn't realized still resonated is gone.

"That feels like an understatement," I admit, earning a half smile from her.

"Accurate." She takes her eyes off me, looking out into the darkness for a beat before she looks back at me. "Do you feel any better since getting here?"

"So much," I admit with a sigh, and she nods.

"Good. Usually, it's just a trembling in your veins until the moon peaks and you shift, so hopefully now you won't endure much else," she explains before she suddenly starts waving her hand at me. "Oh, oh, let me guess your color."

"My color?" I repeat with a frown, and her grin grows wider.

"Your fur," she offers as she slowly walks in a small circle around me. I'm rooted to the spot, my pulse ringing in my ears. I can't figure out why, but I think it's because I'm nervous that she's judging my wolf, and no one is allowed to do that. Ever. "Hmm, I'm going to have to go with white," she declares as she comes to a stop in front of me, and all I can do is gape at her in response.

"How did you guess that?"

She shrugs. "I'm awesome, I can't help it."

This time it's my smile that takes over. I can see why Cassian trusts her, and the closeness I feel between them only intensifies with the knowledge. I can also see a few similar traits between them, like all the time they've spent together has strengthened their bond to make them a true family, thus, they've taken similar traits from one another. It warms my heart knowing Cassian had someone here among all the madness.

"So, you've shifted, dealt with the intense pain and all that, but have you tested out your speed, hearing, and new scent abilities?" she asks, leaving me to gape at her once again when I can't find the strength to say no. She shakes her head with a humoring smile. "I'll take your silence as a no."

Clearing my throat, I give her a playful pout. "I'm that obvious, huh?"

"No, you're new, but we've already established you're a warrior, so you're going to catch on quick," she promises, linking my arm like Flora does as she walks me deeper into the forest area.

"I hope so."

"I know so," she retorts, the promise clear, and I shake the nerves threatening to consume me.

"What now?" I ask when I'm certain I'm ready for whatever she's going to throw at me.

"Now, we have some fun."

"Hey! You're not supposed to be faster than me," Janie exclaims as we both come to a stop outside her restaurant. A grin spreads across my face, excitement blossoming in my gut when I don't feel remotely out of breath.

"What can I say? Beginner's luck?"

Janie rolls her eyes at me as she shoves at my shoulder. "Fuck off, we both know it's not that. Unfortunately for me," she grumbles, making me snicker as her playfulness turns into another arm link as she sighs. "For real, though, that was some awesome shit. Your speed is amazing, and your hearing and sense of smell are on par, too. You're rocking it," she insists, validating me in ways I didn't even know I needed.

"The speed is blowing my mind," I admit, squeezing her arm in a wordless thank you for her help. "When Cassian used his speed to move me, I always wound up trying to hold back a mouthful of vomit by the time we stopped, but now that I'm the one in control of it; it's slightly addicting."

Laughter echoes around us at my admission when words cut through the air, making us pause.

"Having fun?"

I whip my gaze around to find Cassian leaning against the tree to my left. He looks too freaking hot with his shoulder flat against the bark and his legs crossed at the ankle.

"No, I hate her. That's why I'm laughing," Janie says with a snort, earning an eye roll from the man in question.

"Very funny."

"I know," she preens, tugging me along toward him. When it's clear she's not naturally letting go, Cassian cocks a brow at her.

"Can I steal her back now?"

Her grip tightens playfully, but before they can get more into it, a worrying thought falls heavy on my chest.

"Where are the others?"

Cassian sighs, scrubbing the back of his neck nervously. "Beau arrived."

"Beau?" I repeat dumbly, and he nods.

"Yeah, said his white lie was enough to keep the two of us here for the night, but not the others." He says it all calmly, like there's no reason to worry, but I've learned there's always a reason to be concerned.

"Are they going to be okay?"

A smirk dances over his lips as his eyes narrow in on mine. "They might die of jealousy from the night I get alone with you, but otherwise, I'm sure they'll survive."

Janie's hold on my arm relents as she shoves at me, pushing me toward Cassian. "Ew, the pair of you go. I can smell the pheromones from here," she mutters, winking when I glance back at her.

"Janie," Cassian grunts and a burst of laughter parts my lips.

"What? It's true," she insists, heading back toward the restaurant without a single glance over her shoulder.

"I think we've been dismissed."

"I think you're right," I agree, still riding the high from spending a few hours with the crazy woman.

"It's a good thing I got your steak to go then, isn't it?" he states, lifting a paper bag off the ground, and my eyes widen with excitement.

"You're amazing, thank you."

Wordlessly, he takes my hand with his other before guiding me through the trees. He doesn't try to use his speed or question me on mine. Instead, he seems content to stroll through the darkness.

"Where are we supposed to stay?" I ask after a

while, and even though only the moon lights the sky, I see the apprehension in his gaze.

"In my old unit."

Uncertainty twists in my gut. "Is that going to be safe?"

His lips purse for a beat before he nods firmly. "It's the safest place here. I had Brody weave so much magic around it that it's impossible for anyone but us to get in. Which is exactly why it stands untouched," he explains, waving the paper bag in the direction of a small building barely noticeable in the darkness.

I can't tell if it remains as untouched as he says, but he doesn't falter as we near the property. It's a two-story unit with a few windows dotted around the place, but in such low light, I can't make much else out.

He releases my hand to grab the door handle, and I watch in awe as a fizzle of magic dances around his fingers at the connection before the lock clicks open. He waves for me to step inside first, turning the light on as he follows me in, and I take a moment to get familiar with my surroundings.

A small wooden dining table sits to my left, surrounded by a few kitchen cupboards and appliances, while a black leather sofa faces a television to my right. The staircase is against the far wall, breaking up the space as I assume it leads to the bedroom and bathroom.

"It's surprisingly... cozy," I admit, following Cassian toward the dining table as he grins.

"Maybe. It used to be the unit where women would stay in when in heat, but my father decided it was better suited for me."

I can't tell if that fact makes him happy or not, and even though I've been a wolf for all of two minutes, I'm aware of female wolves being in heat and what that can mean. If these walls could talk, I can't imagine how much sex they would recall. I quickly shut the thought down when I consider the fact that Cassian could have had sex here too.

Fuck, who am I kidding? He definitely did.

"What are you thinking so hard about that you're letting your steak go cold?" he asks, breaking my train of thought.

I shake my head, cutting the distance between us as I take the seat he pulled out for me. "Nothing important," I mutter when he continues to stare at me. A stare that only intensifies when that's all I give him, but instead of admitting the little green monster that's perched on my shoulder, I opt to stuff a piece of steak in my mouth before I can make a fool of myself.

Thankfully, he seems to let it slip, getting

comfortable in the chair across from me as I enjoy the best steak of my life.

Sorry, Pearl.

When I can't fit anything else in my mouth, I fall back in my seat, staring around the space again. "This is a full house."

"Yeah."

"How long have you had a whole ass house?" I ask, acutely aware that it's definitely bigger than the home I shared with my father and Nora.

"Since the first day I shifted."

His answer catches me off-guard, leaving me to gape at him before I remember myself. I have to clear my throat before I can speak, which only seems to amuse him. "How old were you?"

"Not old enough." His gaze drops as my frown tightens.

I want to go back to whenever that was and make him feel better, but that's not possible. All I can do now is be what he needs going forward.

"That's insane," I mumble, unsure what else to say, and a sad smile tilts the corner of his mouth.

"That's my father."

"I didn't think it was possible to hate him any more than I already do," I grunt, and he snickers.

"It's always possible."

"Things in this life I didn't believe could be

possible are," I blurt, hating the words as soon as they leave my mouth.

"Such as?" he asks, intrigued, and I shake my head.

"Nothing."

"Don't go shy on me now, Alpha." He leans across the table, sliding my empty plate aside as he captures my hand in his.

Rolling my eyes, I avoid his deep stare. "Sweet words and deep thoughts aren't really what we do."

Silence descends around us, stretching into uncomfortable territory before he speaks. "Why's that?" My gaze flicks to his, but when I don't immediately answer, he cocks a brow at me. "Why?" he repeats, keeping hold of my hand as he rises from his seat, edging around the dining table until he's right beside me. He lifts me to my feet so we're toe to toe, then reaches for my chin with his free hand, forcing my eyes to his.

"You cup my pussy, we fuck," I stumble, the truth tasting like lead on my tongue as his gaze narrows.

"Is that all this is to you?"

"No," I quickly answer, panic flickering through my body, but he seems to believe me.

"But you think that's all this is to me?" he finally mutters, tilting his head as he takes me in, and all I can do is shrug.

Is it specifically what I think this is to him? Maybe? No... I don't know, but we really don't do sweet words and deep thoughts, so I actually have no damn clue.

To drive my point home, he keeps his fingers molded around my chin, holding me in place as he releases my hand with the other, swiftly moving to cup my pussy.

"I can cup your sweet pussy and still talk deep with you, Adrianna," he rasps, sending a shiver down my spine as I gape up at him.

"Adrianna, huh?" I breathe, acutely aware that my full name has never fallen from his lips. Not in my presence, at least, and definitely not aimed at me.

"It seems I need to be clear about a few things with you, and that's absolutely fine by me," he states, tightening his hold on my pussy as his thumb presses harder into my chin. "When I make you admit you're mine, when I take everything you have to offer, and when I challenge you at every turn, it comes from a place deep inside me that *I* didn't even know existed."

His words steal my breath, but the natural need to hide behind humor kicks in. "Your di—"

"Don't say my dick and ruin my wholesome speech, Alpha," he interjects with a knowing glint in his eyes, and I grin.

He knows me better than I can bring myself to admit.

Inching in closer so our breaths mingle between us, he continues. "I fucking love your humor, your secret smiles, your mind, your body… everything, but more than that, I'm obsessed with learning everything possible. And the excitement of exploring you will forever leave me at your mercy. I want to know every part of you, inside and out. With my mind, my body, my everything."

Holy fuck.

"Cass—" I croak, emotions clogging in my throat as I blink up at him, but he presses a finger to my lips, halting me from breathing another word.

"Not yet." A softness settles in his eyes as he presses a kiss to my forehead. But just as quickly as he does it, he retreats, fixating on my eyes once again. "I left my compound before I even knew you existed, but I know it was for you. I know we're nowhere near done on this crazy spiral that is apparently called life, but I know I'm on the right path with you."

How am I even supposed to consider an appropriate response to that? How am I ever supposed to express a single thing after that?

"You sound smitten," I mutter, at a loss for anything else, and the grin that spreads across his face is like nothing I've ever seen from him before.

"I fucking am, but don't use that humor of yours to mask the beauty that rests between us."

Well, damn. Apparently, he's more than a grumpy face and hot body after all. He's everything and more and I don't know how to comprehend it. What I know for sure is he's here with me, for me, and I know I couldn't do this without him.

Words betray me once again as I lift my hand to cup his cheek. "You're a handful."

"Maybe, but as long as I'm yours and you're mine, I don't care."

Morning sun peers through the window as contentment clings to me. I can't believe I can openly admit that Cassian was right, but he was. I needed this. More than he'll ever know. With Janie's help, I'm at peace with my wolf while honing in on my fae abilities, too. To be around another wolf, a female one no less, who withholds judgment and any other bullshit, and instead purposely helps to make me comfortable in my own skin is a rare gift.

With my new abilities, I can hear the fluttering of Cassian's heartbeat from where he lays beside me. His rich, woodsy scent lingers in my nose as my pulse quickens with every passing breath.

Last night was... weirdly special.

I couldn't find a single word last night that compared to what he offered me, and eventually, I gave up trying. It was pointless. I'll know the words when they're there, and they will be, just not when I'm so swept away by him.

For the first time last night, he cupped my pussy and didn't fuck me. Instead, he penetrated me with heartfelt words I wasn't expecting as opposed to his dick. Words that settled any concerns as his eyes bore into mine.

With a full stomach and a full heart, I showered before we slipped beneath the crisp sheets on his bed, and I got to witness the affection of a touchy-feely wolf while having the same need coursing through my veins.

I spent the night pinned along the length of him from head to toe, reveling in our connection as he draped me in his heat. If he moved, so did I. If I moved, he did the same. Instead of blustering under his warmth, I was enthralled by it.

I'm enthralled by him, just as I am with Kryll, Raiden, and Brody. Accepting it more and more every day is both a blessing and a distracting curse, but it's worth it nonetheless.

"How long have you been awake?" His question catches me off-guard as I peer at him. His eyes are shut, but I can sense the slight change in the sound of his heartbeat confirming he's awake.

"How do you know I am with your eyes shut?" I

push back, a soft smile curling the corner of my mouth as I stare at him.

"Because I can hear the cogs turning in your head from over here." *Ass.* His eyes open and he takes me in, cocking a brow a moment later. "What are you thinking about?"

I consider brushing him off, but really, it's futile. Instead, I sigh. "I've just been thinking about the changes I feel."

"Yeah?"

"Yeah."

He seems surprised at the truth sliding from my mouth so easily, but a hint of caution flashes in his eyes. "Good changes?"

I scoff. "They better be because I'm stuck with them whether I like it or not," I retort, earning a half smile before a serious look washes over his features, and he shuffles us around until we're lying side by side, face to face.

"None of it changes who *you* are as a person."

I nod. "I know, I think that's what I'm realizing. None of the changes are about my character," I admit, and a sense of relief washes over him.

"Good, because I kind of like your character," he states, pressing the softest kiss to the corner of my mouth.

"You do?"

His eyes latch onto mine. "Not as much as your pussy but…"

A giggle rises from my stomach, swirling in the air around us as he throws the covers back. A deep rumble from his chest vibrates against the palm of my hand as I keep my skin against his. He doesn't go far, though. The only adjustment he makes is so he's nestled between my thighs.

Desire mingles with excitement, swirling through my body on a mission as the length of his cock presses against my pussy. My heart flutters in my chest as I skim my fingertips over his abs when a distant knock echoes from downstairs.

Fuck.

"Please tell me I didn't hear that," I murmur, already disappointed when Cassian's head lulls with the same frustration.

"I wish."

"Any chance of ignoring it?" I query, but I already know the answer.

"If someone knows to knock, then—"

"I get it," I interject, aware that we're technically on enemy territory, so any noise or movement around the house needs to be taken seriously.

Something tells me it isn't Kenner, though. No way in Hell would that fucker knock.

"Want to race to see who can get dressed quickest?" Cassian asks, a glint in his eyes that sets me alight with the offered challenge.

"You're on," I agree, connecting with my wolf and zipping into action.

All but my boots are on my feet when I lift my hands in the air with glee. "I win!"

A knowing look flickers across Cassian's face, making me pause when he stuffs his hand into his jeans pocket. He's dressed from head to toe, boots included, but that's not what he speaks about when he opens his mouth. "Not when I have your panties in my pocket, Alpha."

My gaze narrows. "Ass. Race you down—"

My words haven't even left my mouth before he's gone.

Fucker.

With my lips pursed and irritation dancing over my skin, I refuse to admit I'm a sore loser and focus on my boots instead. I hear the door creak open downstairs as I lace them up, and the curse that falls from Cassian's lips makes me pause.

Uncertainty washes over me as I creep down the stairs as quietly as I can, and a hint of panic travels down my spine when I hear him bark.

"Leave."

"I can't," the voice is familiar, too familiar.

"I won't warn you again," Cassian threatens as I

reach the bottom step, but the next words make me falter.

"He knows you're here. I'm trying to help."

"Help? You? I don't—"

I step up to Cassian's side, cutting off his tirade as my gaze locks on eyes similar to mine.

"Mother."

FIFTEEN

ADRIANNA

"You need to leave," my mother blurts, not actually acknowledging me in any way.

"No, *you* need to leave," Cassian snarls, his knuckles turning white as he grips the door.

My head snaps between them, watching as anger vibrates between them, and I inch closer to my wolf.

"You don't understand," she persists, waving her arms at her sides. She's clearly frustrated. She was full of emotions the last time I saw her too, when she was waiting for me outside of the fae building on campus. Only that time, Kenner wasn't too far behind her, and I was left injured as she fled.

"You're damn right I don't understand, but if you continue to put Addi in danger, at my father's mercy, then you'll leave me no choice." Cassian's rage is so powerful I feel it surge through my thoughts and limbs, reminding me of all the things this woman has done to hurt me. Not just me, but Nora and our father too.

My mother pauses, her gaze fixating on Cassian as his warning hangs heavy in the air. "No choice for what?" she asks, nostrils flaring with irritation, like there's no reason for us to doubt her.

"For the actions I'll have to take." I still at his warning, my mind tingling with caution as his muscles bunch together with anticipation.

"Which are?"

"Do you really need me to spell it out?" he rasps, a deathly darkness tinging his words.

"Can we *not* do this right now?" I murmur, unsure what I'm trying to stop and whether I even want to, but she's clearly here for a reason, and her presence is a distraction in itself.

My mother offers the smallest smile my way before she takes a step back. "You can hate me later, but if it makes you feel any better, I already hate myself twenty-four-seven, and it's enough to match the hatred of the entire kingdom." Her words are sincere, which makes me pause, but it doesn't seem to affect Cassian in the slightest.

"Are you sure about that? You didn't look all regretful and pained when we spied you getting cozy with Dalton like you didn't leave a trail of disaster in your wake." The venom in his words is palpable now.

"Me and Dalton?" My mother questions, lifting a hand to her chest as her eyebrows gather.

"It doesn't matter, let's get to the point of why you're here," I interrupt, refusing to have this conversation with her now, maybe ever.

"If she's trying to play a sob story, and we're supposed to believe her right now, then we sure as fuck can call her out when her words don't match her actions," Cassian grinds out, irritation flashing in his eyes when he turns to look at me, but the emotion isn't aimed at me. I hope.

"Is this because of your mother?" my mother asks, turning Cassian to stone as his jaw tics and his pupils widen.

"What does my mother have to do with any of this?"

I try to recall any time he's ever mentioned his mother, but I come up blank. What the fuck does she mean? "Cass—"

My words are cut off by the sound of shuffling in the distance, and the three of us whip our gazes to the right, following the sound.

"So it's true, the runt and his bitch are on my land. It doesn't quite explain why you're here, though, Constantine…?" Kenner inches toward us, a little more disheveled than usual, as his gaze narrows on my mother.

I spy a flash of panic in her eyes before she tamps it down, turning to face him fully.

"I wanted to see with my own eyes," she offers, rolling her shoulders back in defiance.

"See what?" he questions, edging closer as he stares her down.

"That they dared be here."

Kenner tilts his head at her, amusement dancing over his lips as he waves her closer to him. "Are you as intrigued as I am?"

"Always," she answers swiftly, not a single pause to be heard, but that's not the truth at all. That's not what she was saying moments ago, or was that part the lie?

Fuck.

What is going on?

"We're leaving now," Cassian states, his voice calm and unfazed, a complete contrast to moments ago.

The withering glare from Kenner confirms his next words before his lips part. "You're going nowhere."

Cassian pinches his nose, exhaling harshly as he tries to rid the agitation from his bones. "We can't keep doing this."

"You're right," Kenner states, making us pause as we stare at him.

That's a surprise.

"Good," Cassian breathes, uncertainty still clinging to him, which is completely valid when his father speaks again.

"Trinity." He calls out the name, and in a flash, the sound of more racing hearts rings in my ear. My senses are overwhelmed as more wolves appear. One, then another, and another, until there's a mini army of them surrounding the unit.

"What is this?" I ask, finally finding my tongue, and his devilish eyes land on mine for a brief moment before he spins on the spot, addressing the new arrivals along with me.

"This is a duel under the blood moon."

Cassian's sharp intake of breath sets panic in my veins. "Father."

"Say it, Trinity," Kenner insists, nudging a girl forward a step.

Her wild eyes find mine before searching Cassian's, but all too quickly, she latches back on to me. She clears her throat, taking a step toward us, and this time the confidence drifts off her in waves.

I know what she's going to say before her lips part. They're words I've heard before, too many times for my preference, but words I'm all too familiar with now. I thought I was done after the first duel. I thought I was done when Cassian dueled. I thought we were past all this shit.

I thought wrong.

"I challenge you, Adrianna Reagan. I challenge you to a blood moon duel for Cassian Kenner."

SIXTEEN

ADRIANNA

This motherfucker is never going to relent. Ever. I'm all for showing resilience, but damn, I'm tired of this man.

"No one is dueling anyone under the blood moon," Cassian snarls, his eyes practically black as he stares his father down.

My lips twist as I take him in, his words swirling around in my head. The way he says it makes me feel like there's more to it than usual. A kind of more that I'm not going to like the sound of.

"My challenge says otherwise," Trinity sings, her voice tainted with vengeance, and I can't help but wonder what the fuck I've done to this girl, what I've done to any of the girls that have challenged me to a duel. My lack of answer makes me feel like it's more because I'm simply breathing and it's inconveniencing them. "Now, stand there and watch as I take down this bitch to claim you for myself," she adds, making my head rear back in surprise.

"Don't you think it's weird that you're trying to fight me for him, yet you show him no respect at all? He's not just a piece of meat, you know. There's more to him than whatever title you're seeking," I bite out through clenched teeth.

"Fuck off, fae," she snaps back, but before I can even react, Kenner's all-out belly laugh echoes around us.

"Ah, but that's not the case, is it, Adrianna?"

My gaze whips to his, my chest tightening with nerves as realization washes over me.

Fuck

I sense my mother's eyes on me, but I don't pull away from Kenner's stare. I'm frozen to the bone. "What don't I know, Kenner?" Her voice is riddled with a tinge of nerves and uncertainty, and I see the amusement in Kenner's darkening eyes.

"I'll let your daughter fill you in. It's quite fantastic if you ask me," Kenner muses, making my nostrils flare with agitation.

"Addi." Concern fills my mother's voice, and I can see her shifting from foot to foot as she waits for my response, but I can't tear my eyes from Kenner.

"Don't speak to her. Crawl back under the rock

where you came from, and you, fuck off," Cassian roars, jabbing his finger in both my mother's and his father's direction.

Kenner laughs, the sound laced with carnage as he steps toward Trinity, inching closer to the house. "Now, now, Son. We're here for fun, and Trinity is waiting," he explains, redirecting the topic and giving me whiplash.

"Trinity can fuck off," Cassian sneers, but I need an answer to the unease settling in my gut.

"What's the difference with it being the blood moon?" I finally manage to shift my gaze from Kenner, taking in Cassian's taut frame as his jaw tics.

"We'll get to that, Pet," Kenner answers, making Cassian's eyes practically glow as he bares his teeth.

"She. Is. Not. Your. Pet."

"What don't I know, Kenner?" My mother interjects, and my brain buzzes from all the different layers of the conversation.

This is all too much.

"I'm a wolf," I yell, sending my mother's gaze my way as her jaw falls slack.

"A wolf?" she repeats, the surprise clear across her features as I sigh.

"Isn't it exceptional?" Kenner adds, with way too much fucking glee in his tone.

"Addi." My name falls from my mother's lips

once again as she steps toward me, but Cassian quickly moves to block me from her view.

"Stay away from her," he warns, anger radiating from him as Kenner continues to enjoy the spectacle.

"I'm sure it will make this duel even more exciting, don't you think?"

I didn't think it was possible, but Cassian stiffens, his muscles bunching even tighter as his head whips to his father. "Was this your plan? Push her to unlock her wolf to force her into a duel beneath the blood moon?"

I take a step back, blinking at the back of his head as I try to process what he's actually saying.

"Someone needs to catch me up. *Now*."

Cassian's head dips as he turns to me, a sigh parting his lips as he brings his eyes to mine. "A blood moon duel has to be between wolves, in wolf form, and you fight to the death."

How does Kenner always stay one step ahead? Why am I struggling at the hands of this man time and time again? He's insane. Completely certifiable. I don't know what his issue is with me, but we need to wrap this up. I've had enough.

I step to the side, revealing myself to the others again, only to find Kenner shaking his head at Cassian's words. "Why would I do that when I need her for greater things?"

Greater things? Fuck off.

"You tell me," Cassian goads, hoping to get some kind of answer. But it goes unanswered as Kenner takes a step back, joining the mass of the spectating wolves as a wicked grin spreads across his face.

"Are we going to cut to the duel now? There's an audience waiting."

"They can fuck off," Cassian barks, clenching his fists at his sides as his father's grin only widens.

"That's not how this works, Son."

"I promise you, if you do this, I won't be responsible for my actions," Cassian promises, and my thighs clench. This is definitely not the time to be getting all hot and flustered over his delicious anger.

Instead of taking the threat for what it's worth, Kenner beams. "Now, that sounds like something a son of mine would say."

The distaste is apparent on Cassian's face, which sets me into action. It's time to put all this shit to rest. I squeeze his arm in what I hope comes across as comfort before I sidestep him and head toward Trinity.

I don't feel it, but the intake of breath that comes from behind me confirms I've slipped through whatever protection Cassian had in place.

"Addi," he breathes, despair etched into every letter as I stare down Trinity.

"I'm not scared of you," she sneers, raking her eyes over me from head to toe, and I shrug.

"Good, because I'm not scared of you either." Disregarding her, I look over her shoulder to where Kenner stands. "So, to clarify, this duel is in wolf form and until death. Is there anything else I should know?"

I don't trust him, not one bit, but it's worth asking.

"No," Kenner confirms, nodding victoriously as Trinity tilts her head to come into view again.

"Do you always talk such a big game?" she asks, trying to provoke me as I shrug again.

"No, I feel like actions speak louder than words."

Without another word, I step back and channel deep down into magic, past every ounce of my fae magic until I connect with my wolf. She dances over my skin, sending ripples of fire through my veins before I feel the first bone break.

The pain is intense, but nothing in comparison to the first time. It happens in the blink of an eye, and I quickly find myself on all fours, paws scratching against the hard ground as I look across the short space to find a cream-furred wolf staring back at me.

Under different circumstances, I'd say she was beautiful, but my wolf quickly bats the thought away as I let her take over. It's the strangest sensation I've ever felt. We're one, but we're still so different.

Before I can overthink anything, my wolf kicks into full force, leaping toward our target. Trinity does the same, charging toward me with purpose until we barrel into one another.

Spiraling through the air, we land with a thud, and she has the advantage. Pinned beneath her, I scratch and claw at her fur, trying to free myself, but it's not easy.

"Get up, Addi," Cassian growls, cutting through my panic, and it's like his words set me alight. With my next kick, my back paw meets her side just right, and she grunts as her hold weakens. I slip from beneath her as quickly as I can until we're both back on all fours, circling each other.

My chest heaves with every pant as Trinity bares her teeth at me. She races toward me in the next breath, and I marginally miss her approach, whirling around only to find her coming back at me with purpose.

This time, she leaps through the air, landing on my back with her teeth on full display, and we both stagger to the ground again. Rolling, the battle for control leaves me dizzy until we come to a stop. I snarl, fury burning through me at the fact that she's on top of me again.

I need to act now. I need to act fast. I need to act like a wolf.

Her front paws press into the ground on either side of my head as she growls in my face, covering me with far too much saliva for my liking, but it only serves to spur me on. Thrusting my claws into her side, she whimpers, but it doesn't stop her onslaught of trying to sink her teeth into my throat.

One nick of an artery, and I'm gone. But now just isn't my time.

Snapping my teeth back at her, I dig my claws even deeper into her flesh, earning a howl of pain this time. I manage to use it to my advantage, twisting us, but instead of trying to lunge for her once I'm on top, I do it in the process.

My wolf takes over, rage, vengeance, and determination flooding me as my teeth sink into her exposed throat.

The howl turns into a gargled cry as I bite, tear, and relish in the copper taste on my tongue.

Any fight from Trinity quickly dwindles to nothing as I let my feral side take over. I have to prove myself. Not to Kenner, not to my mother, not even to Cassian, but to myself.

I see nothing, I hear nothing, I feel nothing but the lifeless wolf in my grasp. Only when hands pin my waist do I remember I'm not alone. My instinct is to fight them off me, but the sound of Cassian's whispers in my ear makes me pause just in time not to rip his throat out, too.

Blinking, I slowly take in his features as he looks down at me with a softness in his pretty stare like I've never seen before. He's given me a lot of firsts these past twenty-four hours, all soft and sweet, while all I'm offering him in return is a crimson trail of blood and chaos in my wake.

"It's okay, Addi. I'm here. I've got you," he murmurs, the comfort slowly allowing me to loosen my grip on Trinity.

Exhaustion clings to my wolf enough to acknowledge I need to shift back. My chest heaves with every breath as I groan through the pain once again. I know I'm back to myself when my fingers curl into Cassian's t-shirt and my body sags with a mixture of relief and disbelief.

An almighty roar echoes in the distance, making me frown as I peer up at Cassian.

"What's going on?" I breathe as he places me on my feet. I keep my eyes locked on his as I get steady, and once I'm stable, I glance over my shoulder to see we're nowhere near the group anymore. "What the fuck?"

"We need to go, Alpha," he states, linking his fingers with mine. "But you'll run faster like this now," he explains, but I'm not following.

"How are we...where's..."

He must sense that I'm going nowhere without answers because he sighs, scrubbing at the back of his neck as he looks deep into my eyes. "You wouldn't stop, and Kenner was mad." I search his eyes for more, making his lips purse as he sighs again. "He was trying to fucking take you, and I needed to get you out of there. She offered a distraction and I took it."

"Who?" My heart races like I already know the answer, and when he stands tall, eyes wide with surprise, I know my thought is confirmed.

"Your mother."

Despite my victory and shifting back, it's impossible for me to shake the blood clinging to my skin. Adding the fact that my estranged mother seemingly contributed to my escape leaves me completely overwhelmed and exhausted.

We run for what feels like hours, my stomach grumbling as the sun inches toward the west. The day slips away from us as we distance ourselves from Kenner. There's only so far we can go, and he's likely going to expect us to rush back to the academy, so Cassian has us running in zig zags across the City of Harrows to make sure we're not followed.

When we take a break at the edge of the city, I feel ready to pass out.

"How much longer, Cassian?"

"I don't know," he admits, pushing a hand through his damp hair.

"Think we've given ourselves enough time to at least consider eating? Because I swear I can't go any further."

His eyes settle on mine, seeing past the blood that stains my skin and reminds me of today's events. He sees something in my eyes because a moment later, he's nodding. "We need to reach out to Beau and lay low until he can let us back into the academy," he states, pulling me into his embrace. I bask in his warmth as his lips brush against my forehead. "Let's stop for food, but don't ask me where to go because everywhere I choose ends up putting you in danger."

He takes a step back a breath later, pulling his cell phone from his pocket and tapping out a message. I gape at him as I pat my pockets, quickly realizing I don't have my own device.

"Are you looking for this?" he asks, pulling my cell phone from his other pocket. Relief floods my veins as I murmur my thanks, impressed that he remembered the damn thing in the carnage.

Looking up at him, his prior words linger in my mind, but the rumbling of my stomach distracts me. I start moving, and Cassian is quick to stay by my side.

"I know exactly where to go," I offer, fixing my hood over my head before I head toward the city walls. I don't use my wolf speed this time; it's impossible. I'm worn out but, thankfully, we don't have far to go.

The familiar door hovers ahead, the chime echoing in the air as I step over the threshold and make my way to my usual booth. I fall into the seat with a sigh as Cassian remains alert, scanning every inch of the restaurant before he drops into the booth across from me.

"It feels like you've been here before," he says, and I nod.

"I have. A lot. Raiden too, apparently," I add, making him cock a brow at me, but I play it off with a shrug. Now that I'm seated in a familiar space, my focus drifts back to him.

"This isn't your fault, Cassian."

His eyes narrow on me for a moment as understanding dawns on him. I see the moment it clicks in his mind. The crinkling of his eyes gives him away before he shakes his head.

"If you say so," he grumbles, and I reach across the table, enveloping his hand in my smaller one.

"I know so," I insist, and he scoffs.

"I know different." His grunt is sharp enough to try and cut me off from going deeper into the subject, but he's a fool if he thinks that will work on me.

"Okay, so explain it to me. Explain what's going through that head of yours."

He purses his lips, avoiding my stare for a beat,

but the moment his eyes finally land on mine, I know I've got him. "I was crumbling at Kryll's, panicked that I needed to give you some time and space to connect with your wolf. I probably should have headed right back to the academy with you, but no, I was stubborn and—"

"You were right," I interrupt, tightening my hold on his hand when I sense him trying to pull away, and he scoffs.

"If I were right, you wouldn't be sitting across from me covered in dried blood."

Cocking a brow at him, I shake my head slowly. "Was it a risk going to Janie last night? Yes. Was it a risk to stay in your old house? Yes. But I can't tell you how much I needed that time." He starts to wave me off, but I remain firm, not giving him a chance to speak. "Truly, and not even just to make you feel better. I can't express what that's done for me, and even now, as I sit here drenched in blood, I don't regret it. I might have only spent a little while with Janie, but hell, the confidence boost is on another level. She helped me in ways I can't explain, and that's thanks to you."

He looks at me. *Really* looks at me. And with every passing second, I feel him soften.

"How do you even exist?" he murmurs, the corner of his lip threatening to tilt up, but he holds it back.

"To torture you," I reply with a wink, and he rolls his eyes at me.

"Daily," he adds, easing the remaining tension that lingers as I release his hand.

"You're welcome," I tease, but the look he gives me is filled with awe.

"You're incredible, Addi."

My cheeks heat under his intense stare and compliment. "I'm not, but I am resilient," I reply, looking anywhere but at him, and to my luck, Pearl finally appears.

Her eyes widen the moment she takes me in. "Do I want to know?"

"Probably not," I admit, and she offers me a tight smile.

"I thought it was Raiden with you. I can get you something else if you don't—"

"That looks amazing, thank you," Cassian interjects, taking the closest plate from Pearl's grasp as she sets the other one before me.

"Thank you," I add, and she nods, but the tightness doesn't leave her face. "What's going on?"

She twists her lips nervously for a moment before she sighs. "Have you seen the media coverage?"

"Media coverage?" I ask, looking as confused as I feel.

"I thought as much. I'll leave it here for some

light reading while you eat," she offers before sauntering off without a backward glance.

"What was that about?"

I shrug at Cassian's question as Pearl places the papers on the edge of the table, and disappears again. Suddenly, my hunger isn't as important anymore. But before I can get my hands on the tempting sheets, Cassian nudges my plate, silently insisting that I eat.

It takes all of my strength not to give in to the paper, but I manage to resist the urge and eat, as if a part of me knows I'm going to need the fortitude once I've read those words. I dig in, eating every morsel until there's nothing left. My fork has barely touched the plate before I reach for the paper.

Dread settles heavily in my gut as I scan the words, reading them three times before I can muster the strength to put them down.

"Care to share, or shall I read it too?" Cassian asks as I try to wrap my head around the situation.

"The media is aware that the campus is on lockdown and has shared it with the kingdom. That's fine, I guess, but it seems my speech about The Council has led to a bit of an uproar. Apparently, there's incriminating evidence against the council, which has the people rising up."

"Addi, that's amazing."

I shake my head at Cassian's delight. "They're

hailing me a leader while some are calling me a liar. The kingdom is divided, people are up in arms, innocents are dying in the chaos, and the frenzied vampires are worse than ever."

He tilts his head, staring at me for what feels like forever before he speaks. "Your speech has caused quite a stir, Addi, but wasn't it supposed to?" My breath lodges in my throat as he gives me a knowing look. "If people are fighting in your name, that's their decision. That's something the heir of the kingdom would receive."

Fuck.

I blink and blink again, lost to his words, as I try to make sense of it all.

"I don't want people to die on my behalf, Cassian."

"I know. Good people never do. But this should prove to you that you're fighting for the right thing." Wow. "You look concerned."

"I've caused a mess."

"No, you caused change."

His words linger, trying to give me strength as I attempt to wrap my head around it.

"I don't know if that sounds positive or not," I admit, and he shrugs, tucking into the steak in front of him with a sense of calmness I could only wish for.

"Positive or not, you're making waves in the kingdom, but they're not for you. They're for the people, and that's being noticed."

"What's being noticed? Ah, the blood, apparently." I startle at Beau beside us, a questioning smile on his lips.

"Good to see you too, Beau," Cassian grumbles, and Beau gives him a pointed look.

"Sorry about the delay, and sorry to rush, but we need to move. I was in the middle of something," he states, pointing over his shoulder toward the door.

It's only then that I notice something about him, too. "Is that blood?" I ask, aiming my finger at his throat, and he shrugs.

"You're not the only one taking names," he says with a grin, but the twist in my gut doesn't let me join in with the humor.

"Explain," Cassian states, rising from his seat and dropping a few bills on the table to cover our meal, and I follow suit.

Beau leads us toward the door without an answer, and I manage to wave at Pearl before we slip outside. The second we do, he turns to us with a darkening expression. Finally, he sighs, taking a step back as he speaks. "I can tell you, or I can show you."

It's not really a question when he already knows the answer.

"Show us."

EIGHTEEN
RAIDEN

Adrenaline pounds through my veins and I relish in the excitement with every drop of blood I claim.

I'd say I'm feral, but that's a wolf thing, and I'm definitely not one of *those*. I'm not frenzied either because that's completely beneath me. I don't know whether I've always been this venomous or if it's worsened since I've been without Adrianna, but either way, I'm owning it.

I don't like being out of control, and that's all I am when it comes to the woman I'm obsessed with.

She'll be back soon.

She better be. If not, Cassian will be the one on the end of my wrath.

"Raiden, watch out!" Brody's voice cuts through the air, alerting me, but the fucker doesn't actually say where to look. I spin to my left, but of course, the enemy is coming from the right. My gaze latches onto the frenzied vampire powering my way, hitting me with their full force before I can brace for impact.

My back slams the ground, pulling a grunt from my lips as I snarl at the frenzied fool. His eyes can't focus, his movements are jagged, and the grip on my shoulders is about as limp as my dick right now. His desire and uncurbed craving for blood leave him at a complete disadvantage against someone like me, who is... far superior.

His teeth extend, the sharp points shimmering under the moonlight, but he's not quick enough. As he leans toward my throat, I buck my hips up, knocking him off balance before I use my speed to regain the advantage.

A sinister grin spreads across my lips as I glance down at the troubled soul. In this state, all they live and breathe for his blood. The frenzied mess is infused into *their* blood, a fact that I only just learned is because of our kind too. It's diabolical.

I should feel sorry for them, but I can't muster the emotion. They're an inconsequential factor in the bigger picture. His Adam's apple bobs against the palm of my hand as I clench my fingers around his throat, tearing him apart before he can even take another breath.

Blood stains my knuckles, pooling around his

lifeless body, but there's no time to bask in the victory. He's not the only vampire we're fighting off.

Rising to my feet, I straighten my shoulders as I shake out my blazer, giving myself a moment to assess the situation around us.

A burst of flames brightens the sky to my left, and I turn just in time to see the glimmer of a white dragon spiraling toward the ground. Four vampires turn to ash under the intense flames before the dragon ascends back into the sky.

Kryll.

Part of me hates how fucking majestic and unique he is, but there's a part of me, clearly not a typical trait for a vampire, that admires him. I'd almost say I'm in awe, but admitting that would turn me into ash, along with the frenzied fools.

Taking a deep breath, I focus on what I can hear, and my attention is drawn to my right, where I find Brody. His hands are raised at his sides, his eyes barely open as his lips move faster than should be possible, especially for someone who doesn't have a speed ability. The chant flows freely from his lips as vampire after vampire is drawn toward him, only to find their almighty death when they get within a foot of him.

We could be done here.

As if hearing my thoughts, a battle cry rings from the dark forest behind me and I sigh.

There's more?

Fuck.

Of course, Beau lures us out of the walls of the academy for a secret mission and then disappears.

Rolling my neck, I brace myself for the new wave of attackers while my thoughts remain on Kryll's older brother.

I'm not sure if he actually wanted the help or if he just wanted us to kill things that actually *needed* killing instead of some fool on campus. Not that anyone on campus has done anything wrong, but we're all wound up and pining for our girl.

A pained cry rings in my ears, quickly followed by another and another. A burst of fire descends from the sky, followed by another, but this time, it's not a white dragon at the other end of it.

No. It's midnight blue.

Massive claws drop to the ground a moment later, shifting as they hit the ground.

"Finally, you're back," I gripe, giving him a pointed look, but Beau ignores the hell out of me. I step toward him, ready to give him a piece of my mind, when movement to his left catches my attention and I freeze.

"Adrianna," I breathe as she saunters toward me with Cassian at her side.

Her blonde hair is braided into a crown on her head like always, but the exhaustion that clings to her features is more intense than usual. My body stiffens at the fact that she's not as relaxed and calm as I expected. But instead of turning my anger her way, I settle my gaze on Beau.

"Why the fuck did you bring her here?"

"What is that supposed to mean?" Adrianna interjects with a raised brow, and I soften—just a little.

"Nothing, Trouble. I've missed you. You look beautiful. Let me just—"

My words are cut short by the racing footsteps that approach from my right. I turn in time to get a hold on the vampire with practiced precision. Eager to get back to her, I make it swift, letting the lifeless limbs collapse to the ground at my feet a moment later.

Turning back to her, I panic when she's not there, but a flash of her blonde hair is like a beacon in the night, drawing my gaze to my left, where she destroys another vampire. A glint of her favorite silver accessories makes me grin as she wipes the blades on her pants, ridding the blood stains from her prized possessions.

A shiver runs down my spine as her eyes meet mine and my feet carry me toward her before I even realize it. She steps into my open arms without pause, settling the worry in my chest as I envelop her.

"Hey, Trouble," I breathe. This time the softness outweighs the stress in my tone and she melts against me.

"Hey, Fangs," she says, peering up at me with a grin. I match it with one of my own.

Life is scattered.

Life is madness.

Life is complicated.

But with her here, in my arms, everything settles, even if just for a moment.

Brody's chants echo in the distance, the smell of burning flesh tingles in my nose, and the roar of Cassian's wolf vibrates the air around us, but between the two of us, the world stops.

"I've missed you." Admitting the fact doesn't cause me the pain I expect. If anything, it eases the weight on my chest.

"I've missed you too."

"Did you ever think you would say that to me, of all people?" I can't tell if the question is to feed my vampire ego complex or to bathe my heart in her, but once the words leave my lips, I don't regret them either way.

"Did you ever think you would miss a lowly fae?" she retorts, the sass shining in her eyes as I shake my head. She's got me there, and she knows it.

"I didn't think a lot of things until you."

"Oh, you've got charming words tonight, huh?" she muses, and I shrug.

The pressure in my chest intensifies again, the weight of my instinctive response growing heavier with every breath. It's so intense it feels like my eyeballs will pop from my skull with the effort of holding them in.

"I love you."

Fuck.

The words blurt from my mouth, relieving the tension consuming me, but the way she blinks up at me with her jaw slack instantly makes me regret them.

Before I can run for the hills, a hand claps down on my shoulder, followed by a knowing snicker in my ear.

"Don't worry, man. When her brain short circuits like this, it takes a minute for her to restart."

I turn to Cassian, who winks at the blonde in my arms. Adrianna's gaze falls to her feet for a beat before she looks at him again. A soft smile ghosts across her lips before she turns the innocent look my way, too.

There's clearly something here that I'm not entirely aware of, but whatever passes between them eases the shock of my words.

"I killed the last one. I win," Brody announces, breaking the moment as everyone turns to look at him. Kryll and Beau are a few steps behind him as we gather together.

"Great work," Beau offers in a clipped tone that is amusing at this point. For a professor, he's the worst at giving compliments.

Ready to get the fuck out of here, especially now that my girl is with us, I release her from my hold to reach for her hand, but she slips from my grasp the second I do, marching toward Beau.

"I'm trying to figure out why you're out here slaying vampires when you couldn't assist the last time we saw a group of them." The disappointment in her tone mingles with the irritation that stiffens her bones.

If Beau picks up on the energy she's giving off, he ignores it as he shrugs. "Because that was official academy business."

His answer does nothing to quell her bubbling emotions. "People were under attack," she bites, hands balling into fists at her sides as he eliminates the remaining space between them.

"Well, Miss Reagan, when you're the one in charge, you can put me to good use. But for now, let's head back before someone realizes we're gone."

Sleep is calling me. It doesn't even have to be my bed, just somewhere I can claim rest for myself. Today has been a whole ass day, and I'm having a lot of those at the moment. My level of exhaustion is starting to reach new heights and I can't seem to ground myself among the chaos.

Between the duel, Cassian making me run all over the city, and a full tummy from Pearl, I'm exhausted. Add the vampire slaying, and I'm wiped out.

I stand with my hands wrapped around my waist as Brody mutters a chant under his breath, shifting the scenery around us to the familiar fountain that sits between the origin houses on academy grounds. A sense of warmth floods my chest at the sight of it, which is weird as hell.

This isn't home, so why does a simple stone fixture resonate with me?

Fuck, maybe I'm just *that* tired.

Beau moves first, taking two giant steps before whirling around to face us. Not a single word has been said since he mentioned following my order when I'm in charge, and I'm still stumped over it now. His lips part, and I've braced myself for his next words when a shrill voice rings from behind him.

"Well, this isn't entirely what I meant by keeping an eye on them, Professor Tora."

Fuck. Bozzelli.

My hands clench as my entire body goes on high alert despite my desire to pass out. As she steps from behind Beau, her expression is neutral, giving nothing away. I'm not surprised to see her illuminated in the night air with her fluorescent pink pantsuit in full view, her makeup just as bright.

Slowly, her gaze shifts between each of us, lingering on me for a moment before swiftly turning back to Beau.

"Dean Bozzelli, I was just on my way to see you."

"You were?" She cocks a brow at him, lips twisting with words unsaid as he simply shrugs in response. When it's clear she's not going to get anything else from him, her sharp stare turns back to me. Her gaze rakes over me slowly, really fucking slowly, to the point my mouth opens to question her on it, but she finds that moment to speak.

"I've had contact with Mr. Kenner *senior* all afternoon." I stiffen, every muscle in my body tightening with tension as she continues to search deep into my eyes. Before I can fathom what to say in response, she continues. "He claims you've found your wolf." I stare at her, not moving a fraction as her assessment proceeds. "He also claims that you were on his land." Her tongue sweeps across her lips as her eyes narrow. "He insisted that we allow him on campus for a meeting to discuss such matters."

Fuck.

I remain silent as she steps toward me, but the moment she does, my Kryptos kick into action, filling the space between us while blocking me from her view.

"That's close enough, Professor Bozzelli," Raiden states, tilting his head at her in a silent challenge as his right arm brushes against my left.

She raises her eyebrows, unwavering under the intensity that is my vampire, before she continues, "I advised Mr. Kenner that if any student of mine was off campus unauthorized, I would deal with the matter myself." Her words linger in the air as everyone braces for the consequences she's prepared. "Lucky for you, authorization was in place." I wait for the joke, or the manic laughter, but nothing comes, and after a few beats, relief floods my veins. I scramble to find something to say to her, but she pushes on before I get a chance. "I also advised Mr. Kenner that no one will be stepping foot on my campus at this time. Not with the media coverage that's exploded." She tilts her head back, looking down her nose at me as Brody steps forward.

"What coverage?"

I rub my lips together, and I could swear Bozzelli smirks, but it's over quicker than I can comprehend whether it's true or not. "Miss Reagan made quite the statement with her speech," she offers, not delving any further into the facts I learned at Pearl's.

"She did?" Brody peers back at me, a grin on his lips as amusement flickers in his eyes, and I shrug.

"A statement that was enough to garner the attention of every member of the kingdom," she adds, and I can't tell if she's pissed or impressed.

"Good," Brody states, nodding in acknowledgment as Bozzelli quickly levels him with a stare that could make a grown man wither and die at her feet.

"Is it?"

"Yes." The agreement comes in unison from Kryll and Raiden, who don't know the details like Cassian and me, but the fact that they're unwavering in their stance beside me only fuels our bond.

"Why is that?"

"Because the kingdom deserves to know the

truth," Brody answers, his tone that of someone discussing the weather instead of the fate of an entire kingdom.

Bozzelli's eyes find mine again. "I think the truth they're not seeing is Miss Reagan here is dealing with matters that aren't even on the academy timetable while everyone else on campus is prompt and ready to learn."

Well, that's not a lie.

"That only speaks to her importance," Raiden states, his fingers ghosting against mine as he stares the dean down.

"Does it?"

I take a step forward, ready to defend myself and explain how I haven't asked for any of this, but I don't manage a single step before Raiden tucks me into his side, leaving Brody to stand toe to toe with Bozzelli.

"Someone here is already dealing with situations that affect the kingdom, that are an attack on their being and a risk to their safety. Someone here is already trying to protect everyone and everything possible." His words are sharp and fierce, leaving my pulse to thunder in my ears as he peers back at me, the following words spoken just for me. "Someone here is already the heir, and we all know it."

TWENTY
ADRIANNA

The shower beats down on me as exhaustion continues to linger along my limbs. My brain is mush and I no longer know which way is up. Words are being tossed around, words with a lot of strength and meaning behind them, and they're all in regards to me, yet I can't seem to make sense of them.

This is all I've ever wanted, all I've ever known. My father was training me to be *his* heir long before the announcement of the Heir Academy was made. It's all I've believed for myself, and the academy was an easy gateway, but now *everything* has changed.

The first time I walked through the city gates, my focus set on the academy walls, I was a wallflower, floating through the City of Harrows without garnering so much as a sideways glance, but now... people are noticing—not just me, but my actions and my words.

Maybe it's the reality of all of my wishes coming to the forefront, or perhaps it's my strength wavering under the pressure. Either way, I sat down on the bathroom tiles some time ago and I haven't been able to stand since.

Thankfully, Raiden gathered us all back in his room so I could enjoy the privacy of his bathroom instead of the shared option in the fae building. I'm washed, scrubbed clean to the bone, but I can't bring myself to stand up and shut the water off. The feeling of it hitting my shoulders is somewhat soothing.

My mantra of calm and collected feels like it has gone completely out the window at this stage. Too much is happening all at once, and all I feel is a sense of numbness that I can't seem to shake.

It seems that my speech is sending shockwaves through the kingdom. I spoke those words a few days ago and I've been distracted by some issue or another since then. I haven't attended a single class since the speeches were given, I honestly don't know what day it is, and Brody's words from earlier repeat in my mind.

"Someone here is already dealing with situations that affect the kingdom, that are an attack on their being, and a risk to their safety. Someone here is already trying to protect everyone and everything

possible. Someone here is already the heir, and we all know it."

I had braced for impact at Brody's words, but to my shock, Bozzelli said nothing. There wasn't even a disapproving glint in her eyes at his words. Instead, she waved us away dismissively, and now here I am, taking a moment to wallow.

Wallow? I don't know if that's precisely what I'm doing, but it's making me it's bitch nonetheless.

I'm in a daze, and the reality is that everything is messy because I face these challenges. Challenges that aren't necessarily out of my depth, but they are surely meant for someone with greater experience to deal with it. I don't have any experience. I just have new abilities and a ton of people with my name at the top of their shit list, yet I'm supposed to attend classes tomorrow like my world isn't spinning out of control.

I only have the power over myself and every ounce of it is being used to keep me alive at this point. Brody is right. I don't see this being an issue for everyone across the board. I'm not facing trials under the academy's control. I'm facing real-life trials that come with cut-throat circumstances.

"Hey, Dagger."

I startle, blinking at Brody, who leans against the glass panel, secluding me from the rest of the room. There's a look in his eyes, one I can't quite decipher, but my gut tells me it's sympathy. An emotion I want nothing to do with.

Clearing my throat, I straighten my spine and start to stand. "Hey."

"Stay," he breathes, making me freeze and my eyebrows bunch together in confusion.

Before I can question him, he closes the glass door behind him and enters the shower. He doesn't seem to acknowledge the water as he inches closer to me, fully clothed. Crouching, he captures my chin in his grasp.

"How hard are you struggling with looking vulnerable right now?"

His question floors me, leaving me to gape at him for what feels like forever before he offers me a knowing smile. The curl of his lips settles something inside me and I sigh.

"I forget you're all wise and shit," I grumble, rolling my eyes as he winks, swiftly discarding every item of clothing from his body. Each one hits the tiled floor with a slap before he's at eye level with me again.

"Don't worry, Addi. I can be vulnerable with you."

My tongue feels like lead in my mouth for a moment as I struggle to think, but when my eyes reach him, I find exactly what I need.

"Maybe I wanted to come and be strong with

you instead," I offer, earning another one of his killer smiles.

"Dagger, I'm never strong. Not when it comes to you." His lips press against my forehead for a split second before he takes a seat behind me with his back against the tiled wall. His legs spread enough to pull me into an embrace, my back to his front as he sways me slightly.

His lips whisper by my ear, but I don't know what he says. A moment later, I notice the water shutting off. "Do you want to talk about it?" he offers as I sink further against him.

"About what?"

"Whatever is going on up here," he replies, tapping at my temple before replacing his fingertips with his lips.

I hum, lost in thought, but when I can't break it down, I try to explain where I'm at. "I don't know how. I feel it, I know that, but expressing it is hard. Cassian asked me the same question, but..."

The words die off. I don't usually express how I'm feeling like this; I typically hole myself up alone and exert my stress before building my walls back up and facing the world. Things are different with him. They're different with all of my Kryptos. Trying to be vulnerable with any of them isn't easy, especially when a sense of embarrassment threatens to creep in.

"I can't even imagine where your head is at,

Addi. You can't catch a break. We tried to escape all of this at Kryll's, but then your body began to react to the start of the blood moon. You went to see Janie, which Cassian insists was amazing for you, but you woke up to being challenged to yet another duel. I'd offer you a carefree night here, but I don't want to risk another surprise for you in the morning," he admits, recalling the past forty-eight hours as way simpler than they've felt.

"That sounds accurate," I mumble as his fingers soothingly trail over my skin. "Why isn't it getting cold in here?" I ask, failing to expose myself anymore with him, focusing on the fact that a cool chill hasn't taken over now that the water is off.

"Because you're a wolf, Dagger. Hot-blooded, remember?" he muses, letting me change the subject without a single complaint. Silence dances around us for a beat, but it's comforting in a way that can't be explained, only experienced. "You know, I've never been with a wolf before."

My heart stills at his words, breaking the silence so casually I have to twist my head to look into his eyes. "Is that supposed to excite me? The thought of you with someone else?" I bite, my hands flexing with irritation as a smirk grows across his face.

"No, but your jealousy excites me," he replies, way too pleased with himself.

"You're an ass," I grumble, inching to move out of

his hold, but he locks his arms around me, pinning me to his chest.

"I'm a ray of sunshine, and don't you deny it," he insists, his lips grazing my ear with every word. My mouth opens, but nothing comes out, which only seems to please him even more. "I love it when you're speechless, but if you don't shut your mouth, I'll find something to fill it with."

The carnal twinkle in his eyes takes my breath, and a sweep of my tongue over my bottom lip does nothing to moisten the dry spot.

"You're asking for it," he rasps when I don't clamp my lips shut at his sensual threat. His eyes find mine and I nod. My body takes over, letting the thoughts and worries that flood my mind rest as tingles shoot down my spine at the intense look in his eyes. "Dagger."

"Please."

H er big eyes search mine, a desperate need consuming her as she leans into me.

She has a lot going on, more than anyone really should, but she's resilient, that's for sure. She's not sinking under the pressure, but it's giving her an internal challenge that she's never faced before.

Doubt.

I don't know if she knows it, but I can feel it in the air around her. Every turn, she has a hurdle; every hurdle makes her stumble. What she doesn't realize is that with every fall, she gets back up, dusts off her knees, and carries on.

I don't want to wash that all away with a fuck session, yet it's impossible for me to deny her. Especially when she's sitting here all cute and shit with her vulnerability laid bare. I think this might be the hottest part of her.

Her flaws.

We all have them; shit, I'm drenched in them, but Addi wears them so beautifully.

"Please." Another plea falls from her pretty lips and my restraint wavers. The threat was supposed to stop her from making my dick unbearably hard, but all I seem to have done is spark a heat she's unable to deny.

Stroking my fingers over her soft skin, I feel goosebumps prickle at the touch. My hands drift from her sides to her thighs, then all the way up to her shoulders before I grip her chin and tilt her face toward me.

Her gaze flits between my eyes, dancing with hesitance and desire, and I diminish the former the best I can with my lips against hers. Our mouths move together, claiming and giving lazily as we take a moment to savor one another.

"I could drown in you forever," I breathe against her parted lips, and she stifles a moan as she peers at me with a heated gaze.

"More." It's not a plea this time; it's an order. One that makes me smirk.

"You'll get me as fast as I give myself to you or not at all."

She gulps, sweeping her tongue over her bottom lip as she stares deep into my eyes, trying to see if I'm lying or not.

Fuck.

She'll make a liar out of me if she keeps looking at me like that.

All sin, yet demure. Pent up with desire, yet delicate in my grasp. Innocent at first glance, but devilish beneath the surface.

It takes everything I am to hold true to my word. To give myself a chance of surviving the intensity in her eyes, I inch her forward just enough for me to stand. Her jaw falls slack when she stares up at me, but before she can question me, I hoist her in the air.

The second I pin her chest to mine, her legs wrap around my waist and her arms tighten around my neck. I stride out of the shower with purpose, but my steps falter the moment I edge toward the door.

I can't go back in there. Back in there... I'll have to share her, and right now, I'm feeling selfish as hell. This is for me, all for me, just like I'm all for her.

Changing direction, I swiftly move us over the vanity that sits along the left wall, our reflection giving me the perfect view of her ass as I approach. My fingers flex against her thighs before I lower her to the surface, watching her shiver at the cool contact.

Her thighs instinctively part and I take a step back, drinking her in like the delicious potion that she is. She could be laced with poison and I'd still take every sip she has to offer.

"Brody." My name, nothing more than a whisper on her lips, makes my cock jut toward her as my chest clenches.

"Patience, Dagger," I reply, making her eyebrows furrow in irritation, but they swiftly relax the moment I drop to my knees.

Her pussy is at the perfect height propped up on the vanity for me to feast on.

As if sensing my thoughts, her thighs part a little more, offering me even more access to her needy core.

Reaching for her ankles, I ghost my fingertips up her legs, swirling over her knees and consuming her thighs before I yank her forward enough to splay her pussy at the edge of the vanity.

I run the pad of my tongue from her core to her clit in one slow, delicious move. Her sweetness already glistens along my tongue, her arousal evident as her palms fall flat on the vanity beside her.

"Fuck, Brody," she rasps, a twinkle of the devil flitting in her gaze among the innocence that drapes over the rest of her. "More, please more," she begs after one small move, and I feel like a fucking king.

When a woman like Addi begs you, no matter what patience you're trying to exercise, you deliver. Because fuck is she worth it.

Repeating the motion, I add a little more pres-sure this time, doing the same thing again and again until her fingers find their way into my hair. I groan against her pink flesh as she tries to grind against my face, but I grip her thighs, holding her in place as I swirl my tongue around her sensitive nub, relishing in the gasp it earns me.

Once I'm confident she's not going to move, I release her right thigh and drag my fingertips to her core. It's not a gasp that echoes around us next; it's a cry. Grinning, I double my efforts, plunging two fingers into her pussy as her head falls back.

Sucking on her clit, I swirl my fingers in her core, finding the exact spot that I know will make her detonate at my command. The second I brush over the magical place, her hips flex and her ass lifts off the vanity, desperately seeking more.

Needy for the taste of her release on my tongue, I do it again as I rake my teeth over her clit. Four strokes of my fingers and her pussy clenches around me with a ferocity that can only mean one thing. The nip of my teeth gets tighter as I bite back a groan and her moans bounce off the walls around us.

Slowly, she untangles her fingers from my hair and I relent, easing out of her core as she shudders at the loss. Her eyes find mine, wide and desperate, and I grin.

"Don't worry, Dagger. I'm not done with you yet," I promise as I lift her off the vanity. Her hands skim over my chest as she rises on her tiptoes and presses her lips to mine. The kiss deepens with every swipe as she tastes herself on my tongue.

I'm gone for her. Completely fucking gone.

Before I come without touching her with my cock, I grab her waist and spin her around so she's facing the mirror. With her back against my front, I feel her heat everywhere as my eyes meet hers in the reflection.

Incantations tingle in my mind, ideas blossoming at what we could do as my body pleads for its own release, but I hold my magic back, eager to please her just as I am. The fun stuff can come later.

Stroking a hand from her face, over her shoulder, and down her arm, my teeth sink into my bottom lip when her back arches at the sensitive touches, pressing her ass against my dick.

With my free hand, I align my cock with her entrance, and she leans forward, bracing her hands on the vanity as she offers me better access. Trailing a hand down her spine, I sink deep into her core. I don't know who groans first, but the sound from both of us lingers in the air as my heart races. Her tits bounce with the force and it's a sight I'm desperately aware I won't forget anytime soon.

Gripping her hips, I tear my stare from hers in the reflection and look down at where we're connected. My fingers flex against her skin as I pull out until only the tip is nestled in her folds. I stroke my thumb over her ass before I plunge deep inside of her again.

Her pussy molds around my dick, making my vision blur as I repeatedly take what's mine. Peering back at her in the mirror, her eyes are black, pent up, and desperate for another high, but I need to let her know this isn't a distraction from what's happening around her.

I need her to know everything inside of me.

"What do you see in the mirror, Dagger?" I rasp, my pace unrelenting as I fuck her with a desperation that comes from somewhere deep inside me. She shakes her head, confusion apparent in the crinkle at the corners of her eyes. "Tell me what you see when you look in the mirror, Addi," I repeat, using her name instead of her nickname this time in hopes of making her see.

She gasps and groans, clenching the edge of the vanity like her life depends on it, and a beat later, she shakes her head again. "I don't know."

I scoff, my fingers digging deeper into her flesh as I lean in closer, thrusting my cock into her sweet pussy. "Shall I tell you what I see when I look at you?"

She pauses, a flash of uncertainty flickering in her eyes before slowly nodding.

Wrapping my arm around her front, I press my palm against the center of her chest, pulling her to me so her back is flush against my chest. I shift my angle so I can still claim her, my dick pummeling in and out with need as I press my lips to her ear while making sure I can see her in the mirror.

"I see the heir of the Floodborn Kingdom."

She gasps, her cheeks gaining a pink hue as her eyes roll to the back of her head and she comes. Her pussy clenches so tight around my cock I'm sure I'm going to pass out, but instead, I'm dragged into the most intense orgasm of my life.

Wave after wave of ecstasy roars through my veins as I chase after her in pursuit of our mutual pleasure until we're both spent. Our panting breaths mingle together as perspiration clings to every inch of us.

I've never been more certain of anything in my life. Those words; they're true. I know them in my mind, in my heart, and in my soul.

I may have come to the academy with a different purpose, but it's all about her now.

I'm at her mercy. We all are, and we all know it.

It's time we start admitting it if we plan on surviving the madness that seems to surround us.

The reflection that stares back at me this morning is nothing like the one from last night. The heat, the passion, the desire; it's no longer written all over my face. Instead, my lips are pursed, my eyes are narrowed, and my shoulders are stiff.

If I could hit the rewind button and lose myself in the moment again, I would. Unfortunately for me, I have classes to attend.

"Ready?"

My gaze finds Kryll in the mirror, a soft smile on his lips as his eyes rake over me from head to toe. "I'm as ready as I'll ever be," I murmur, turning toward him as I try to alleviate the weight pressing down on me.

The second I'm beside him, he pulls me in, pressing me against his side in a half hug that warms me all the way to the bone.

"Are you sure? You seem tense, and we all know Brody fucked the tension out of you last night." The knowing smirk on his face makes me lower my gaze, hiding the heat in my cheeks.

"Honestly, I'm fine. The tension is probably because a simple day of classes feels weird at this point. In comparison to everything else we've had going on, it should be a breeze. What could go wrong on campus with a few lessons and a meal here and there, right?" I bounce on the balls of my feet, plastering a smile on my face, and he takes the opportunity to kiss my temple before guiding me into Raiden's lounge area.

"Don't jinx yourself," he says with a grin, giving my arm an extra squeeze, and I hum in agreement. That'd just be the cherry on top of everything else.

Cassian, Raiden, and Brody are all dressed and ready for us. I find myself frozen in place as I take each of us in, soaking in the fact that there's a room draped in red, green, brown, purple, and gray cloaks, yet so much emotion and feelings, too—not of the angry, war-inducing kind, either. Despite our different origins, our unity signifies everything our kingdom needs and deserves. It's a beacon of hope among every single person that the origins can come together and overcome any bad blood.

The *L* word keeps being tossed around casually, and as much as it panics me, I know I feel it too.

Saying it out loud, however, is a different thing entirely. Acknowledging it, though, it becomes abundantly clear that it's not just about us and what it means to me, it's what it signifies for the kingdom too.

We're bigger than us, we're brighter for them.

Eager to get my focus back on track, I nod toward the door. "I want to stop by the fae building and check in on Flora. It feels like forever since I last saw her," I admit, acutely aware that it hasn't been that long, but I definitely miss her presence.

"Lead the way, Dragon Princess," Kryll whispers against my ear, threatening another deep tinge to my cheeks as we pile out of the room, down the stairs, and outside into the cool morning air.

Instinctively, I draw my cloak tighter around my body, feeling the press of my blades hidden beneath my t-shirt.

"Does anyone else feel all anti-climatic this morning?" Raiden asks, hands tucked in his pockets as he keeps a step ahead.

"Oh, is this morning not all grand and exciting for the infamous vampire?" Cassian grunts, trudging a step behind him. He's been quiet this morning, no quieter than usual, but I kind of feel jealous of his natural ability to just... be.

"No, asshole, I mean, the three of us have been back on campus longer than you two pesky wolves," he grumbles, waving a hand between Cassian and me as he peers over his shoulder. "But even though you weren't here, we were all pining like losers. At the same time, you were off dealing with dickhead dads and wolves and shit. This morning feels..."

"Calm?" Brody chimes in when Raiden trails off, and he simply hums in response.

"I think you need to acknowledge what calm feels like and enjoy it. We don't need drama every day. It would be nice for us to make it a day, a week, damn, even a month or year without someone coming at us," Kryll states, and I nod. That would be nice. I'd settle for an hour, or making it till lunch at this stage.

We're quiet the rest of the walk, locked in our own thoughts as we head over to the fae building. We see a few students, and even though we get the odd look here and there, it's uneventful as we approach the doors and step inside. I slip out of Kryll's hold and take the stairs two at a time. Reaching the end of the hall, it feels strange as hell being here, even though my room is here, too.

I consider sneaking inside and taking a moment, but opt against it when I realize there's nothing in there that I actually miss. Instead, I rap my knuckles on Flora's door and wait.

And wait, and wait, and wait.

My eyebrows bunch together when it feels like

an eternity has passed, and I knock again. My concern only worsens when there's still no answer.

"Maybe she's already at breakfast," Brody offers, scrubbing the back of his neck as he steps toward me. I get the feeling he's worried for me and not for the same reason as I am. Probably because I'm over-reacting.

"Likely," I murmur, stepping back from her door. "Was she on campus yesterday?" I ask, my gaze skimming from Brody to Kryll and then Raiden, who all nod in response.

"She was raining Hell on us for leaving you 'unprotected,' as she put it," Raiden explains with an eye roll.

"Unprotected?" I ask in confusion, following the four of them back toward the stairs.

"Yeah. Apparently, you should be surrounded by all of us at all times," he adds.

"Ignore him. She cares, and she was worried you two wouldn't be safe on your own," Kryll chimes in, and Brody scoffs.

"I mean, technically, she was right."

Technically, I can't argue with that.

Feeling a little more at ease, we leave the fae building and hurry over to the dining hall. I'm eager to see her with my own two eyes just to be sure. My steps falter when I walk through the double doors, the smell of bacon in the air, and there's no sight of Flora or Arlo.

My muscles tense, apprehension coiling through my body as I scan the room twice to no avail.

"Let's sit down and we can strategize, okay?" Brody murmurs, stepping up to my side before guiding me toward the center table.

I can feel eyes on us, but there doesn't seem to be anything out of the ordinary. The weirdest thing is my wolf senses are going into overdrive from all the noise. I'm sure I can hear the people chewing their food five tables away, and it's not a good vibe.

Dropping into my usual seat between Raiden and Kryll, Brody takes the seat across from me with Cassian right beside him, but the noticeable absence of Flora and Arlo makes my gut twist.

"Maybe she was in Arlo's room? They should be here soon," Kryll states, squeezing my thigh in support, and I nod in agreement.

"You're right. I'm definitely overthinking it," I mutter as food is brought to the table.

"Maybe, but nothing is a surprise around here anymore," Raiden adds, reigniting my concern as he tucks into his food casually, like he didn't add to my distress with his statement.

Fuck.

"Eat, Princess. You need the energy. If they don't show, we can hunt them down later, but I'm sure it's nothing," Kryll whispers, offering another reassuring squeeze before he digs into his food.

I stare at the stack of pancakes and bacon smothered in syrup and sigh. The niggle in the back of my mind leaves me with no desire to eat, but he's right, food is fuel, and I'm going to need it to get through the day.

The first bite is difficult, my stomach twisting in protest, but by the fifth mouthful of deliciousness, my concern calms enough to let me proceed. The moment I lift my fork to my lips with the last bite attached, my wolf senses perk up, and I know with raw certainty that the footsteps, which are getting louder, are heading our way. But more than that, I know exactly who they belong to.

I turn to my left just in time to see her palms slam on the table beside Raiden. Anger blazes in her eyes, and even though they're not aimed at me, I know the rage is *for* me.

"Is it true?" Each word is snapped through bared teeth as she narrows her eyes on the man beside me—the same man who doesn't even bother to look in her direction as he continues to eat.

"Is what true?" He sounds even more bored than he looks. That doesn't hide the fact that she's garnering attention like always, and all eyes in the dining hall are now turned our way.

Vallie's bullshit, in the grand scheme of things, is

nothing compared to what else we may face, but she has such a way of getting under my skin that it's impossible to ignore.

"That you're fucking a half-breed."

My eyes bulge out of my head as my wolf rears to the surface. Fury consumes every inch of me, rendering me volatile as I slice my gaze to hers.

Despite my inner turmoil and the impending threat of my bones cracking because my wolf is ready to slay, Raiden sighs, completely unfazed.

"You're here for some drama, Vallie, and I'm not about it. So, fuck off." He finally glances at her and sighs the last part, but she's not done.

Far from it.

"No, Raiden. I demand an explanation," she insists, standing tall and folding her arms over her chest as she flicks a sneer my way before refocusing on the man she still thinks she deserves.

"You deserve nothing," he replies calmly, turning back to his food, which only serves to piss her off, and she's reaching for his arm in the next moment.

"How can you say that? I love you, and you're fucking some half-bred whore," she growls, and I'm up on my feet, lurching through the air in her direction.

I'm ready to slaughter her.

I'm ready to be done with her incessant bullshit.

I'm ready to bathe my claws in her blood.

Much to my wolf's dismay, hands catch me around my waist, pulling me back before I can make any kind of contact. Black ink peeks out from the sleeves of the man holding me hostage, confirming it's Kryll, but that doesn't stop my wolf from bucking in his grasp.

"Let me down. Now," I growl, my nostrils flaring as my chest heaves with every breath.

"Look at her. Such a fucking mess. Get a rein on her," Vallie says with a snort, causing me to try to rush her again, but Kryll's hold only tightens.

"You're poison, Vallie. To the bone. You're just sad because nobody fucking likes you, let alone loves you. Not for your status, not for your name, and definitely not for the person you are. Killing you, whenever that day comes, is going to be the best day of my life." The words are dark yet light on my tongue. I don't even know what I'm saying or where it's coming from, but I get the sense my wolf is way more invested in killing this bitch than I am.

"Get her out of here," Cassian grunts, and I smirk, ready to wave this cunt off, but to my utter surprise and horror, it's me that's being carted from the room.

"Put me the fuck down, Kryll. Right now," I snarl as he spins me, tossing me over his shoulder despite my best efforts.

"It's for the best, Addi. You'll thank me for it

later," he promises, but the words go right over my head because they're a load of crap, just like Vallie and her shit.

I will never thank him for pulling me away from her. Over my dead fucking body. Although, preferably hers.

The audience doesn't register in my brain as Kryll stalks to the exit, and just before we step out of the room, Vallie gets the last fucking word.

"That's right, take your bitch for a walk. She needs one."

Kryll ignores my protests as he heads outside, taking the long way around to our first class. The second my feet touch the ground, I point my finger at him.

"Don't ever do that to me again!" My chest heaves as the words part my lips, but as I stare into Kryll's expectant gaze, my fury wanes.

Fuck.

Swiping a hand down my face, I turn away.

"And don't do that either," I grumble, trying and failing to take a deep breath.

"I have no idea what else I just did, Princess, but—"

"Don't call me that. I'm mad at you," I interject, still refusing to look at him, but it's pointless. I'm already softening, despite the demand from my wolf to barge back in there and tear that bitch to shreds.

"Are you mad at me?"

The question comes from Raiden. There's a pointed look on his face as he assesses me and my shoulders slump when my eyes meet his.

"No."

"Good. Then I'll be the one to tell you that he did the right thing. I know you want her gone—shit, so do I—but I was certain you were about to shift and tear her throat out."

"I don't see a problem with that," I bite, my wolf right back at the surface again, and he understandably takes a step back.

With his hands raised in surrender, he opens his mouth to speak, but I wave him off. Turning away from him forces me to come face to face with Cassian instead.

Why are there so goddamn many of them?

His eyes stare deep into mine, holding me hostage as I will my breathing to level out. He takes a slow step toward me, then another, and another, until we're toe to toe. Just as slowly, he lifts his hand to cup my cheek.

"It's okay, wolf. She's safe. The rage isn't needed... yet," he murmurs, making me frown, but to my surprise, each breath becomes easier as my wolf simmers down inside of me. He must sense the shift because a victorious grin spreads across his face. Irritated by his glee, I whack his hand away and step back. "You're welcome," he grumbles with a raised brow, leaving me reeling with more agitation. I feel like I'm one step away from stomping my foot and sticking my tongue out at him.

"It's okay, Dagger. Your wolf is new, and she's going to want to protect you. Not just from physical threats, but verbal ones too. Besides, we all know Vallie is a bitch." My gaze snaps to his, nostrils flared in irritation, and he lifts his hands in surrender. "Not that it justifies anything. Her death is coming, and her blood is yours, you just have to make sure it's done at the right time for the right reasons," he finishes with a shrug, like we're not talking about killing someone right now.

I sigh, dipping my head so my chin rests on my chest.

If I want to be the heir of the kingdom, I can't go around killing people just because they piss me off. That's obscenely controlling and something The Council would do. I refuse to be like them. I can't. If things are going to change, they need to start with me. Not just in the words I promise but in the actions I take too. Otherwise, the role won't ever be mine, and it has to be.

"Thank you," I rasp, using all my strength to lift my head and face Kryll. A soft smile ghosts his lips as he nods.

"No thanks necessary. Honestly, it was more for

me than you. My dragon was one step away from doing the exact same thing," he explains, eliminating the distance between us. The second he's within arm's reach, he engulfs me in his arms, squeezing me tight for good measure before releasing me again.

"So, are we ready for class?" Brody asks just as the bell chimes, answering for me.

Wordlessly, the five of us head inside, through the student-filled hallways as we walk toward History class. The mess in the dining hall earns me a few wary looks from others as we pass, but thankfully, no one says anything to piss me off. Or more importantly, my wolf.

The moment I step inside, my back stiffens at the sight of Vallie in the front row, but at least for now, my wolf doesn't rise to the occasion. Taking my seat, Kryll flanks my right side and Brody my left, nestling me between them as the professor turns to face the class.

Her eyes snag on mine for a beat, a hint of surprise at my arrival, but she quickly shakes it off as she shuffles a stack of papers and addresses everyone.

"Good morning, students. I hope you've all had a pleasant start to your day. We're going to spend the next lesson going over how The Council came to be." Her smile widens, and I can't tell what part of her sentence intrigues her. Does she like The Council, or is she simply a history buff?

Fuck if I know, but I don't need any more surprises.

Stop overthinking everything, Addi.

With another deep sigh, I force myself out of my head and focus on the professor. My eyes track her hands, noting how animated she is when she talks. It takes me a moment to realize I'm not taking in a single word she's saying.

Fuck.

Exhaling again, I try harder.

"The people voted for The Council, a chosen democracy that was agreed upon by every origin," she explains as a projection appears in front of her. It symbolizes each origin and the colors we're wearing as it spins slowly like an orb between her hands. "Each origin selected their own representative, and not a single one has changed throughout that time."

"That doesn't make sense. Whose idea was that?" someone calls out from the back row, but I don't turn around to see. The thought triggers something in my brain, forcing me to glance back to my right, where Flora and Arlo's seats sit empty.

Shit.

I was so caught up in Vallie's drama I forgot to reach out.

Kryll's hand lands on my thigh, drawing my attention to him. He must sense my distress because he offers me a squeeze as he mouths. "We'll figure it out."

I nod, but the uncertainty doesn't dissipate. My pulse thunders in my ears as I focus on the professor again, trying to listen as she speaks. "To some, it doesn't make sense, and many have different opinions on the matter, but I think what surprises me most is that it was never considered to actually find new representatives; the Heir Academy was the only option considered."

That surprises me too.

"Now, the struggle for power grows greater every day, which is why the academy was even considered at all. It outweighed the continuation of The Council by astonishing results. Why do you think The Council agreed to it if they were going to be removed from power?" she asks, her gaze trailing over the room as Brody clears his throat beside me.

"They didn't." All eyes turn his way as he shifts in his seat.

"They didn't?" the professor repeats, tilting her head for him to proceed.

"My father explained it to me," he says with a shrug, as if trying to deflect focus away from him, but instead, he seems to hold everyone's attention even more.

"What did he explain?"

Brody's lips purse, a hint of irritation flickering in

the corner of his eye when Vallie's shrill voice cuts through the air.

"Well, my daddy, long rest his soul," she sneers, glaring over her shoulder at me before turning back to the teacher. "Told me that the vote was orchestrated among the people. That those who made the vote had no power to do so, so really, we shouldn't be here, and we should be thankful they didn't opt to slaughter us all as an example instead of giving us the opportunity to explore an academy." She sits back in her seat, folding her arms over her chest with a smug look on her face, leaving me completely bewildered.

The realization I had earlier over killing for killing's sake suddenly feels pointless as I glare at the back of her head.

"That has got to be the most fucked up Council offspring vampire shit I've ever heard," Kryll mutters under his breath, and I can't hold back the snicker that ripples from my stomach.

Thankfully, I'm not the only one making noise, so I don't earn any additional stares.

"Thank you for that opinion, Miss Drummer," the professor says, clearing her throat as she waves her hand to the rest of the class. "What do the rest of you think of The Council and how the academy came to be?"

"I think there have been enough power-hungry people in control of this kingdom for too long.

Someone with no special abilities as the heir would create the safest surroundings, providing equality to all and preventing the magic from corrupting us any further."

Glancing back, I stare at the human guy in his cream cloak. His words are firm, his jaw is tight, and it's clear he's truly locked in on his beliefs. In some respects, I see what he's saying and how that may give the illusion of a better kingdom, but the way he speaks sends a shiver down my spine. I get the feeling his first call of action would be to kill every magical being in the kingdom, which would only bring his demise.

"Perfect contribution, Niall, thank you. How about a wolf? Give me a wolf's opinion on the matter," the professor calls out, scanning her eyes over everyone. She lingers a beat on Cassian, but the glare he gives has her moving on to the next girl in a green cloak. "Lola, please."

The girl sits farther down my row, shifting in her seat nervously as she laces her fingers together. "I think that the people in power need to change. It doesn't even have to be a wolf. I believe the kingdom deserves someone who puts this land above themselves. That takes others into consideration, not in a people-pleasing way, but in a way where we feel valued and safe. I'm exhausted, and I'm barely old enough to know what that word means, but people are dying and lives are being destroyed. Not just by the frenzied vampires that are still somehow allowed to terrorize our streets, but by decisions made by others." Pain shimmers in her eyes. There's a lot she's not saying, so much more than just the face value of her words, and it makes my chest clench with a mixture of compassion and vengeance.

"Thank you, Lola. That's perfectly expressed. Now, how about... a fae." My spine stiffens with panic. Since Flora and Arlo aren't here, the number of fae present is already low. My chances of going unnoticed are slim. Her eyes meet mine a moment later, as if sensing my thoughts, when her lips twist. "I think we all know what you think, Miss Reagan."

My mouth falls slack, unable to process what she means by that statement because it can be taken in so many ways, but before I can question her on it, another shrill voice cuts through the air once again.

"I think we all know that the fae are the last origin that should be in power. Especially not some half-bred bitch who kills innocent people without consequence." Vallie's pointed look is aimed right at me, but I don't turn to face her. Seeing her in my peripheral vision is enough for my wolf to rise to the surface again.

"I don't recall any innocent people dying at the hands of Miss Reagan. Does anyone else?" the professor asks, her question stilling my racing heart as she scans the class.

Not a single person utters a response, earning a huff from Vallie as she flicks her hair over her shoulder in disgust.

The bell tolls, drawing the class to a close, which only spurs Vallie on to stomp toward me. With her palms braced on the table in front of me, she all but sneers in my face. "You're all going to regret your decisions when my uncle officially takes my father's place on The Council. You're not even ready for the power that he has promised me."

My mood doesn't settle all morning. It doesn't help that Flora and Arlo don't appear, continuing to stir the uncertainty weighing down my stomach. There's an explanation, there always is, but I've sent a few messages Flora's way and heard nothing in response.

Nothing.

Flora is too chatty for that. Even if she were sick, Arlo would surely message on her behalf.

The second the bell rings for lunch, I'm out of the classroom and trudging toward the fae building. The guys don't question it, keeping a step behind me as I race up the familiar stairs and slam my fists against her door again.

I wait a beat. Maybe half, if I'm being honest, before I do it again.

"Maybe you're overthinking it. Whatever she's

doing is her business," Raiden states, and I turn to face him. He leans back against the wall, foot propped up as he stares me down, and I narrow my eyes.

"I didn't say it wasn't."

"I know. I'm just also saying that you've been on and off campus a few times now, and this isn't how she acted when that's been the case."

I cock a brow at him. "I get messages, and she talks your ear off to make sure I'm okay. The only person I can pester about her isn't here either, and she's not responding to my texts," I ramble, arms flying around with each word as worry continues to boil deep in my blood.

"Maybe you could talk to Fairbourne," Brody offers, redirecting my attention as he steps toward me with a soft smile in place. "If she's not here, she's either somewhere on campus or off-site. The only way they can leave the academy is with approval from Bozzelli."

"It doesn't seem likely they'd be off campus, though. Does it?" I ask, lips twisting in thought as I try to figure out where the hell she is.

"Does she matter this much?" The question comes from my stone-faced vampire. It's no surprise, really; even when I think he's softening. I guess it's difficult to overcome a lifetime of being selfish.

"Yes!"

He shrugs, pushing off the wall as he heads toward the stairs. "I was only asking. If it really matters this much to you, why don't we go and eat and then hunt Fairbourne down? If he doesn't have the answers, he may be able to help us search," he offers, and I instantly feel bad for snapping at him.

My mouth opens, but before I can say a single thing, Cassian steps between the two of us. His hand grabs mine, tugging me after him as he peers at Raiden. "It's hilarious that you think she will eat before seeing Fairbourne."

Kryll snickers, patting the vampire on the shoulder before following us down the stairs. It's not until we're outside that Raiden summons a response. "I'm just saying food first is always good, and I'm starving."

"Then you go and eat. We'll meet you there," Cassian snorts back, not bothering to turn around.

"Fuck that. I'm coming with you."

"Well, shut up then," he barks before taking off.

This time, we don't stomp through campus. Instead, he uses his wolf speed, which triggers my own. I've barely taken a full breath before I find myself outside Fairbourne's office. A pleased smile spreads across my face, relieved I no longer have the nausea coiling in my stomach from the movement.

I can hear Brody grumbling about Kryll helping him keep up, but it's not entirely audible over the pounding in my ears. Knocking on Fairbourne's door, I bounce on the balls of my feet, waiting for it to swing open. When it doesn't happen instantly, I do it again, with more urgency to the action this time, but it still doesn't summon the man I'm looking for.

"He might not be in there," Raiden offers with a sigh. "This is why we should have gone for food first," he grumbles, earning a shove from Cassian beside him as my shoulders slump in defeat.

"Someone has to help me."

"Who?" Kryll asks, concern swirling in his eyes as he looks at me, and I shrug helplessly.

"Bozzelli?" Brody offers, and my gaze swings to her office door at the end of the hallway.

It's worth a shot.

I'm moving without an answer, but it seems he wasn't expecting one because he's right at my side as I knock on another door, pleading for this one to open.

One breath. Two breathes. Three.

I rub my lips together, my desperation rising with every inhale when the door finally swings open, but it's not Bozzelli.

"May I help you?"

"Who are you?" Raiden grunts as I take her in.

Blond hair frames her heart-shaped face. Large-framed glasses are nestled on her nose, encircling her blue eyes as her smile struggles to meet her eyes. "I'm the dean's assistant."

Huh. I didn't know she had one of those, but I guess it makes sense.

"Is she free?" I ask, not caring to say anything else when I have more pressing matters at hand.

To my dismay, she steps out of the room, shaking her head and closing the door behind her.

"I'm not sure where she is. Maybe pop back after final lessons for the day," she offers before squeezing through the gap between Brody and me, strolling off without a backward glance.

The five of us stare after her, at a complete loss, until Brody turns to me. "I thought her assistant would know her whereabouts at all times."

I hum in agreement, but Kryll shrugs. "This is Bozzelli we're talking about. I don't think anyone can keep up with that woman."

"That's true," I agree, the defeat feeling more prominent than ever.

"So..." Raiden begins, but I wave a hand, cutting him off before he can speak.

"Food. We're going, but this isn't over," I promise.

This time, I take off through the hallway on my own, eager for the adrenaline to pump through my veins as I turn up my speed. I relish in the vibration through my chest as I bypass the dining hall, opting to do two laps of the outer perimeter before slowing my pace at the entrance.

I expect to see my Kryptos at the table already, but instead, they're a step behind me. Nobody says a word, and I fight back a smile as I wind my way through the tables, taking my usual seat as the guys drop down into their spots around me.

My stomach grumbles, earning me a knowing side glance from Raiden, who smothers the grin on his lips. I pretend I didn't hear it as a plate of food is placed in front of me.

Agitated, more at the helplessness that still consumes me than the food, I part my lips to give them some shit lecture about not knowing what I actually want to eat. But I manage to clamp my mouth shut again quickly as a steak comes into view. The mashed potatoes and vegetables make my stomach growl even louder.

Damn.

"Thank you," I grumble, not lifting my gaze as I tuck in.

With every bite, the frustration inside of me dims, but the worry only rises.

I don't make it halfway through my meal this time before my wolf senses pick up.

Fuck.

The ridiculously sweet scent is the first thing I notice, followed swiftly by the click of shoes. The space between each step, mixed with the sugary notes of whatever perfume she drowns herself in, confirms the person prowling toward our table without lifting my gaze.

"Give me strength," Kryll breathes, his irritation mirroring my own when I catch a glimpse of her out of the corner of my eye.

"What was that, Kryll?" she asks, tapping her fingers impatiently on her sleeve.

"I'm asking someone for the strength to deal with your presence. Don't worry yourself. You could help by walking away, but we both know you're not going to," he grunts, making my eyes widen in surprise.

I'm used to Raiden giving her shit, but a snarky tongue from Kryll is something else entirely.

Her nostrils flare as her lip curls in a sneer.

"Why are you here again?" I ask, cutting in before she can say something to offend my dragon. That's only going to piss me *and* my wolf off. Nobody wants that, not when I'm already out for her blood to begin with.

"Get to it, Vallie. I'm hungry," Raiden grumbles, laying his fork on his plate as he looks up at her with a heavy sigh.

"I'm not here for you, Raiden. I'm here for her," she grinds out, aiming a perfectly manicured nail in my direction.

Excellent. At least she's getting straight to the point this time.

"What do you want, Vallie?" My eyes fixate on hers, waiting for whatever bullshit is about to follow.

She scoffs, pursing her lips as she rakes her eyes over me. "Don't sit there all high and mighty when you're a lowly fae."

I roll my eyes at her constant crap. If she thinks calling me a lowly fae is going to hurt my feelings, she's in for a shock. "A half-breed. That's what you called me earlier, right? Maybe stick with that slur instead; it might cut a little deeper." I reach for the water bottle at the side of my plate, taking a sip as I keep my eyes trained on her.

Apparently, that's not the response she was looking for.

She leans closer, waving her finger more firmly in my direction. "You are nothing but trash. Everyone knows it. It's embarrassing that you're here. You need to run back to wherever your cowardly father is hiding and never come back."

My spine stiffens, my wolf ready to take control as my eyes narrow. "What did you say about my father?" The words are dark, the tone even darker as my hands ball into fists on my lap.

I hate the grin that splits across her face. She knows she has wormed her way under my skin with the mention of my father. Fuck.

"I'm not repeating myself. You heard me," she goads, planting her hands on her hips as she rakes her deathly gaze over me.

"Don't. Ever. Speak. Of. Him. Again."

Calm and collected. Calm and collected. Calm and fucking collected, Addi.

"Or what, whore?"

My teeth grind together as Kryll leans into my side. "She just wants to cause a scene, Princess."

He's not wrong. That's all she has ever done, and I'm over it.

Taking a deep breath, I turn away from Vallie and focus on my food. Her eyes burn into the side of my face, and I'm acutely aware of the audience she's conjuring for the second time today.

"That's right, simmer down, bitch. Learn your place while the important people speak."

I drop my fork, turning back to her with narrowed eyes. Is she dumb as fuck, or is she dumb as fuck?

Exhaling, I force the muscles in my face to relax as I try to breathe through the growing rage. "I'm going to kill you one day. Do you want today to be that day?"

I mean it. I fucking mean it. Screw calm and collected. It gets me nowhere with assholes like her.

She cackles at my warning, inching closer to the table as she snarls at me. "Fuck your threats. They won't amount to anything, just like you. Your mother didn't want you. The state of the entire kingdom has been because of you. You were never going to be a true heir to your father, not as a half-breed bitch. Your sister would have been no possible replacement either. I wonder if she's as much of a whore as you or if—"

Her words are lost as I launch through the air. My bones crack and pain ripples through me from head to toe, but the ache is nothing in comparison to the damage her words cause.

She can come for me and snarl at my father, but my sister... Nora... fuck, no.

I refuse, but my wolf refuses even more.

A yelp parts her lips as my claws connect with her chest, knocking her to the ground. My heart ricochets in my chest with every breath as my vision burns red.

Growling and snapping my teeth in her face, I curl my claws deep into her flesh, earning a shrill cry of pain that rings sweet in my ears.

It's not enough.

The fear in her eyes isn't enough.

The tremble in her limbs isn't enough.

The torment I want to plague her with isn't enough.

Nothing will be enough.

No other thoughts filter into my mind as I succumb entirely to my wolf.

My teeth sink into her neck, ripping and tearing. The taste of copper registers on my tongue, her panicked screams getting louder, then gurgly, then nothing at all.

Nothing at all.

She doesn't writhe beneath me.

She doesn't taint the air with her squeals.

She does nothing.

But for good measure, I sink my claws into her chest, ripping her heart from her chest, and lay it at her feet.

The world stops. The intoxicating weight of my worries depletes to nothing more than a distant memory as my wolf finally calms.

Blood stains my paws as I slowly inch away from Vallic's lifeless body and the truth of what I've just done threatens to take over, but my subconscious keeps it at bay. For now, at least.

"Addi." I blink up at Cassian as he calls out my name, but I continue to retreat. "It's okay," he promises, dropping to his knees, and the movement makes me pause. My wolf senses are in overdrive. The noise is too much, but all I can focus on is the smell of blood in the air. "Let me help you, Addi," he encourages, inching toward me.

He doesn't stop until his hand reaches for my fur, running his fingers through the blood-splattered matting at the side of my face. Not that he seems to care. If anything, he digs his fingers in deeper.

His touch releases something inside me, and I lean into him, finally seeing through the fog that's clouding my vision. Two deep breaths and the familiar pain that comes with shifting spirals through my body as I transition back into myself.

My clothes are in place, but blood tinges my skin and stains my hair as a reminder of my actions.

"There's my alpha," he murmurs, pulling me against his chest in the most heartwarming move I've ever felt.

I melt in his hold, taking strength from him as my mind continues to spiral with the world around me. "Cass," I breathe, unable to complete his name, let alone express what's happening inside me. His hold only grows tighter as I sense a shadow cast over us.

Tilting my face, I look up to find Brody, Kryll, and Raiden hovering above us protectively.

I don't know what's wrong with me. I've killed before. I killed her fucking father, but this... this feels different, and I don't think it's the good kind of change.

"Over there, Professor. Hurry!" The cry rings through the dining hall. The voice is unfamiliar as I lean back out of Cassian's hold to find the entire student body gathered around the carnage splayed across the floor.

Horror dances in some of their eyes, fear in others, but what startles me the most is the respect that vibrates through the air.

It can't be for me.

That's not possible.

Before I can think any more about it, Professor Fairbourne appears. He looks down at Vallie on the floor before his gaze travels to me. I'm only now aware of the fact that I've just confirmed I am half-breed to the entire audience hovering around me, but the worry I expect to come with it doesn't register in my mind due to everything else going on.

"Adrianna, what is this?" Fairbourne tries to keep his voice even, but the surprise is evident.

"Just do your job and clean the mess up," Raiden snarls, stepping around to block me from Fairbourne's direct view.

Fairbourne is my origin leader. He's not a danger to me.

Or he wasn't.

Who is the origin leader of half-breeds?

"Mr. Holloway, stand down. Miss Reagan, come with me," Fairbourne demands, his tone leaving no room to question him as my body stiffens.

"She's not going anywhere," Cassian bites, his fingers curling around my arm to keep me at his side for good measure.

"He's right." I frown at the voice, the girl unfamiliar to me as she steps from the crowd. I stare at her in confusion. Her eyes are locked on mine as she approaches, expressing something, but I'm unsure what. All I see is her jaw tightening before she spins to face Fairbourne, a step off from Raiden and her shoulders roll back. "There's no way in Hell you're taking a wolf without *our* leader present."

A wolf? Does she mean me?

Before I can formulate a single word to start the question, another girl steps forward, followed by another and another. Guys join the mix, creating an entire shield around me in defiance, each one draped in a green cloak.

"Stand down, wolves. This is above me. I'll only be the messenger. Bozzelli is going to want to see her," Fairbourne explains, sending a shiver down my spine as I process his words.

My father told me he was trustworthy, but I've yet to see that for myself since I arrived on campus. I can't remember a moment from my childhood with him in it, but I honestly can't think of anything right now. Maybe later, I might come up with something.

"I said you're not taking her anywhere. You can try, but you're going to have a lot of fun getting through all of us first," she promises, folding her arms over her chest.

Her sass is impressive. Her swagger is something else entirely.

"It's—"

"Face it, Fairbourne," Raiden interjects, pointing at the girl beside him. "She's not messing around. Neither am I, or anyone else. You're not taking Adrianna anywhere. Do you need me to spell that out for you?"

I don't need them to fight this for me, but I'm frozen in awe at the fact that they're willing to stand by my side.

"What are these screams I'm hearing? Who is... dead? My... who did this?" Bozzelli's voice carries through the air, stilling me as I brace for the onslaught of anger.

Refusing to hide, I finally stand, straightening my spine as my eyes latch onto Bozzelli's. "It was me."

She rakes her gaze over my face, acknowledging the blood that is drying onto my skin, and sighs. "I won't be able to get you out of this. Someone already called—"

"At ease, civilians."

All eyes spin to the double doors as rows and rows of men filter into the room, each one dressed in black cloaks with gun-metal gray armor fitted beneath them.

They're not just men... they're soldiers.

"Who the fuck called in the military?" Cassian

snarls, tucking me behind him as they swarm the room.

The military? The fucking military? Where the hell have they been since the academy opened? There's been more trouble than this, but *now* they show up? What about the frenzied vamps? Where are they when we need them to handle *that* shitstorm?

Now?

Why?

"Make way. We're here for a Miss Adrianna Reagan, but we're more than happy to take the rest of you if necessary," the leader calls out as he inches closer. I try to take a step, not wanting to cause any more of a scene than there already is, but I don't move a single inch before the students are causing a stir.

Everyone is frantically trying to move, pushing me farther into Cassian's side as I feel Brody step to my left and Kryll crowd me from behind.

"Look," Brody whispers, linking his fingers with mine. I frown at him, barely able to see a damn thing with Raiden standing right in front of me, but when I realize what he means, I don't have to.

It's not something specific he wants me to see. It's everywhere.

The sea of green cloaks is suddenly mingled amongst various grays and blues.

Faes and shifters.

Holy shit.

"You can't just take her. An explanation is going to be needed, and even then, the Princess of Dragons isn't to be manhandled." The statement comes from a guy in a blue cloak. I can practically feel Kryll beam from behind me, but something twists in my gut.

I want people to trust in me, believe in me, but not like this. Not when I literally killed someone for... mentioning my sister's name?

Shit.

The reminder flares my anger to life again, my wolf ready to burst free once more, but another part of me is disappointed. Everything my father taught me... it wasn't for this.

I could blame my wolf, but shifting or not, I would have used my fae magic to slaughter her otherwise.

I don't regret my actions, not when it comes to Nora, but deep down, I know they're not the actions of the next heir, the future leader of the Floodborn Kingdom.

It's not me.

I can't be it.

I want to feel worthy of these people standing beside me, but instead, I only feel deserving of the fact that the soldiers are here to take me away. I can't see past that fact, and before I realize it, I'm slipping from the safety blanket of my men. Squeezing through the crowd is just as easy until I'm standing face to face with Bozzelli, who now has the soldiers beside her.

"Is this her?" the leader asks, glancing at Bozzelli. She stands speechless, her jaw slack as her fingers grip the hem of her bright orange blazer. I save her the hassle.

"I'm Adrianna Reagan," I confirm, taking the final step toward him as protests begin to ring out from behind me.

I can hear the anger in Cassian's shouts, Raiden's growls, Brody's snarls, and Kryll's bark. I understand their concern, but it's futile at this stage. There's just one lingering thought that I can't seem to shake.

"I'll come with you, no fight necessary. But what confuses me is the fact that I killed her father on property in front of The Council. Why weren't you called then? Why wasn't I detained then?"

The leader steps toward me, a crook to his smile as he shakes his head. "Unfortunately for you, I don't give a shit what confuses you. All I care about is my job, which is to detain you until The Council is ready to see you."

"No way! No fucking way," Raiden snarls from behind me, but the slap of magic curls around my wrists, stiffening my body from head to toe.

I can't turn, I can't blink, I can't breathe.

Magical bindings secure my hands together and render me helpless.

It's too late to step back and undo everything unfolding here. I'm at their mercy.

TWENTY-SIX

KRYLL

Fury burns through my veins as the fucker practically lassoes Addi's wrists together, freezing her in place before he disappears into thin air.

Not alone.

No.

With her.

The sea of people who stand in our way is supposed to be a band of support, but instead, they serve only as a blocker between her and us, rendering us helpless to protect her.

Not from them, from herself.

"Why the fuck would she do that?" Cassian snarls as the students start to disperse slowly. The murmurs are all centered on the girl who no longer stands beside us, making the ache in my chest worsen with every passing breath.

"Because she's Addi. I think I would have been more shocked if she didn't," Brody states before grinding to a halt as Raiden whirls around on him.

"Then why the fuck didn't you stop her?"

Brody doesn't take any of his shit, shoving at his chest with a sigh. "I didn't know she was actually going to hand herself over, but she slipped between all of us before we could do anything about it. Besides, I've heard and been a part of the conversations when she gets mad at being controlled. I won't push her away by smothering her."

"It wouldn't have been smothering her. It would have been protecting her," Cassian interjects, raking a hand through his hair as desperation thickens the air.

"How the fuck are we supposed to protect her now? We don't know where she is, and we're practically trapped here," Raiden snaps, his eyes almost entirely black with rage as a thought comes to my mind.

"For them to have gotten in, the magic holding the lockdown in place must have—"

"Been lifted," Brody states, finishing my sentence, and I nod.

A look travels between the four of us before we take off. We don't need to take off like fools to the gates, but somewhere a little more private so Brody can work his magic and get us out of here the quickest.

Raiden rolls to a stop as soon as he steps out onto campus grounds, stepping behind a tree as we gather around. "Where to?"

"The Council," Brody grunts in response. "If she's not there, my father will be, and I can push him for answers. Either way, it's a start," he adds, making total sense as the three of us reach out to touch him. A whispered chant falls from his lips, but after a few moments, the usual tingles of magic aren't traveling over me as we shift locations. Instead, we're left with... nothing.

"Hurry up, Brody," Cassian growls, earning an eye roll from the mage.

"Does it not look like I'm trying?" he snarls back, irritation stiffening his shoulders before he sighs. "The lockdown must still be in place," he finally admits, and we all step back.

"How?" Raiden asks, but I shake my head.

"The how doesn't matter right now. What matters is what other options we have," I grumble, scrubbing a hand down my face as I try to remain focused instead of letting myself succumb to the worry that threatens to take over.

"We need to get off campus. That's the main point," Brody explains, and we all nod.

"If we can't use magic, let's try on foot," Cassian

states, turning toward the winding path without another word.

The three of us hurry to keep up as Raiden huffs a sigh. "If we can't use magic to get the fuck out of here, how do you think it's going to be possible on foot?" he asks, earning a grunt from the wolf storming ahead.

"I would rather fail trying than not try at all."

Well, then.

"That's the wisest thing you have *ever* said, and I should know because I'm wise as shit," Brody declares, amusement in his tone, but when I glance at him, the grin on his face doesn't reach his eyes, confirming the worry that's settling over him too.

We need to get to our girl, and we need to get there now.

As if the thought runs through all of us, I grab Brody's arm and take off at speed for the gates. He grumbles his thanks as we slow to a stop at the unmanned post, but when we attempt to cross the barrier, we're met with an invisible wall.

We're not getting out of here.

Fuck. Fuck. Fuck.

The tension thickens between us, worry morphing into anger and frustration as we try with all of our might to get the hell through the magic, but it's pointless. We're locked in.

"What now? There has to be something," Raiden states, his words more like a plea than anything.

"Beau. We need to find my brother," I insist, whirling around on the spot as I try to gather myself before I take the lead. The others don't say a word as we head back toward the main academy building.

I all but skid to a stop outside my brother's office as I rap my knuckles against the wood.

Open the door. Open the door. Open the door.

My begging goes unanswered, but instead of walking away, I try the handle. To my surprise, it opens, but it doesn't reveal my brother on the other side.

Fuck.

"What now?" Cassian grunts, running a hand through his hair before tugging at the ends in desperation.

"Could he be in class?" Brody asks, and I shrug.

"I don't know, but it's worth a try, right?" I can sense the uncertainty in my own voice, the hope dwindling as we keep facing barrier after barrier, but I still head toward my brother's classroom.

Students still line the halls, no one actually moving on from the scene in the dining room, and it makes my gut twist.

Addi, she... fuck. She did what all of us would have done in that moment. Vallie has done nothing but torture and torment our girl, and she had it coming, but I could feel the distress seeping from my princess. She may not have regrets over doing it, but she regrets something.

The second I heard the mention of Nora from Vallie I knew she had pushed too far. I faltered when I sensed Addi lurching from her seat, but this time, I didn't stop her. I couldn't, not after this morning.

Should I have? Maybe, but there's no changing that now.

Checking the classroom my brother sometimes occupies, we come up empty, so I barrel out to the fields where he spends more time, but still nothing.

"How is this even happening to us right now? I feel like we're running around in circles. We're wasting time," Raiden snarls, his words resonating in my chest as I nod in agreement.

Pulling my cell phone out of my pocket, I try to call him, hating the fact that I didn't think to do this first. But as is my luck right now, he doesn't answer. I try once more for good measure but still come up empty-handed.

Desperate, I fire off a message.

Kryll: Call me. Now!

TUCKING my cell phone back into my pocket, I make sure it's on loud so I can hear any incoming calls before I turn my attention to Brody. "Reach out to your father. If he has answers, he can give them to us over the phone," I insist, and he swiftly digs out his device, too, and brings it to his ear.

I can hear the rings from here before they drown out and the call is cut short. He tries a second and third time before sighing with defeat.

"Do we take it to Bozzelli?" Raiden asks, making my eyes widen in surprise as I note the seriousness on his face.

"Is that going to be a waste of our time? She's never helped before," Cassian grunts as the four of us start to head back to the main academy building.

"That's true for the most part, but since Addi's speech, she's been... different," I admit with a shrug, my muscles bundling tighter as I try to remain as calm as possible.

"Different doesn't mean she's going to be of any use," he bites back, and Brody sighs.

"Right now, she's the only chance we've got," he adds, making a point. "Besides, what did she say back there to Addi? *I can't get you out of this.* Would she have tried?"

His question lingers in the air, and none of us are able to answer. Bozzelli is exhausting, and I don't know where we stand with her. She was a bitch, until she wasn't. I think we're all waiting for the reality that she's going to snap back into her asshole role and we can't trust in a single thing she says or does.

She did allow Addi and Cassian to stay off campus for an extra night at Beau's request, and she did defend Addi against Kenner when shit hit the fan, but now? We can't be sure.

Stepping into the main building for the hundredth time, we barrel through the hallways, but just as we turn down the corridor that leads to Bozzelli's office, we're stopped in place by Professor Amos.

"You're not in class," he states, casting a wary gaze over the four of us as I fight off the eye roll.

"How good of you to notice. Now, fuck off," Raiden grunts, stepping around him, but he doesn't make it far before Amos reaches out, grabbing his arm as he holds him in place.

His jaw tics, his Adam's apple bobs, and his shoulders tense.

Raiden could wipe the floor with this fuck in one breath, but the professor doesn't seem to care. "Get your fucking hand off me before it becomes the only part left of you," he growls, his anger flashing through the air at his threat.

Professor Amos shrugs, a curl of a smile on his lips as he stands taller under Raiden's intense stare.

"As a human, I've been threatened with much worse. Now, if you're quite done, I was wondering if you were in need of any assistance. But watch the next words out of your mouth because if you upset me, I won't help at all."

"What makes you think you can help to begin with?" Cassian interrupts, folding his arms over his chest as he stares Amos down.

With a simple shrug, he releases Raiden's arm and dusts off his cream cloak. "Are you attempting to get out of here?"

"What makes you say that?" I ask, confused, and he shrugs.

"I'm a human. I might not have magical powers, but I'm not dumb. Adrianna Reagan was just escorted off campus, and the four of you have been fighting over her attention from the get-go," he retorts, making Brody scoff.

"Please, there was no fighting involved. We're excellent at sharing, I'll have you know. Also, not from the get-go. For me, maybe, but these assholes needed a moment to catch up. Some might still need an extra push, but we're getting there. Now, how is it you think you can help?"

"I know where the infused relic is kept that holds the lockdown magic in place."

"Why the fuck didn't you lead with that? Let's go, now," Raiden growls, arms out wide in a mixture of anger and frustration as the professor whirls around and charges toward Bozzelli's office.

"Ungrateful assholes," Amos mutters under his breath, doing little to keep it to himself as we hurry after him.

Stepping into Bozzelli's office, she's nowhere to be found. Being here without her present feels awkward, but the professor doesn't seem to mind. Uncaring, he swoops around to the other side of her desk, pulling open the third drawer without a flourish before waving the small relic shaped like an anchor.

"How is it just lying around like that?" Cassian snaps, eyebrows furrowed in confusion as an uneasy feeling washes over me.

The door slams shut behind us, the sound echoing on repeat in my mind as the professor transforms before us. "Not all shifters are dragons, handsome," the woman before us says with a wink. Her eyes are blacker than black, and her hair is even darker as she lifts the relic in the air, looking nothing like the professor she had moments ago.

A blinding light takes over the room, claiming my vision until there is nothing.

The stained walls behind me only look slightly clean in comparison to the state of the bars that frame me in the rest of the cell. It's almost ironic. The metal cage that holds me captive is the same one we freed my father from. It seems fitting.

Maybe they could name the space after my family, call it a tradition, and be done with it.

There's a woman in the cell across from me. She's turned away, leaning against the wall as she seemingly sleeps or chooses to ignore my existence. I'm okay with it either way. The guard station is empty, all of the soldiers residing on the other side of the door that acts as an additional layer of security between them and us.

There are no beds, toilets, or even sheets, but I don't know what I expected. I'm locked up here as a criminal; I don't deserve those things.

Bending my knees, I sigh, letting my head fall against the wall as I brace my arms around my legs. One thing this place does is leave you with nothing but your thoughts, and mine are going around and around, wreaking havoc inside of me.

Vallie is dead... because of me. It's a fact I'm not sad about, and I definitely don't regret putting an end to her. It may have happened over her provoking me, but she's done worse and I should have acted sooner. I just shouldn't have done it like that. Filled with rage and barely in control in front of a full crowd.

No one is ever going to believe in me now.

Everything I've worked tirelessly for, everything my *father* worked himself to the bone for, was all for nothing.

Guilt doesn't plague me. Disappointment does.

On top of all that, I have four men who I am entirely obsessed with, and know in my gut that they deserve better than this; than me. Maybe I was put in their path to show them what not to do, how to be better and not make such foolish and selfish decisions.

I wouldn't be surprised if they were realizing all of this now, in my absence. As much as it hurts my heart and soul, it's probably the best. For them at least.

My head falls forward, my chin resting on my chest as I take another defeated breath. I need a break from my mind. I need the soldiers to get their asses in here and get on with whatever they have planned, which I'm sure is nothing compared to the feelings eating away at me.

I feel like I'm stuck at the bottom of an old well. There's no hope of getting out, the sunlight above barely more than a dot, I'm so deep. When I think it can't get any worse, water starts to rise from the ground, soaking my boots.

I'm drowning in my own anxiety.

My fingers wind their way into my hair, clinging to the messy braid as I will the pent-up strain to fuck off, but I get the feeling I won't be so lucky. Not anytime soon. My self-loathing has reached new heights and there's nothing I can do about it.

There's always something that can be done, Addi.

I push the thought from my mind. I've been programmed to fight, to take the hard road if there's hope waiting at the end of it. But right now, sinking in the inky black water and letting it consume me feels less painful.

"Your thoughts are giving me a headache."

I startle at the statement as my gaze whips to the cell to my left. The woman straightens her legs, slumping back against the wall, and tilts her head in my direction.

Her ears aren't pointed, which makes me think she's not a mind fae, but I'm acutely aware of my ears, so I don't want to assume. Yet I can't see how else my thoughts would be causing her distress. I also have my own mind magic gridlocked so no one can see into my head. It's one of the first things my father taught me, and I need that ability now more than ever.

I'm aware I'm just staring at her, but she doesn't falter under my gaze. Her hair is a chestnut brown, swept back off her face in a neat bun at the base of her neck. Her eyes are as rich as her hair, but there's no light behind them, like she's given up on many things before she got here.

"My thoughts?" I finally manage, keeping my voice even as I peer at her, and she shrugs.

"I'm familiar with internal pain. It's drifting off you in waves." *It always takes one to know one.* I nod, not bothering to summon a response, but that only seems to encourage her more.

Shifting, she turns to face me, crossing her legs as she laces her fingers together. "Get it off your chest. It always makes me feel better." I'm shaking my head before she's even finished, which makes the corner of her mouth tip up in amusement. "Built like a fortress, huh? I used to be like that. Now, I'm free."

"You don't look free," I retort, pointing at the bars, and she snickers.

"In here," she replies, tapping her temple like she knows something I don't, and she's right. I'm lost in my mind. I don't know anything. I hum, not sure what she's seeking from me, but she doesn't leave me guessing for long. "Once upon a time, I was a small girl, idolized by my family and loved deeply by my brother, mother, and father. Everyone of importance thought I walked on water," she muses, a flash of something in her eyes before it quickly diminishes. "Some might say I abused that with them, used it to my advantage, played them, but I was just a girl, you know. No one wanted to rein me in, so I did what I wanted when I wanted."

"Sounds like fun," I murmur, wondering what it would have been like to grow up without the pain of being a fae girl. Considering who my father is, we were hiding more than most of our kind. He sheltered us, slowly letting us venture deeper into the small village we took refuge in, but not beyond that, *never* beyond that.

I am and always have been, however, treated like royalty among my family. Between the three of us, we hold each other on pedestals, which isn't all that healthy, I'm sure, but the love we have for one another is unbreakable. I can understand the pull of that feeling. I've felt it myself.

"It was excellent until it wasn't." I can't tell if she wants me to ask, to let her delve deeper into her past, but it seems she doesn't need the prompt. "I overstepped, winding up trapped at their mercy and against my will."

"In here?" I ask, and she shakes her head.

"No, this is nothing in comparison," she states, a ghost of a smile on her face before it quickly disappears. "I was banished, like *banished* banished."

I know that feeling. Well, kind of. I saw my father, that was bad enough. "That must not have been nice."

She scoffs. "Some may say I deserved it, but I'm not some." A darkness creeps into her eyes, leaving them almost entirely black as she gets lost in her thoughts for a moment. With a single blink, she's present again, eyes meeting mine as she sighs. "I spent almost twenty-five years encapsulated in a crystal."

"A crystal?" I repeat with a frown. How is that even possible?

She hums, pressing her lips together with distaste before she sighs again. "There were once magically infused crystals known as 'the kiss of death,' that were made entirely from amethyst." My heart rate spikes, but I keep my features neutral. I know what she's talking about, but she doesn't need to know that. "Before they were banned, they were used to basically immobilize magical beings. The only way for such a powerful item to work was to use the soul of another magical being to fuel its power."

My eyes widen. "So the crystal worked by the soul tethering the magical being's powers?" I ask, trying to wrap my head around it, and she nods, her smile growing wider.

"Exactly that."

Holy fuck.

I gulp, shaken by the memory of the very stone that was embedded into my flesh not so long ago. "It's a good thing they banned them then," I murmur, while also wondering what someone could do that would warrant such a punishment. Having the crystal embedded into your body is one thing, but to have your soul held captive in one of them feels like a whole new level of consequences.

"It is," she confirms, eyes locked on me, and it almost feels like she's searching for something—something that would prove I know all about them, but I tamp my emotions down. "So, what has you in here?" she asks, sensing the connection dissolving between us.

I shrug. "I did something I shouldn't have," I admit, and she cackles with amusement.

"Haven't we all? But it must have been a doozy; otherwise, you wouldn't be here."

I look at her, like really look at her, and consider the conversation she's offering. I don't want to boast. I don't want to be glorified by another criminal, but I also understand what she means about getting things off my chest.

The chances of ever seeing this woman again are very unlikely, and that's if I make it out of here at all. With that, I take a deep breath and answer her. "I killed someone."

She tilts her head, assessing me. "You don't seem mad about it."

"She deserved it," I reply, recalling the time Vallie bit me and the other time she tried to crush me beneath a sheet of ice, plunging me into the frozen depths below.

"So what's running through your head if it isn't guilt?" she asks, and I rub my lips together, giving myself a moment to figure out the right words without giving too much away.

"She was a constant burden, but my actions only served me when I wanted to be more than that."

"More than what?"

I shrug. "More than selfish. More than me. More than a broken fae."

The ache in my chest at the truth of my words hurts like a bitch, but saying it out loud also comes with a wave of relief I didn't know I was chasing.

"That's a lot of more you're after."

I shrug. "I'm not seeking more from anyone else, just myself."

"It must be exhausting."

It's something, but I can't deny how much I want it. To be something, to be someone, to be fucking heroic when the grounds on which I was born were anything but.

"If you could have all of the mores that you wanted, where do you think that would lead you?"

"To be the person I was always meant to be," I answer without missing a beat.

"A thought that has always amused me is who I'm meant to be. Maybe I was never meant to be a villain to many." Is that what I am now? A villain? My gut twists, hating the thought of it as she looks away, staring at the door instead. "I always wanted to be a leader; I wanted to be more than myself, but it was never my fate."

I can only assume that's why she wound up inside a crystal, but I keep my thoughts and lips firmly shut.

Our conversation is drawn to a complete halt when the turn of the lock echoes through the room, drawing my attention to the four soldiers piling into the cell. Their eyes are set on me and I know my time has come. I'm ready to face whatever they want to throw at me.

I don't bother to stand, determined not to look like a fool while I've still got the magical binding drawn tight around my wrists. Silently, the soldiers take great pleasure in hauling me to my feet, and my gaze travels toward the woman who has fed me more knowledge than I was expecting, but her cell is empty.

"Wait. Where did that woman go?" I ask as they head for the door with me in tow.

The guy on my left scoffs, entertaining me for a moment. "What woman?"

"The one that was in that cell," I bite back, confusion and panic shooting through my body as I blink at the empty space.

"I don't know what the fuck you're talking about. You've been in here alone. Did you bang your head or something?" he grunts, thrusting me through the door with more force than necessary as the guy on my right huffs.

"How about she shuts the fuck up so she can get on with her punishment."

My confusion is short-lived as I'm tossed to the floor in a familiar room. I grunt as my knees smack against the harsh stone beneath me, my hands doing little to break my fall.

I expected to find myself in front of The Council, but I didn't think it would be in the same room where they used Nora as a threat against me, attempting to force me to become a fated mate in their desperation for control.

Fuck.

Wetting my lips, I look at the audience I've been granted. It's only natural my gaze lingers on Kenner first. He may not be a member of The Council, but his presence is always too close when I find myself in trouble, usually because it's his doing. The smug look on his face is nothing new, but how defenseless I feel is.

My nostrils flare as irritation threatens to get the better of me, so I turn my attention to the next person: Mrs. Holloway.

I can see where Raiden gets his arrogance; she's smothered in it. Her pencil skirt falls just short of her knees, elongating her legs as she stands tall, her silk shirt tucked in, and her brown hair curling around her face. She's a total vision of demure, but the curl to her lips tells an entirely different story. She's been behind the frenzied vampires this entire time, which was a shock to Raiden too, but as I stand before her now, I don't know how I didn't see it before.

Finding another parental figure to one of my men, my gaze latches onto Mr. Orenda. He pushes his glasses up the bridge of his nose as he assesses me. Every part of him screams that he's a mage. From the messy hair, a by-product of raking his fingers through it while deep in thought, to his disheveled clothing, also an afterthought in comparison to the books in his hands. He's desperate to chase the idea of fated mates or anything else that may create greatness in his eyes, no matter the consequences. He's the definition of a mad mage, focused only on what magic can do, and I don't see it as a positive attribute from this angle.

Finally, my gaze shifts to the final person in the room, and even though I've never seen him before, I know exactly who he is—Mr. Drummer's brother, Vallie's uncle.

He shares the same eyes as his late brother, and the crinkle of anger around his mouth is a look I've seen many times on Vallie herself. Anger vibrates from him, but there's a smugness there that only a vampire can emit. He's furious with me, madder than mad, but once again, someone's desire for power outweighs the blood they wish they could spill.

He wants me dead, but the idea of using me to obtain greater power outweighs it all.

"On her feet," he snarls, not turning his gaze from mine as he orders the soldiers. I grunt as they yank me to my feet, my hands hanging bound and helpless before me, but I refuse to falter under his intense stare.

His movements are measured, cutting the distance between us with slow, purposeful strides before he slices his hand through the air and connects with my cheek. I brace for impact, managing to maintain my balance from the force, but my head still swings to the side.

Fucker.

My skin burns from the contact, and as I look him square in the eyes, I watch as a shit-eating grin spreads across his lips. He gets a kick from slapping women around. Noted. I already thought he was scum, but that simply confirms he's so much worse.

I might be a murderer to two of his family members, but I at least have standards.

"Feel better?" I goad, tasting copper as I offer him a wide smile.

He snarls, ready to attack again, when Brody's father cuts forward, grabbing his arm. "We haven't got time for this just yet."

I almost thought he was coming to my rescue, but it's all about a greater purpose. Silly of me to forget. I sigh as Vallie's uncle steps back. "Excellent; if time isn't on our side, does that mean you're going to cut to the chase?" I ask, cocking a brow at each of them.

It's Mrs. Holloway who steps forward next, arms folded over her chest as she sneers at me. "Is it true? Are you a wolf?"

My gaze flickers to Kenner. I don't know what I was expecting her to say, but it wasn't that.

"Go on, Pet, tell them what you are," Kenner says to my stare, a grin splitting his face as he waves for me to follow his instruction.

"I'm. Not. Your. Pet," I bite out through clenched teeth, just like Cassian did the last time he used that damn nickname on me. His grin only spreads wider, pleased he's gotten under my skin.

"Tell her you're a wolf."

I sigh, settling my gaze back on Mrs. Holloway, who stares at me expectantly. Looking at her reminds me too much of Raiden. It pisses me off. "You already heard him," I say with a sigh, and she shakes her head.

"I want to hear it from you."

I roll my eyes, irritated with this bullshit, but curiosity has gotten the better of me. "I'm a wolf and a fae." She purses her lips, a flash of something crossing her gaze, but it doesn't last long enough for me to decipher it completely. "Why does it matter?" My question hangs in the air for a moment before she drops her arms to her sides with a sigh.

"To you? It doesn't. To us, it makes a huge difference." She slips her hand into her pocket, pulling a small coin-shaped object out and placing it into Kenner's outstretched palm.

"What am I missing?"

She looks away, disappointment and irritation coiling through her. When it's clear she's not going to answer, I look to the others. More specifically, Mr. Orenda. Kenner will be smug as fuck, and I don't know who Vallie's uncle is, but his handprint still burns on my cheek, so I'm not looking to him for answers.

To my surprise, he offers me a tight smile as he slowly edges toward me. "The last center of our fated mates was a vampire, which gave Holloway the power of control; now you're part wolf and part fae. With no fae leader in the room; the control goes to Kenner."

"You're still going on about that?" I ask, blinking at him.

"About what?"

"Fated mates?"

"Of course. Why else would we have you here?"

I try to step back as he continues getting closer, but I'm blocked by the soldiers still standing behind me. "Didn't you learn the last time?" I grind out, earning a snicker from Vallie's uncle.

"Of course they did. Hence, the extra men, the magic rendering you useless, and alternative leverage."

"Leverage?" I repeat, my heart skipping a beat as my pulse thunders in my ears. "What leverage?"

"That will come in due time," Orenda offers, pulling something from behind his back. "But for now..." His words trail off as he stabs the needle into my neck, earning a grunt from my throat as I feel a burning sensation travel through my veins.

I'm bound, with the soldiers grabbing me as if they were expecting his move, rendering me power-less to his will. "What are you doing to me?"

"Making you as pliant as possible." He turns without a backward glance, shuffling toward the edge of the room as he places the syringe on the tabletop.

I feel light-headed, my limbs floating as I try to blink through the discomfort.

"After your last capture, resulting in my brother's

untimely death, I felt it was best we take all precautions possible," Vallie's uncle states, but I struggle to settle my gaze on him.

"What. Leverage?" I bite, the words still lingering in my head, and even with my blurred vision, I see the sinister smile creep from ear to ear across his face.

"Of course, bring them in," he orders, and I scoff.

"If you were going to drug me, why get leverage? And are we going to clarify who the fuck you're tethering me to?" I spit out, aware that there's a slur to my words but refusing to let it get between me and the answers I need.

"Like I said, Miss Reagan, I didn't want to end up like my brother. I made sure *every* precaution was taken."

Shuffling sounds from behind me, but I'm at the mercy of the soldier holding me in place as I struggle to remain on my feet. I'm practically splayed against him, eager to hit the floor, until the sight of two people being dragged into the room forces me to be more alert.

My heart seizes, pain and panic making me even more delirious as I gape at them.

Their leverage is Flora and Arlo.

Flora and Arlo.

Leverage.

The panic in Flora's eyes resonates deep in my bones while the rage radiating from Arlo pounds through my veins, pushing me to shake the drugs swarming through my body.

I blink repeatedly, trying to see straight when all I feel is sluggish.

"Flora," I breathe, my heart clenching at the sight of her watery eyes and red, blotchy face. She's been crying; even in this state, I can see that.

I feel like I've been teleported right back to when it was Nora being leveraged against me, but there's something different about today. I'm not getting out of this mess like I did then.

"W-whatever they say, Addi. Don't d-do it. D-don't do it. You hear me?" Her whimpers twist my gut as her bottom lip trembles. "Promise me, Addi," she adds, her words firmer as she tries to get me to agree.

I gape at her helplessly before my stare turns to Arlo. I find the same resolution in his eyes. His jaw is tight, his nostrils flared, and his eyes narrowed as he nods at me, pushing for me to give Flora the response she wants.

The issue is... I can't.

I thought we had kept The Council at bay. I thought wrong. I should have realized that their silence only meant they were working harder to try again. I hadn't scared them off. I hadn't done anything but give them the time they needed to set this all in motion, then I gave them the perfect opening when I killed Vallie.

The soldiers' response to the matter was quick. Maybe *too* quick. Maybe there's more to that situation than I first thought, but thinking about it now is pointless. It's not going to save me from what they have planned next.

My gaze flickers back to Flora, but when my lips part, my words aren't for her. "What exactly do you want from me?"

"No, Addi. No!" Flora yells, trying to fight out of the hold the soldier has her in. My teeth clench as the soldier kicks her legs out, sending her to her knees with a crash.

"Don't. Touch. Her," I bite, my face pulsing with

rage as I sneer at the soldier. I'm aware of the slur that still lingers in my voice, but I refuse to let it weaken my words as well as my limbs.

"It's simple," Kenner states, stepping in the way of Flora so he has my full attention. "You will agree to become the center of our fated mates."

"Why?" My eyes narrow on him as my body relaxes further into the soldier that's keeping me propped up.

"You will become the new heirs of the kingdom."

"Why?" I push, aware of the conversations I've had with the guys over the matter, but I want to hear it from these fuckers too.

"That part doesn't matter," Vallie's uncle chimes in, earning a deathly glare from me once I can actually set my sights on him. "Fuck, Orenda, how much did you give her? She has to be awake and have some control over her magic for this to work," he adds as Brody's father stumbles toward me again.

"I used as much as you said," he mumbles under his breath, avoiding my stare as he steps in front of me. "I can extract a little of it. Give me a minute."

"We don't have time for this," Holloway grumbles, tossing her hair over her shoulder with a sigh.

What's the rush? They've got me cornered, and no matter how I try to run through scenarios in my head, none of them lead to me escaping.

"Please, Addi. Don't do this. Not for me, not for

us. Please," Flora cries, making Kenner roll his eyes, but he at least moves out of the way so I can lock eyes with my friend.

"It's going to be okay, Flora. It's going to be fine," I promise, attempting a smile, but I know it falls flat.

Before I can offer any other comfort, a sharp sting burns at my throat again as Orenda pumps something else into my body. I groan at the burn, but as he steps away, syringe in hand, he takes most of the discomfort with him.

Before I can attempt to gather myself, the soldier propping me up pushes me to the floor. Thankfully, this time I manage to catch myself with my bound hands before face-planting the stone beneath me.

Flora yelps in panic as I try to take a few deep breaths. With each inhale, I feel my focus coming back as the world stops spinning. Mostly.

My fingers curl into fists against the harsh floor, the bindings of the magical restraints around my wrists keeping my rage burning inside of me. I huff a sigh as I push myself to my knees. "If I agree to this, I want to know what comes from you doing it. What are you gaining?"

Rising to my feet, I sway a little, but I don't feel half as bad as I did a moment earlier. Although, I can still feel whatever he injected in my veins.

Kenner snarls, irritated with my persistence, but instead of charging at me, he turns for Flora. In a flash, his fingers are curled in her hair, yanking her head back as he holds a blade to her throat. "You're forgetting who has the power here, Pet. You're forgetting you don't have a choice."

"Then why aren't you just fucking doing it?" I snap back, trying to hide the trembling in my bones at the sight of Flora in danger.

I'm pulled back by my hair as the door swings open behind me. The woman who leads the way isn't someone I recognize, but my muscles ease at seeing who follows her.

Raiden. Kryll. Brody. Cassian.

My Kryptos.

Fuck.

Fuck. Fuck. Fuck.

I didn't want to need them like this. Not after today, after what I did. But seeing them makes all the pain go away.

"Addi, baby—"

"Ah, ah, ah, Dragon Boy. Step out of line and she gets punished," the woman sneers, aiming a black fingertip my way.

I turn to Kryll, noting the rage boiling beneath his skin, but he clamps his lips shut and falls in line.

"What the fuck is going on here?" Raiden's voice booms through the room, earning an eye roll from his mother, who seems less than impressed with his outburst.

"Raiden, shut up. The quicker this is over with, the quicker I can get out of here," she grumbles, making my vampire sneer.

"Is the wine calling, Mother? Any work is too hard for you. Even something like this is incomprehensible to you. I should have guessed."

"Watch your mouth, I—"

"Enough! I sacrificed my niece for this. Now, do it," Vallie's uncle snaps, pointing at Brody's father, who quickly steps into action.

"Boys, if you don't mind, hands on the globes," he murmurs, placing the familiar sphere-topped stands in front of them. He comes to me last as I try to ignore the quiet *please* and whimpers from Flora, but when she only gets louder, I can't take it anymore.

"I'll do this without a fight and make your life a hell of a lot easier, but just let me speak with her and calm her down first," I insist, looking at Orenda and no one else. He might be just as mad as the rest of them, but he's the most likely to have a hint of compassion in the room.

He pushes his glasses up the bridge of his nose, considering me as Holloway scoffs. "No. Don't be fooled by her bullshit. She's up to something."

"I'm trying to calm her down. I'm not asking for you to remove my restraints; just let me console her. How are you going to focus on your chants if she's making so much noise," I hiss back, hoping Flora doesn't take offense because that's really not my intention, but I'm trying my best here.

"Fine. Quickly," Orenda mumbles, waving his hand at me.

I move before he can change his mind, stepping around Raiden and Brody to find her still on her knees. I drop down in front of her, lifting my joined wrists in the air before pulling her in the best I can, given the circumstances.

"Please, Addi. Don't do this," she pleads, and I take a deep breath.

My eyes settle on Arlo over her shoulder as I all but breathe into her ear. The words on my tongue are so quiet I'm certain she won't hear them, but when I stand again, I see the fight in her eyes. The pleading is long gone.

"It's okay, Flora," I state, and she nods, keeping a straight face as I make my way around to the remaining stand.

"Addi," Brody murmurs, pulling my gaze to his, but I don't respond. I offer him the smallest smile I can muster as nausea roils in my stomach. All I want to do is crawl into myself, curl up into a ball, and forget the world exists, but I don't have a choice in the matter.

"Do it," I order, placing my hands on the stand before me. It's more to keep me stable than anything, but Holloway was right: the quicker they get on with it, the quicker I can face the next onslaught from them.

Orenda stands center to the five of us, palms facing up as he starts to chant softly. It almost sounds like a lullaby, but in reality, it's far from it. My grip tightens on the sphere under my palm, not by choice but by magic, followed swiftly by a sharp sting as if the damn thing is cutting into my flesh.

Magic bolts through my body, claiming me in every sense of the word as a scream parts my lips and everything turns white.

White light explodes in my vision, and I'm lost, feeling like I'm free-falling into an abyss. Only, there's no fear or panic etched into my every breath. Instead, it's almost comforting.

There's a familiarity to it. One that envelops me in a warm embrace, and although I feel like I'm spiraling, it feels guided.

Safe.

Until I blink, and the white light is gone.

It's not the room at The Council that comes into view, though.

It's worse.

Much, much worse.

The weight of the drugs has lifted, the worry over Flora and Arlo has evaporated, and even though my Kryptos do not surround me, I still feel at ease. A sense of contentment tries to wind its way through my bones, but the sight that greets me makes it impossible.

My boots settle on the grass beneath me, the moon glistening like a beacon overhead, but the chaos in the distance holds my attention. I'm carried toward it, whether I like it or not. My feet ghost over the ground as the noise gets louder, and the pain I once felt grapples to capture me once again.

The castle looms in the distance, the cries of my sister hang in the air, and my nightmares of that night hold me captive like they always do. Only, it's not quite the same as usual because I'm still me, conscious and aware of everything that has happened since the night this all took place, but there's a smaller version of me standing a few feet away.

It can't be a nightmare, but what else could it be? A vision?

I shake my head, willing the scene to change in front of me, but it doesn't. As always, a younger version of Kenner sneers down at my smaller self, filled with rage and destined to change my life forever. Along with Nora's.

Nora.

My gaze shifts to where she stands, my heart racing in my chest as I gasp. I need to move, and I need to do it now before he can act. I will my feet to move, but nothing happens. I try to scream, try to get his attention and bring his focus to me, but it's futile. Whatever this is, wherever I am, I have no control over any of it.

Not even myself.

I'm pinned in place, watching the terrors unfold from a new angle, still incapable of making it all disappear. As if my thoughts are realized, I'm drawn closer, standing shoulder to shoulder with my younger self as Kenner takes off toward Nora.

Horror burns through me, but the scream that howls into the night isn't mine; it's hers—my smaller self.

The noise rattles the very air as the almighty blast of white light consumes my vision once again.

This is why it feels so familiar. It's what I felt that night too.

Fuck.

I don't know what any of this means.

Until the white light dims again, everything moves in slow motion, my worlds colliding as I charge toward Nora, both me now and me then, barreling toward her in a fit of rage. But I'm not the only one with my sights set on her.

There's a boy. He's barely taller than me, but he's definitely faster. His eyes are narrowed, but not at Nora, at Kenner.

"Daddy, stop!" His plea rings in my ears and my body grows stiff.

Cassian.

"Stay back, Son."

"No, Father. No!" he yells, getting closer to them as the child version of me glows.

I wasn't blinded by the light... I *was* the light.

I watch as I stutter, tumbling over my feet as I near the boy that I now know is Cassian, along with Nora. He stands between his father and my sister, fury etched into his features as he lifts his hands in protest.

"Out of my way, boy," Kenner snaps, swiping at his son without care, sending him careening into the bushes that shelter us from the wind. "See to it that Orenda clears his memory of this night. No son of mine shall remember this moment and not believe in me," he snarls, as malicious as ever, as I stumble the last few steps toward them.

The panic and need to protect them both doesn't just swirl in my thoughts here, but the tingling in my bones tells me I felt it then, too. My smaller self leaps through the air just as Kenner gets within arms reach of Nora, pummeling me into her as my magic bursts from my body.

My scream turns into cries of horror as Kenner is blasted back, lost to the darkness as I lay in a crumpled heap on top of Nora. Magic oozes out of me in every direction, shimmering in bright lights as it connects with each wolf in the field.

Howls of pain echo in my ears as every wolf falls to the ground, stopping their assault on my father, Nora, and me.

The wind picks up as I try to stand, effectively knocking me back off my feet and onto Nora as I hear my father call out my name. By the third shout, the lights dim and my scream turns into a muffled whimper, that night playing out in high definition as I succumb to the hidden truths.

I reach them as soon as my father does, seeing the truth of that night through his eyes.

Nora is passed out beneath me as I groan and writhe to try and stand, but all I can do is blink up at my father with pitch-black eyes and black singed fingertips, waving for him to help.

Is this what happened? Is this what happened to me? Is this what I did?

I look down at my hands now, noting the lack of black tips as my father falls to his knees at my side. Blood gushes down his face, staining his skin as he soothes me.

"Oh, Addi. It's okay. You're okay, I'm here, I'm with you. It's all going to be alright." His words barely register in my mind as I stare, completely enraptured as he speaks to my younger self.

He rubs my hands with his, promising to take it all away as a soft glow washes over me again. I'm warm, happy, calm, and tingling with excitement, but I can't process where it's coming from. It's like I'm feeling everything I felt then and forgot. I didn't forget of my own accord, though. It was my father's doing.

I watch as he repeatedly drapes his magic over me until my eyes are back to normal and my fingertips are no longer dipped in black ink. It's then that he sees Nora, and it's then that it's clear it's too late to prevent any serious damage.

Because he was saving me. From my own magic.

It's heartbreaking and soul-shaking all at once. I see now what I never saw then, what my father shielded me from.

My darkness.

"You're welcome."

I snap my gaze to my right, noting the silhouette of a woman in the tree line. It's impossible to make her out, but the cackle that rings in the air before she disappears is familiar—I heard it earlier today.

In my cell.

The woman.

The same woman who wasn't there when the guards took me.

What does all of this mean?

Before I have a chance to contemplate any of it, the world shifts around me. I choke on my breath, which is securely lodged in my throat, as dizziness washes over me.

"Adrianna, answer me right now!" The order comes from Raiden, and it takes everything in me to look his way. "Oh, thank fuck," he rasps, his hand still imprinted on the stand before him.

Returning to the present, I feel a telltale shiver run up my spine as a gush of magic coils in my gut. It forces a snicker to my lips as it intertwines around the magical binding securing my wrists together.

With a snarl, I tug at the binding, watching as it clatters to the floor in a heap. My pulse thunders in my ears as my head falls back and a surge of magic cascades over me.

A bright light beams around the room, but it doesn't blind me. Not even a little.

Not this time.

THIRTY-ONE

ADRIANNA

Chanting rings in my ears as my body vibrates with the remnants of the magic coursing through my bones. It's all I feel, all-consuming, and completely out of control.

One word repeats in my mind.

Protect.

Protect. Protect. Protect.

I must protect Flora.

I must protect Arlo.

I must protect Kryll.

I must protect Raiden.

I must protect Cassian.

I must protect Brody.

I must protect the kingdom.

My sense of purpose is grounding even as it leads me into the depths of an unfamiliar darkness. The light courses through my veins as it projects around the room, engulfing those whose names swirl in my thoughts with a beam so bright that it's almost blinding.

I'm rooted to the spot, fingers tingling with my fae magic as Flora calls out my name, breaking through the fog I'm engulfed in.

My gaze snaps to hers, watching as she squints, and I quickly realize it is only me who can see through the light I'm generating; the rest of them are completely lost to it.

"Do it, Flora," I yell, my chest heaving with every word, and even though she can't see me, she doesn't waste a moment before springing into action.

Raiden, Kryll, Cassian, and Brody are still connected to the stands, locked in, with a sense of bewilderment tainting their perspective along with the light.

"Do what?" Brody hollers, wanting to be a part of whatever the fuck this is, but there's no time to answer. Flora is already swirling into action.

Her hands lift at her sides, her fingers twitching, and I immediately recognize the move for what it is. She's searching through the minds she can reach around her. As if sensing my thoughts, screams break through the air a moment later, and I watch in satisfaction as Holloway, Kenner, Orenda, and Vallie's fucking uncle, whose name I don't even know, drop to the floor.

She sifts through their minds enough to break them into squealing animals writhing at the intrusion, but stops before she might regret it. I've watched her slay frenzied vampires, but this is different. The Council isn't supposed to be the enemy, yet here we are.

"Holy fuck," Raiden grunts, jolting back from the stand as he shakes his hand, and my shoulders sag in relief. She broke whatever magic was holding all of them in place.

Without missing a beat, the four of them start to charge toward the fuckers holding us captive again, but my magic doesn't like that. It swells through my body, making me grunt as I lift off the floor. The light extends from me, projecting into a physical bubble that wraps around not just me, but those I want to protect.

I'm nothing more than a vessel for the protection my magic insists upon, but in doing so, it protects those on the outside of the bubble from feeling the wrath of my men.

"What the fuck?" Cassian snarls, practically punching at the light engulfing them before he whirls around to look up at me. "Make it stop," he barks, his anger not at me but at The Council as they slowly start rising to their feet outside of the protective bubble.

My response lodges in my throat, every inch of my body lost to the magic that burns to make them disappear, simply to protect.

That damn word.

Protect. Protect. Protect.

"Alpha," he warns, but Kryll quickly shoves him to the side, looking up at me in concern.

"Knock it off. She's not in control right now," he bites, his worried eyes crinkling further as he takes me in before he turns toward where The Council stands cornered in the room.

"We need to do something. My father is still chanting, likely trying to place the puppet magic over our fated mates bond," Brody states, raking his fingers through his hair nervously as he watches his father's eyes close and his lips move.

"That's what she's protecting us from," Flora states, earning a whimper from my lips, and I finally understand the magic floating through my body.

That makes a lot of sense, but I'm much more used to defending myself physically, not like this.

"It's okay, Adrianna. We've got you. Just like you've got us," Raiden breathes before nodding at Kryll. One movement between them and a whole conversation is held without a single word being spoken.

I blink once, my magic trying to decipher what's needed of me, when Kryll stretches his arms out wide, shifting into a beautiful white dragon before my eyes. A piece of me warms at his presence, as if I've been longing for him, but as his wings expand in the small room, he knocks me to the floor. I brace for impact, but arms pin me to a hard chest before gravity does its job.

My glow is gone, the barrier between us and the enemy vanished, but the magic is still simmering inside of me, coiled tight around my bones.

Gaping up at Cassian, his eyes burn deep into mine as he remains silent. A harrowing noise comes from Kryll as his claws scratch against the floor.

"Now, Kryll!" Raiden shouts, pulling me from my intense stare-off with Cassian as my dragon stretches his wings out wide, sending the walls blasting into rubble effortlessly.

"No!" Holloway cries, scrambling toward her son with her vampire speed, but she quickly drops to the floor, another crying and writhing mess, as Flora steps out from behind Raiden.

My vampire stares at her with slightly widened eyes, finally realizing that it was her that brought them to their knees to begin with. "Thanks," he breathes, the impressed tone undeniable, making Flora smirk.

"Let's get out of here before we start thanking each other, yeah?" Flora says, amusement coloring her words.

"Once they're dead, we'll have a fucking party," he retorts, turning back to his mother with a snarl on his face, but I can still hear Orenda.

His chants vibrate in my ears, broadcasting their plans on a loop, and it reignites the light inside of me. I already know what's going to happen, and my vengeance isn't going to be satisfied. The thought is another reminder that my magic is in control and I'm just here to be used at its will.

I'm nothing more than a blinding light a moment later, only this time, I can move, but the pull is out of my control as I barrel toward Kryll. The second I touch his scales, a warmth blossoms in my gut.

His eyes find mine and his soul connects with the swirling mess inside me, and it's as if he understands completely. Hands upon hands touch me despite the burning light and I gasp, losing my balance at the euphoria that dances through my body.

I can feel them. I can feel them all—my Kryptos.

The tingles zapping through my bones intensify as my mind is overwhelmed with an array of thoughts until the chants I hear are no longer Orenda's but Brody's.

A weightlessness washes over me as my mind goes quiet and the world around me shifts. Everything is a kaleidoscope of colors, flickering through my senses until it all goes dark.

As I fall into the depths of exhaustion, my light accompanies it.

I see it the moment her light dims and her body becomes heavy. Curling her farther under my wing, I don't dare shift back until Brody has us on safe ground. Not that I think something like safe ground exists anymore, but we need to be as far away from The Council as possible.

Today is... fucked. Well and truly fucked.

I don't know how we got here, but ever since we stepped through the academy gates, it's been nothing but carnage. We've been drawn to it. We've been drawn toward *her*. Right now, in this very moment, as we flee from yet another relentless danger, it all makes sense.

My soul is complete, even more so than when my dragon claimed her for his own. It's euphoric, tingling down my spine, through every nerve ending as the magic connects and claims me all at once. It leaves me breathless, yet disappointed because the stark reality is: their magic worked. They fated us together, a fact I can't truly wrap my head around yet. The mention of their magic taints the magic curling through my body, claiming me like a brand. I want it written all over me. I want it etched into the ink that already stretches across my skin.

She is mine, and I am hers.

Nothing and no one is ever going to change that. I will fight for her, accepting any order or command required to hold her on the pedestal she deserves. Adrianna Reagan has spent enough time hiding due to the actions of others. Now, as our connection grows stronger with every passing breath, I know it is my duty to help her get where she belongs.

On the throne.

Our surroundings settle, pulling me from my thoughts as I stare down at Addi's sleeping form. Only when I see the others take a deep breath and relax a little do I shift, managing to keep *my* princess in my grasp as my wings disappear and my scales return to flesh.

"Why the fuck have you brought us back here?" Cassian snarls, standing toe-to-toe with Brody, who doesn't back down under the intense glare-off.

"Where else are we supposed to go right now? The compound? That's a *no*. Raiden's house, or mine for that matter? Definitely not. You saw our parents back there," he grinds out, pointing his thumb over his shoulder. "Sure, the clouds with all the dragons and shit would be protective, but I didn't want to risk Addi because of the damn moon that hurt her last time." His chest heaves with every breath as his shoulders stiffen. "So, tell me Cass, where else was I supposed to fucking go?"

The echo of everyone's panted breaths is all that can be heard as his words hang heavy in the air. Glancing at our surroundings, I quickly understand Cassian's concern.

We're at the gates of the academy.

Where all this began.

But Brody's right. Where else are we supposed to go? I don't want to risk Addi in the Dragon Kingdom again. Not after last time. It's too soon.

"Addi isn't safe here," Cassian finally grunts, stepping back with a hint of defeat in his movement as Flora immediately appears at his side, placing a hand on his arm.

"I mean this in the most polite way possible, but that woman isn't safe anywhere. I guess that's what comes with being the heir of the kingdom. Danger seeks her out no matter what she does or where she goes. At least here we're in familiar territory, and she's got all of us to help." Her soothing words calm the storm threatening in my muscles, easing the tension creeping up my spine, but it doesn't have the same effect on Cassian.

"Why are you helping? I thought the fae ran from danger."

Flora steps back, surprise etched across her features as she folds her arms over her chest. It's not a surprise that Arlo appears at her side a moment later, his jaw ticking with irritation as he glares at Cassian.

"Watch yourself. You don't get to speak about being a fae when you have no clue," he bites, blindly searching for Flora's hand behind him. "The only person Flora ever has to explain herself to is herself. Well, probably Addi as well because that's important to her, but you can mind your tone and take your pent-up stress out on someone else. *Anyone* else, but not her." He cocks a brow at the growly wolf who simply waves him off with a grunt.

Any other circumstances, and I would pat the fucker on the back for standing up for her best friend, but right now, my priority is helping the unconscious woman in my arms.

"This whole thing is great and all, but should we actually focus on getting somewhere a little more protected?"

Cassian stares at me with narrowed eyes, as if I asked a question in a different language. "You want to go back in there?"

I shrug, but Raiden answers before I get a

chance. "Brody is right. Flora too. But don't get used to it," he adds, wagging a finger at both of them as he moves to my side. He strokes a finger down the side of Addi's face with a sigh. "Nowhere is safe, but if I had to take a guess, this is where we're most likely to have the upper hand."

"You mean like when the soldiers just showed up on the other side of those gates and took her? Fucking took her, and there was nothing anyone could do," Cassian snaps back, nostrils flaring as his hands ball into fists at his sides.

"That's only because she offered herself up," I murmur, voicing the words swirling in my head.

"Whatever. If this all goes to shit, I'm not taking the fucking fall for it," Cassian grunts, storming toward the wrought-iron gates without a backward glance.

"Grumpy much?" Brody muses, trailing behind him, and I shake my head.

We can't weaken ourselves from the inside. That will only leave us vulnerable to people who wish us harm, and that's the last thing we need. We have to stand together now more than ever.

Raiden indicates for me to let him hold Addi as we follow after the stomping wolf, and I scoff, shaking my head as I carry on. "You have to share, Kryll," he grumbles with a pout, but I don't bother to engage with him and his dramatics.

As we approach the gates, Flora clears her throat, glancing at me from the corner of her eye. I tilt my head at her and she offers a tight smile. "I know there's a lot going on, which is probably why everyone's extremely aggravated, but do you think it could have something to do with the new magic?"

"New magic?"

She nods, glancing at Addi's face before sliding her focus back to me. "The fated mates. I can feel it around the five of you. Damn, it's so strong I'm certain if I squinted, I'd see it too."

My eyes widen in surprise. It takes me a moment to connect the dots. She's a mind fae. That's how she made The Council crumble back there. I hadn't considered the fated mates being a factor, but there hasn't been a moment to think.

"Possibly," I breathe, and Raiden scoffs.

"I feel like my blood is literally thrumming with every breath I take. It's definitely doing something," he states with a shrug. "But we're not all that good at talking about shit without our girl grounding us and making us see sense," he adds, earning a hum of amusement from Flora.

Joining Cassian at the gates, there are no guards spread out like usual. Only one man stands with his arms folded over his chest as he glares at me.

"Where the fuck have you been?" he snarls, making my back stiffen as my grasp tightens on Addi.

"I could ask you the same question, Beau," I bite back, furious to see him standing here so expectantly when we desperately searched for him earlier.

He frowns at me, making it clear that he has no clue what my issue is, but he thankfully lets us through the gates. Once he's locked it behind us, he finally takes note of my girl in my arms and her friends who are with us on this little adventure.

"Catch me up to speed," he orders as he waves for us to follow after him. Despite my irritation at him, I do. I tell him everything. From the fight with Vallie in the dining hall, even though I'm sure he's heard all about it, to the human-origin leader luring us off campus. His facial features don't change when I explain what The Council has done or the extra steps they planned to take with the puppet magic shit. To his credit, he just absorbs it all.

"I think that about sums it up," I state with a sigh as he continues to walk us around the grounds' perimeter. However, despite my ramblings, I'm still aware that he's not taking us toward the main academy, nor the origin buildings.

"You're forgetting the glowing part," Brody states, raising his eyebrows at me, and I roll my eyes.

"I'm pissed at him. I was withholding," I grumble, which earns me another pointed look, except this one is from Flora.

"Now isn't the time for sibling squabbles," she

states, earning an amused smirk from Beau for a split second before it quickly disappears again.

He doesn't say a word like I expect him to. Instead, he waves us down a dirt path. "Follow me."

"Where are you taking us?" Cassian asks, also aware that we're on the opposite side of campus compared to our rooms.

He glances back over his shoulder, his eyes searching mine out first before he answers. "My house."

"House? Why?" I ask, acutely aware that he's never let me go to his place on campus. Some bullshit about space and the fact that he's a professor here.

"Because everything is a shitshow here, and you clearly need time since you're the center of it all," he offers, which makes sense, but it startles me that he can see that too.

As we veer to the right, following the dirt path, a house comes into view and my eyes widen.

"That's some house," Raiden states as I simply gape at it, and Beau chuckles.

"I'm a dragon prince. What else were you expecting?" he retorts, making me roll my eyes.

House is an understatement, but more so, I'm questioning how I've never noticed it on the grounds before. It's a two-story monstrosity with pointed rooftops that are segmented into wings with long, stained-glass windows. The frames are black and the walls are even blacker, with a view over a stream to the right. Even with the height, it seems to be shielded by the trees that line the dirt path.

He leads us inside, the colors not getting any lighter, and it weirdly suits my brother. He's fun sometimes, but otherwise, he's an enigma. He has layers of darkness and pent-up emotions and nobody to share them with.

The entryway has a staircase leading up to the right, with doors framing the rest of the room. He heads toward the back, waving for us to continue following him until the kitchen comes into view. It has black marble floors, black gloss cabinets, and a black dining table.

"Your eye for color is... something," Flora muses as she takes it all in and says exactly what I'm thinking.

My brother doesn't offer a response, not that she seems to mind. Instead, he double-checks that the back door is secured before leading us to the left. "There are two rooms here. Make do with them as you please. Just don't go upstairs. The bathroom is through there, and you know where the food is. The living room is the other door off the kitchen. Again, just don't go touching my shit upstairs," he repeats with a grumble before he starts back toward the front door.

"Where are you going?" I ask when it's clear he's not openly offering an explanation, and he shrugs, a tight smile ghosting his lips as he grabs the door handle.

"To cover for you."

"Cover for us?"

"Oh, you won't know. You were off on your adventure, which definitely makes sense now, but, uh... Vallie's not dead. She never was."

Visions flutter in my mind. Whispers of fated mates, whimsical magic, and white dragons dancing through my dreams. Every breath I take makes the visions weaker as my body wrenches me from the depths of unconsciousness. My muscles ache as I stretch out beneath soft sheets, a hum ghosting over my lips as I sigh, a hint of contentment nestling deep in my gut before I pry my eyes open.

Black curtains flutter in the wind, making my eyes crinkle with confusion. My contentment is halted as uncertainty rushes over me. Pressing my palms against the mattress, I shuffle back until I'm propped against the headboard, which gives me a better view of the unfamiliar room I find myself in.

The sheets spread beneath me and over me are as black as the curtains, which match the carpet, headboard, and every piece of furniture in the room.

Where the fuck am I?

A ripple of magic shivers down my spine at the thought and a split second later, the bedroom door bursts open. I lurch forward, hands patting at my ribcage to find none of my daggers within reach, but my burst of panic quells at the sight of Kryll in the open door frame.

His auburn hair is swept back off his face, finger trail marks running through the lengths as his wide eyes search mine.

"Did you feel that... whatever it was?" I rasp, wetting my dry lips as he nods. He steps into the room, clicking the door closed behind him as he approaches the bed.

"It's like it was telling me to get in here now, making me aware you were awake," he explains, and I take a deep breath. A reminder that the dreams that plagued my vision weren't make believe, but reenactments of the last thing I remember before the world went dark.

It really needs to stop doing that. I'm supposed to be alert and ready to act at any given moment, but it's as if my mind, body, and soul know that I'm safe in their arms.

"Is everyone okay?" I ask, hoping to distract myself from the magic that trembles through my veins.

Kryll sits beside me on the bed, his thick arms

coiling around me in a warm embrace before he tucks a loose tendril of hair back off my face. "Everyone is fine. What about you?"

I shrug, which earns me a pointed look before I even speak. "Where are we?" My attempt at distracting from the topic seems to work when he shuffles to get comfortable on the bed.

"Beau's," he offers, making me frown.

"On campus?"

"We didn't know where else to go and you were passed out," he mutters, uncertainty flashing in his eyes, and I shake my head.

"No, you did the right thing. It just seems so..."

"Black?" he finishes, a hint of amusement in his words as I nod in agreement.

The tension eases a little from my limbs as my stare locks on his. "This feels weird," I admit, earning a knowing smile from my dragon.

"I agree. It's like we're jacked up with all of this tension and emotion." I nod, feeling the exact same thing in my veins too. "Brody said it's because the magic worked. They made us fated mates."

I nod, my breath parting my lips in a whoosh as I ask the one thing I'm still a little uncertain about in my tired state. "The puppet—"

"They didn't achieve that," he interjects, and the remaining stress that was clinging to me eases.

"That's a relief, at least," I offer, wiggling my

fingers when the tension doesn't ease from the magic pulsing through my body.

He reaches for my hand, encapsulating it in his own as he runs his thumb over my skin. "Take a deep breath. Brody helped us figure out how to keep it at bay. For now, at least," he explains, pressing his lips to my knuckles before he continues. "I'm sure it will be a thousand times easier for you with your fae mind, but it's all about focusing on your feelings among the madness in here," he states, tapping at his temple with his free hand. "The tingling and over-whelming sensation is because we feel everything. We're all tethered to you, but we're all affected by each other too. The bond between us now is simply strengthened by the magic."

My eyes widen, surprise coating my thoughts. "That's... a lot."

"Yeah. I guess because it's all new, we don't know what it is we're actually feeling. That's prob-ably why it's so manic, but if you can take a deep breath, connect with your center, and focus on your own thoughts and feelings, it should allow you to separate the others. At least enough to put them behind a closed door so it's not so overwhelming," he adds, his smile turning to one of encouragement.

"How did you feel it and know to come in here then?" I ask, intrigued, and he shrugs.

"I kept opening the imaginary door Brody told

me to imagine so I could be alert for you," he offers, avoiding my stare with what looks like a hint of embarrassment, and it destroys my heart in the best way possible.

"Thank you. You didn't have to do that," I murmur, leaning into him as he presses another kiss against my skin. This time, it's at the corner of my mouth.

We sit side by side as he gives me a moment to wake up and try to process everything that's happened. I have no idea what time it is, how long we've been here, or anything else besides the two of us sitting here, but it's enough. For the first time, I trust in the foundations surrounding me instead of bulldozing everything to regain control.

If Kryll is sitting calm and collected, then I should take that as a sign that there's no immediate danger to be concerned about.

Time passes and I don't even care about the pace of it. Fast. Slow. It doesn't matter. I take the time to focus on my breathing and my thoughts, slowly separating them from the carnage in my head before invoking the imaginary door in my mind. It works enough to calm the simmering in my veins, and I release a breath I didn't even realize I was holding.

"Better?" Kryll asks, shifting to wrap his arm around my shoulders, and I hum in agreement.

"Much."

"I know it won't last forever, but I'm sure it will be a fun exercise for us to all figure out together," he states, and I stare at him in disbelief.

"That doesn't sound fun."

"It doesn't? I love the idea of the five of us having something special like this. Even if it wasn't our doing, we should focus on the positive. Otherwise, the darkness will consume us, and there's enough of that going around already," he explains, squeezing my arms supportively.

"Oh, I agree on that part. I don't like change, and this feels huge, no matter how much I try to play it down in my head, but my concern is more with having to handle Cassian and Raiden. Between those two, the fight for control is going to be real."

He snickers at my statement. "That is *very* true. I feel like we should take bets on who will blow first."

"That would be mean, wouldn't it?" I say, amusement lifting the corner of my lips as he shrugs.

"Scared to lose?"

"Me? Never." A lightness settles on my chest, and it practically feels like I'm floating on a cloud.

"Can I ask you a question?"

Nerves threaten to steal the lightness away from me. If he asks about the light, I don't know what I can say because that will take some time. "Of course," I rasp, despite the panic I can feel creeping just beneath my skin.

"Are you ever sad about your ears?" I blink at him. Then I do it again. And again. Startled by his question. To the point where he quickly starts to backtrack when all I do is stare at him. "I'm so sorry. I shouldn't have asked that. I just—"

"It's okay. I just wasn't expecting *that* to be the question. You could have given me five hundred guesses and that still wouldn't have been one of them," I admit, swallowing nervously as he whispers another apology under his breath.

"You don't have to answer," he adds when I still stare at him, my mind swirling with thoughts, but I shake my head.

"No, I can answer, and I want to, I'm just trying to find the right words," I offer, and he nods, stroking his thumb over my arm as I think. He doesn't rush me. He gives me even more time to process my thoughts before I finally clear my throat.

"Fae ears are unique, not just from any other origin, but from each other. They're a symbol of who you are and where you come from, and I love that. I love it *so* much. You have to watch their mannerisms to detect a shifter, a wolf, a vampire, a mage, or a human. With a fae, it's right there for everyone to see. To wear with pride. When I was small, I remember asking my father why our ears were pointed, and he said, 'The fae are blessed with pointed ears to symbolize our love for magic and the possibilities that behold us. But they also allow us the privilege of being able to spot someone of our kind in a crowd and seek safety.'"

"That's beautiful," he offers, and I smile despite the sadness causing an ache in my heart.

"I remember running my fingers over them every time I was nervous. That was the first pain I felt when they were taken from me. Running my hands over the scars definitely didn't feel the same," I explain, sharing more of my story than I've ever spoken aloud before. "My father saw the effect it had on me and taught me how to see the positive in the scars, that now my ears symbolize a survivor, that they show my resilience. They represent the pain I experienced and withstood to rise above it. He confirmed that the trauma traumatized me, never diminishing that fact, but he ensured that I didn't let it bring me down, explaining that it made me whole in a completely different way than before."

"Fuck, Addi," he rasps, his watery eyes wide as he searches mine. "Remind me to pat that man on the back the next time I see him," he adds, a shaky smile on his lips as he tries to lighten the mood, and it works. It feels freeing to speak about it with someone, to lower my walls and let someone witness my vulnerability.

Maybe Brody was right about talking about my feelings all along.

"Why do you ask?" I rub my lips together, searching his stare as my words hang in the air.

"If you had a choice now, would you project to the world that you're a fae or a survivor?"

His retort knocks me back a breath as my eyes widen. That's another profound question, one that takes me a hot minute to process before I can even consider an answer.

"If I had the choice, I would proudly wear my ears. I don't need anyone but me to know I survived. The fact that my soul was broken and I pieced it back together is something that only I need, no one else." The words ache as I say them, the truth tasting like acid on my tongue, as if it betrays all of my father's encouraging words that followed the attack that night. But it's the truth and doesn't take away from what I've been through. It never will. It's who I am but not who I choose to be.

Trauma is a dangerous thing. It can wire you to want to right all the wrongs in the world, creating a hero in its wake, or it can sink you into the depths of despair and create a villain as you try to take everything and everyone down with you.

I refuse to be the latter. Always.

Kryll ghosts his hands over my cheeks, turning to face me fully as he searches my eyes. They're frantic and dancing with an uncertainty I've never seen before as he lifts his left hand to his lips, nipping at his fingertip in one swift motion.

Before I can question what he's doing or why he's harming himself, he strokes his finger over my scars, the droplets of blood cool against my flesh as my pulse rings in my ears.

Understanding washes over my soul as my breath stutters in my chest. My nostrils flare as I bite back tears, all while his eyes search mine, a hint of panic in his gaze as I choke out a sob and lift my hands to my ears, ghosting the trail he just took.

My heart ricochets against my chest as my eyes fall closed. I search for the scars that are burnt into my mind as well as my flesh, but that's not what my fingers find.

I gasp and choke as tears stream, unabashed, down my cheeks, staining my skin for all of eternity as I feel the tips of the ears I thought I'd only ever recall in dreams.

"I can change it back if you like," he rasps, the emotions swirling in the room merging from the both of us.

I'm lost in the moment, running my fingers over the pointed tips that sit on either side of my face as tears burn in my eyes and leave my cheeks damp. I can't put into words or even a thought what this means to me.

Opening my eyes will take away from this moment and I want to cling to it forever. My skin tingles from head to toe, but this time, it's for an entirely different reason; no fated mate magic necessary. I feel hot all over, drenched in emotions I can't even fathom as the quiet dragon sits patiently for me once again.

I should look at him and show my gratitude, but I don't know where to begin.

I sense the warmth from him as he lingers close to me, but I can also feel the uncertainty rising in him, and I can't put him through that. Especially when it's completely unnecessary.

"Thank you," I whisper, prying my eyes open, and his shoulders sag in relief.

"Are you sure?"

I nod, a watery smile spreading across my face before I launch myself into his arms. He catches me, and it's a miracle we don't go tumbling to the floor as he wraps me up in his grasp and turns us so I'm in his lap, thighs on either side of his as I hide my face in his neck.

A thought suddenly sinks in my gut. "Will people know about you? If they see my ears? I don't want to put you in any danger. I—"

"Princess, even if it did, I would still do it a thousand times over to see that look on your face. Besides, we can say it's from the fated mates spell or something," he offers, melting me even more as I tighten my hold around his neck.

He holds me, rocking gently from side to side as my emotions slowly settle. Finally, I lean back to look him in the eye, but before I can speak, he lifts his palm to my cheek, a stunning smile spreading across his face.

"You were beautiful before, Addi, but now?

Wow, just wow," he breathes, making me shake my head in disbelief.

There are no words in my brain that can give him anything even remotely as special as this, so I do the only thing I can think of and fuse my lips to his. It's gentle, whimsical, and full of love as I brush my lips over his again and again.

He remains still, letting me take the lead as his fingers dance over my waist. My hands move from around his neck to cup his cheeks as I deepen our connection. His groan vibrates against my lips, a sound that only serves to fuel my own fire, and I instinctively grind down on him to feel his cock hard beneath me.

Fuck.

I lean back, startled. I don't want to repay something so wonderful with sex. I don't want him to think this is what I'm comparing it to because it's so far from the truth it's not even real.

"Fuck, Addi. Don't stop. I can feel it in here," he explains, tapping his finger against my chest, right where my heart is nestled beneath my ribcage. "Give that to me," he breathes, eliminating the distance between our mouths once again as I do just that.

My lips grow firmer and firmer against his until his tongue slips out, dragging along my mouth, and I gasp. "Holy shit," I rasp, my body on fire for an entirely different reason as I curl my fingers in his hair, tugging desperately as our kiss deepens.

His hands shift down to my hips, dragging me along his cock, which sets me alight, even with the layers of clothing between us.

I don't know how to say the affectionate words he seems to know resonate inside me, so I show him the only way I can; with how my body craves his. Tugging at his t-shirt, it tears beneath my grasp before he can aid me and the material is quickly discarded.

A second barely passes before my t-shirt finds the same fate, but he's quicker than me, bucking up in the air to turn us both and splay me out on the sheets beneath him as he tugs at my pants. When I'm left in nothing but lace underwear, he looms over me with a satisfied grin on his lips and desire in his eyes.

He reaches for my ankle, ready to bring his lips to my flesh, but I'm not done playing for control yet. Yanking my ankle from his grasp, I wrap my legs around his waist and use my wolf speed to spin us again. We tumble to the floor in the madness, the thud echoing around us as I settle on top of him.

"Oh, this is going to be fun," he murmurs, squeezing my waist in the most delicious way possible before I'm tossed in the air.

My back hits the wall with enough force to make me gasp. Kryll towers over me, his body pressed to mine from head to toe, forcing me to tilt my head back so I can see into his eyes.

"You like the fact that I have to strain so much to look up at you like this," I state, running my hand over the seam of his pants where his thick cock is enclosed, and he groans, nodding with delight. "What if I like it when you look up at me?" I challenge, taking a deep breath before I push off the wall, spiraling us both back toward the bed.

He hits the mattress with a grin, confirming that he's not putting up much of a fight here, but the grin quickly drops when I continue up the length of him, bypassing his lap as I settle my thighs on either side of his face instead.

"Just. Like. That," I rasp, desire tingling over my limbs as he brings his hands down on my bare thighs, squeezing for good measure.

Before I can even bask in my fake triumph, his hands shift to my ass, bringing me closer to his mouth and raking his teeth over my core.

"Oh, fuck," I groan, my head falling back as I rock against his face.

My bones are already tingling, the desire coating my veins is impossible to deny as the whisper of an orgasm already skates across my skin. But when the moment ecstasy coils in my core, he stops.

I gape down at him as he pushes me back an

inch, but before I can utter a single word to him, we're moving again. I feel his fingers dig into my thighs as we spin, my back colliding with the wall once again, only this time, his face is between my thighs.

He snags at my panties, the lace fluttering to the ground on a forgotten whisper as he feasts on my pussy. My palms press flush against the wall, desperately seeking something to hold on to, but I come up empty, leaving his hair as my only option.

I hold on for dear life as he rakes his teeth over my clit, swirling his tongue in my core and lapping at my folds like a starved man. The tingles grow tighter, my thighs clenching uncontrollably around his face as he hums against my flesh.

I slump back against the wall, no longer able to put up a fight as euphoria climbs through my body. Once again, I'm just a vessel, but it's with pleasure this time. I fall apart, tearing at the seams as his tongue delves into me repeatedly.

Even when I'm spent, he doesn't relent, coaxing my body to life despite the exhaustion that threatens to overtake my limbs. I'm on the verge of begging him to stop when he nips at my clit, his teeth on the brink of pain, and it ignites my need once again.

Determined to regain some control, I twist my fingers tighter in his hair, his name all but a breath on my lips, but it's enough for him to pause long enough to look up at me.

I don't think, I just act, tipping my body forward before I launch toward the floor. Even with my wolf speed, I manage to gather myself enough to soften his fall to the floor before I catch my footing. I'm a mess of limbs, spinning so my pussy is still in his face while I can stare down at the length of his cock.

"That was some fucking move, Princess," he grunts, splayed out on the floor beneath me. I preen at his compliment, but I don't waste any time as I seek out what I want. Ripping at the button of his pants, they spring open, revealing his thick length draped in his black boxers. The color is fitting for this room, but I still claw at them until his cock glistens under my watchful gaze.

Precum shimmers at his tip and I lean forward, running my tongue over the salty essence that leaves me eager for more. As my tongue swoops over his cock for a second pass, he presses two fingers at my center, teasing me with the remnants of my first release.

Desperate for the upper hand, I take a deep breath and swallow as much of his cock as possible. It's embarrassing how little I actually take, but it's not my fault the quiet dragon was built with the most enormous cock in all of existence.

Breathing through my nose, I try again and again until he's so far down my throat it's physically impossible to move another inch. My eyes roll to the back of my head as he fucks me with his fingers, taking everything I have to offer as I suck at his cock like I'm preparing for the afterlife.

I feel his pulse quicken against my tongue and excitement coils through my veins, but before I can bask in the release I'm desperate for him to give me, he lifts me in the air. I'm helpless in his hold, letting him move me like a puppet set for his entertainment.

He settles me on top of him still, enjoying his view from the floor, but now I'm facing him.

"Ride me, Princess."

Fuck.

My core clenches as I press my feet into the floor, lifting my ass enough for him to line his cock with my entrance.

"I want to see your tits bounce with every move."

Fuck.

He offers me his hands, lacing our fingers together as I use his strength as leverage before I impale myself on his cock.

"Oh my..." My words fall off the cliff I'm dangling over, the room spinning as he fills me completely. He gives me a beat, a whole ass second to succumb to the size of him, before he snickers.

"I don't see any bouncing, Addi. Do you need me to assist?" he breathes, his words raking over me like a sultry caress as I shake my head.

Finding a response to him is impossible, I do the only thing I can as words betray me yet again.

I ride him.

It's different. Immediately, I know it's more.

Our eyes are locked and our fingers are inter-twined as our skin slaps repeatedly.

I can't breathe, I can barely see, and all I can feel is him. Not just at my core, but everywhere.

"Fuck, Princess. That's it. You're so fucking beautiful," he breathes, his words leaving me light-headed as I somehow up my pace.

It's close to torture, dragging my pussy off his cock, but the excitement of him slamming back inside me makes it all worthwhile.

My orgasm is close. I can feel it. My moves turn ragged, my breaths coming in short pants as he grabs my hips and thrusts up into me.

Slam after slam after slam.

It's not long before I feel his fingers bite into my hips and his cock twitch in my core, detonating me. Wave after wave of pleasure crashes over me as stars burst in my field of vision like swirling galaxies being born before my very eyes.

I feel so much, not just with my body but also with my mind, and instead of burying it down, I embrace it. Feeling everything is bliss, like I'm floating in the afterglow.

The first sign I notice we've moved is the soft touch of sheets beneath me as I blink up at the man who changed everything for me. A soft smile floats across my lips as I touch the sides of my face again, confirming the reality that is now mine.

He looks down at me in what I hope is a mirror of how I'm looking at him because it's beautiful.

It's love.

Even if I don't know how to say it.

It's there.

He strokes a hand over my cheek and I lean into the touch as the door bursts open, breaking the moment.

"Holy fuck, you two," Brody says, panting for breath with blazing eyes. "You just made me cum," he adds, pointing down at his pants, where you can just about make out the outline of a wet patch.

Holy. Fuck.

Kryll laughs first, his head dropping between his shoulders as he shakes his head in disbelief. "Fuck off, Brody," he grunts, peering up through his lashes at me as I chuckle.

"I think you've done enough fucking for the both of us." I laugh louder, basking in the madness that is my life, when his chuckle comes to a halt. I peer at him, confused at the sudden shift. When my eyes latch on to his, a smile transforms his face and I can feel a blush creeping over my cheeks immediately at the understanding of what has his attention. Then he speaks and my heart soars. "Your ears are beautiful, Dagger."

K ryll lies with his head against my stomach, stroking gentle circles over my skin as I lean against the headboard. Post-orgasm bliss is my new favorite place to be. Every five seconds, I lift my hands to my ears, double-checking they're real, but I haven't built up the courage to go and look in the bathroom mirror yet.

A part of me wonders if I'll even recognize myself, but I think what has me rooted to the spot more is the impending expectation to bawl my eyes out. Again.

As if sensing my thoughts, hunger gets the better of me, but before I have a chance to verbalize it, my stomach does the complaining for me. Mortification heats my cheeks as Kryll stares up at me with a knowing grin.

"I need to feed my princess," he states, pushing

off me as he stands at the side of the bed with his hand extended for me to take.

"You don't," I grumble, lacing my fingers with his before he tugs me to my feet.

"I do, but I think you've put it off long enough. Why don't you take a minute in the bathroom? I'll go and see what there is to eat," he offers, pulling me into his warm embrace.

I both love and hate that he knows what I'm thinking. I love it because it makes me feel connected to him on a higher level, but I hate it because that also lets him call me out on my shit.

He's right. I have been putting it off, but we don't need to both know that.

"Fine, I'll meet you out there," I grumble, squirming in his arms as he squeezes at my sides and presses a kiss to my temple, earning a soft giggle from me despite my attempts at being grumpy.

He leaves without a backward glance, sadly, dressed once again, giving me the moment I need as I slowly approach the attached bathroom. Taking a deep breath, I run my hands over my t-shirt, which has definitely seen better days. Using it as my excuse, I use my magic to clean myself up, right to the top of my head, where I fix my crown braid into place.

When there's nothing left for me to do, I bite the bullet and step over the threshold. As if sensing my nerves, a colossal mirror faces me, making it impossible for me to hide from my reflection.

My feet are carrying me toward the vanity that stands before it, my brain awash with disbelief as I stare at myself. Thankfully, a light switches on as I walk halfway into the room, making it easier to see among the all-black aesthetic that consumes the space.

The decor is long forgotten as I twist my face from side to side, taking myself in as warmth rattles in my chest.

This is me.

This has always been me.

Now, my symbol has been restored.

I feel complete, in a way nothing else could make me feel. I feel like I'm glowing. I feel like I've won, even though there's still so much uncertainty in my life. The restoration sprinkles me with each spark as my belief grows.

To be here, with my men, my friends, and my ears, it's special. All I need is my family and I can never want for anything else in my life.

That's my reality.

I was chasing a dream: to be the heir of the kingdom that failed my father. Even though it's still a dream, it's not what I've been hunting for all this time. It's this. To be where I am at this moment, knowing there are people out there willing to stand at my side, so much so that it's impossible not to trust them while they choose to trust me too.

I belong.

It's not a place I've been searching for, not a physical one, at least. It's the feeling I get when contentment washes over me—a rare but distinct feeling nonetheless.

Running my fingers over my ears one last time, I roll my shoulders back and head for the hallway. I have no idea where I'm going, acutely aware that I did, in fact, arrive here completely passed out, but as I follow the murmured voices, I wander into the kitchen where everyone is sitting.

Flora is the first to notice me. She jumps up from her seat, where she is curled up beside Arlo, and storms toward me with purpose. She darts through the air, almost knocking me off my feet as she holds me in a deathly tight grip.

"I don't know whether to kiss you or kill you," she squeals, earning a huff from Cassian, who leans against the fridge with his arms folded over his chest. She waves him off with an eye roll, making it abundantly clear that this isn't the first time he's been an ass to her, but she continues to ignore him as her giddiness pauses for a beat, her eyes finding my ears before they grow watery. She sinks her teeth into her bottom lip, shaking her head as she tries to contain her emotions.

"I'd like to see you try," I rasp, trying not to make a big deal about it.

"You shouldn't have done that," she says, grabbing my arms as she gives me a pointed look, which I match with one of my own.

"I wouldn't have done anything else," I answer honestly, and her shoulders slump before she drags me in for another hug.

"Can you at least share her for ten seconds so I can have a hug too?" Raiden grumbles, appearing beside her, and she giggles, stepping out of his way so he can swoop me up off the floor.

"Hi, Raiden," I whisper against his ear as he swirls me around, peppering kisses over my skin before I'm placed back on my feet.

"Hey, Troublemaker," he answers, offering me a wink before he's shoved aside and replaced by Cassian.

The grumpy wolf pins me to his chest, breathing me in, and I feel his chest loosen and his body relax with every beat that passes. He doesn't offer me any words, just a stroke of his thumb over my cheek as he assesses me. With a nod, he steps back, making room for Brody to fill the now-empty space.

An infectious smirk plays on his lips, making my own pop as a reminder of his interruption earlier plays in my mind. He kisses me softly, just as wordless as Cassian, before he steps back again.

My gaze turns back to Flora. "What happened, Flora?"

She understands exactly what I mean and points for me to take a seat at the dining table. I follow after her as Kryll places a plate of food down in front of me, and I murmur my thanks.

Margherita pizza for the win.

I take my first slice as she sighs, getting comfortable in her chair before she speaks. "It happened in the night," she admits, lacing her fingers together nervously in her lap until Arlo moves to the seat beside her and intertwines them with his own. When it seems like it's too much for her, Arlo clears his throat.

"They stormed her room in the middle of the night. You would think the fact that I was there would have helped, but I was incapable of doing anything against them. The human origin professor came in, so we didn't realize what was going on until we found ourselves captive."

Fuckers.

"Did they—"

Flora shakes her head, waving me off before I can finish speaking. "They didn't do anything to us. They didn't even bother to bind us or anything. The only fae they're worried about magically is you, which worked in our favor eventually, right?"

"Why didn't you attack them straight away so

you weren't taken prisoner?" Cassian asks, making me glare at him.

"What the hell is up with you?" I blurt, clearly sensing some animosity from him, and he shrugs.

"No, it's okay, Addi. He's only asking because he cares about you, and I get it. That's why I stayed, and it's exactly why I didn't put up a fight. They were going to get you there regardless of whether I stayed or not, so I wanted to be of use when the time came, even if the chances were slim," Flora states with a shrug as Arlo pulls her into his side.

"Don't make me warn you again," he states sharply, eyes fixed on Cassian, who ignores him.

Whatever this is, it needs fixing.

"I'm sorry any of this happened to you, Flora," I breathe, the truth flowing from my lips as she shakes her head at me.

"Don't you dare apologize. None of this is your fault."

She squeezes my hand in comfort, drawing a smile to my lips as a door swinging open echoes from down the hall. Kryll is the first to move, skidding to a halt by the door as his brother walks in.

His eyes take us all in, assessing us individually until his gaze settles on mine. "I'm glad you're awake."

"Me too," I retort before he turns his attention to his brother.

"We've got a situation."

My spine stiffens at his statement, locking me in place as everyone else waits with bated breath too. Kryll curses under his breath, rubbing at the back of his neck. His gaze flickers to me for a brief moment before seeking out Beau again.

"Ah, shit. She hasn't been awake all that long. We haven't told her about that yet," he states cryptically, and if I thought my spine was stiff before, that was nothing in comparison to now.

"Told me what?"

All eyes turn to me, and Kryll's face shows a hint of guilt as he braces for impact, but the flourish of someone else entering the room pulls my attention away from him.

I know who it is immediately from the lilac outfit she's wearing, but the crinkling of her eyes and pursed lips give her away too. She plants her hands on her hips, her eyes drilling into mine before she speaks.

"Then the pleasure of telling her is mine." Her shoulders stiffen as if she needs a moment to say the words too, and I start to think the worst. My father? Nora? Fuck. It's on the tip of my tongue to tell her to get the fuck on with it when she finally does. "Vallie isn't dead, but she needs to be."

"You're going to have to slow down if you want us to hear a word you're saying," I snap, irritation coiling through my veins as Bozzelli marches out of Beau's house just as quickly as she arrived.

Adrianna was the first to move, her jaw slack as she chased after the woman. It feels dumb now, not telling her at the first opportunity, but in my defense, I'm trying to figure out all of this fated mates shit because my body feels completely out of whack.

I don't know what I expected. I don't think any of us did. Yet here we are, confused again, but at least this time, the five of us are together. Extra footsteps confirm the addition of Flora and Arlo.

Everything unraveling around us is the polar opposite of what I expected academy life to be like. This shit happening so quickly in succession has thrown us, but we will rise above it. Today, we plan and strategize. We need to use our allies to get ahead of The Council. Fighting against the tide of this madness isn't an option. We have to adapt and survive.

My steps falter, my gaze shifting to Adrianna as she keeps one step ahead of me, forcing herself to remain at Bozzelli's side.

Is this what her life has felt like? No breaks, no coming up for air, no understanding which way is up?

Fuck.

No wonder she's so strong. She's had no choice but to be. Anything else, and she would have wound up dead by now. My gaze flicks to her ears, noting Kryll's magic and smiling at the restored tips, pointed and perfect.

A shove from behind, encouraging me forward, pulls me from my train of thought. I glare back at Cassian, who doesn't even bother to look my way before I quicken my pace and turn my look of disdain on the dean.

"What's all this about?" I ask, aware that Vallie apparently isn't dead, but that doesn't explain the urgency. "And either slow down or speed the fuck up so we can have an actual discussion," I add, and she sends a withering stare my way.

I don't back down. She's a vampire; I'm used to

their wrath more than anyone else. Fuck, has she met my mother?

"There's no time to slow down," she bites, her nostrils flaring with irritation as I shrug.

"That's fine. I said you could speed up too," I add, tilting my head at her, but she ignores me.

"Someone needs to tell me something," Adrianna states, her eyebrows furrowing with confusion. My concern for her only grows as she rubs her lips together nervously.

Bozzelli sighs, her pace unwavering as she continues toward the academy building. "They know you're here, and they know their plan didn't work. I've been ordered to take you to the dungeon," she states, her tone giving nothing away.

What the fuck?

"Then let me stop you right the fuck there. We're not going," I snarl, furious to think this woman would expect us to go willingly. Not again, not after last time.

"Does she look like she's being held against her will?" Bozzelli asks, halting as she glares at me, and I shrug.

"That's not what I said. But you sure as hell are not putting her in any more danger. She's not a toy for you to use at your leisure," I bite back as Adrianna cuts the distance between us, planting her hand firmly on my shoulder. I can't decide if it's to comfort me or shut me the fuck up, but either way, I'm silenced.

A soft smile teeters over her lips as she stares at me for a moment, making me assume that I'm not in any immediate trouble with her before she turns her attention to Bozzelli. "He's right." *Ha.* "And he's wrong." *Fuck.* "I'm going to need more information here before I take another step. I'm not a puppet on a string. That's what they wanted, and that's what they're pissed about. I'm not going to offer you the reins instead."

Fuck yeah. My dick chooses the perfectly inappropriate moment to stir to life, but she's hot as fuck when she's assertive and bossy. I like it. I like it a lot.

"We don't have much time," Bozzelli starts, but Adrianna waves her hand, interrupting her without care.

"I thought you didn't take orders from anyone?" She cocks a brow at the dean, her words hanging in the air as Bozzelli searches her eyes. It takes a moment, but I see it—the fear.

My lips part as I take a step toward her, but before I can push her on it, she explains.

"They have my niece."

Shit. Does this woman have a family? I never considered that. Not that it matters to us.

"I'm sorry for that," Adrianna breathes, a softness to her tone that makes it clear she feels more compassion than me right now. "I understand the weight of someone using your family against you, but I'm still going to need you to explain things a little better," she adds. Her posture is relaxed and her chin is up high as she waits for Bozzelli to make a decision.

The stare-off breathes from one moment into another and I take a second to assess the crowd that stands in silence with me. Kryll's staring at Adrianna, watching her every move, while Brody is fixated on the dean, waiting for a single move out of place. Cassian is a mixture of the two, his eyes dancing between our supposed leader and our actual leader. Flora, however, stands back a step, nestled between Arlo and Beau, as their stares bounce back and forth.

Circling back to the two women, my gaze lingers on Adrianna just as she purses her lips and Bozzelli relents.

"Fine. Quickly, but please keep walking with me," she asks, earning a nod from Adrianna as they fall into step once again.

"The soldiers arrived quickly. *Too* quickly, and the second you were out of there, a mage who works directly with The Council hurried into the room, chanting under their breath as they approached Vallie. She took a breath thirty seconds later."

"Where is she now?" Adrianna asks, her pupils wide as she takes in the information.

"Likely with her uncle, who is the one demanding I get you in the dungeon."

Fucker.

"I'm assuming they want us contained because their plan to control our magic didn't work," Kryll clarifies from a step behind me and Bozzelli hums.

"I believe so," she admits as the academy building comes into view. She continues to scurry along until she reaches the door, where she pauses, her gaze finding Adrianna's. "I'm sorry they did that to you. I'm sorry I didn't do anything to stop them from taking you. Had I have known—"

"Don't apologize for something you didn't do. What is meant to be will be, this is one of those things," Adrianna states, interjecting with a hint of pride in her words, and it makes my cock twitch again.

Bozzelli nods, worry flashing across her eyes for a second before she pushes at the door and steps inside. The rest of us follow her. The hallway leads to a winding set of stairs that head underground.

"Are we actually willingly going to the dungeons? For them to do what? They're not going to be painting our nails and shit, Adrianna. They're going to want to kill us. The chance to control us has passed. Now, we're too powerful, and they're going to want to put a stop to us by any means necessary," I state, raking my fingers through my hair as Adrianna looks back at me with a soft smile.

"They asked me to bring you to the dungeons, Mr. Holloway. They didn't say anything about making sure you were detained," Bozzelli states as she inserts a long golden key into the lock at the end of the hall to reveal a dark and dreary room on the other side.

I was hoping the dungeons would be a little more fanciful than what one would typically picture, but no. This is somehow worse.

"What are you saying?" I grumble, hating that she's giving me hints instead of getting straight to the point.

She rolls her eyes at me, keeping her stare fixed on Adrianna instead. "If you want to save the kingdom, start with them."

Adrianna nods, rolling her shoulders back before she steps into the dungeon.

"Adrianna," I plead, hurrying in after her.

"It's going to be okay, Raiden," she states, a smile on her lips as she turns to Bozzelli. "Just the five of us. That's who they want. Beau, take Flora and Arlo somewhere safe. I don't want them to be used as pawns in someone else's game again," she orders, and both Beau and Bozzelli nod in agreement.

The door is closed without another word, trapping Cassian, Brody, Kryll, Adrianna, and me.

Complete darkness engulfs us until Brody begins to chant under his breath, and a moment later, a soft glow flickers from the four corners of the room.

"What now?" Cassian asks, hands on his hips as he stares at the small confines we now find ourselves in. But Adrianna doesn't falter; if anything, she stands taller.

"I have a plan."

A plan is a plan. Strong and decisive until you're left to sit and rot away in it. I have no idea of the time. I foolishly chased after Bozzelli without considering my cell phone, but none of that really matters when there are bigger things at play. It's not like I could call for help from down here. That's the whole point: Shut us off from the rest of the world and take our lives in the darkness like we mean nothing.

It's almost funny. *Almost.*

I spent hours upon hours losing myself to the actions I took. I killed her, and for a moment, I regretted it. But now that I know she's alive, planning some cunning shit with that damn uncle of hers, I know I've wasted too much time churning over what I did.

It seems I'm all set to do it again.

Her words from the dining hall replay in my mind. *You have no idea of the power.*

Fuck her and fuck her uncle's promise of power. The Council is corrupt beyond words and we need to put a stop to it. Killing Vallie so they don't kill me is only fitting. Besides, it's clear now that she was purposely goading me to attack her. Shit, they even had a mage on standby, ready to revive her.

Bozzelli was right. If I want to save the kingdom, we must first save it from them. No one else will, and I refuse to allow the kingdom to continue to crumble under the weight of their desire for more and more power. The Council has to be disbanded, even if it's not me who replaces them. I know I will have done what I was meant to do if I focus all my efforts on stopping them.

That's my core purpose.

I know it.

What's not my core purpose is waiting. My patience is running thin.

All the rushing Bozzelli had getting us here, and now we're waiting. Hours. My mind and body know it has at least been hours; I just don't know how many exactly.

"Are we going to address the beacon in the room?" Raiden asks, cutting through the silence, and my gaze snaps to his. We're each nestled against the wall. Kryll is beside the door, opposite me, Raiden along the left wall, while Brody and Cassian take up the right wall.

All perfectly in position for when the time comes.

Raiden cocks his brow at me and his comment finally registers in my brain, making me roll my eyes as a sarcastic laugh parts my lips.

"Ha ha, very funny," I grumble, stretching my legs out in front of me, but when none of the others laugh along with me, I know it's a topic that does actually need addressing. What better time than while sitting patiently, waiting to be attacked. "Fine," I mutter, nervously rubbing my hands down my thighs.

"If you don't want to talk about it yet, then you don't have to," Brody insists, making me smile as I shake my head.

"I'm good. We do need to talk about it. I'm just not in the best zone to find all of the right words," I admit. "The light... I remember it from one other time in my life," I start, avoiding their watchful stares as I look down at my lap. "It happened the night Kenner took my ears," I add, a shiver running up my spine and making my pointed tips tingle at the memory. "I didn't realize the light was coming from me at the time. I didn't realize much about it at all until earlier, but when our magic connected, it came to life again, like it was protecting me. Just like it had all those years ago."

"I'm sorry you had to go through that, Princess," Kryll murmurs, his hands twitching as if he wants to reach out for me, but the comforting will have to wait in case our long-overdue guests join us.

"It's okay. When our magic connected, the memory from that night played out in my mind, only this time, I wasn't blinded by the light. I saw every-thing; crisp and clear. You were there," I state, turning to Cassian, who frowns.

"I was where?"

"At the castle that night."

"No, I wasn't," he grunts, his defenses rising as I shake my head.

"You don't remember, and you won't because your father made it so." His brows furrow deeper as my words linger in the air. "You tried to stop him," I admit, a sad smile tainting the corner of my mouth as I intertwine my fingers. "You tried to stop him from getting Nora. You defied him, and I'm sure you can guess how well he took that."

He stares at me, his jaw slightly slack as disbelief washes over him. "I don't remember."

"And I'm glad you don't," I insist. "I felt a connection to you that night," I add, wanting him to understand the best I can. "I couldn't explain it, and I still wouldn't be able to now, but I felt it deep in my veins. A tug pulled me toward you just as fiercely as it screamed for me to protect my sister."

"Maybe your heart knew he was your mate. Well, the wolf one," Brody states, a wink accompanying his play on words.

I hum in acknowledgment. That would make sense.

"Did anyone else have a vision when our magic collided?" I ask, receiving four blank stares in response. I nod in understanding when another thought comes to mind. "There was also a woman," I explain, bending my knees as I wrap my arms around them protectively.

"A woman? The same one who led us to you?" Brody asks, and I shake my head, recalling what she looked like.

"No. She was... technically in the cell beside me—until she wasn't, " I say, earning four confused stares.

"You're going to have to explain that a little more, Alpha," Cassian grunts, scrubbing at the back of his neck, and I nod.

"She was in the cell beside me with her back turned to me for ages. Then she apparently could sense I was overthinking, and she started to talk about herself cryptically."

"Did she say anything exciting?" Raiden asks, a

bored tone on his tongue as he tries to see the point of her, and I shake my head.

"Not really. She talked about wanting to be a leader, her family abandoning her after treating her like a princess, and how an amethyst kiss of death works, but when the soldiers came to take me to The Council members, she was gone."

"Gone?"

"Yeah, and I even asked the soldiers to make sure I wasn't losing my mind. They made it clear that I was because no other prisoners were being held in those cells."

It sounds dumb now that I'm saying it out loud.

Raiden clears his throat, glancing at the others before turning back to me. "Maybe it was—"

"She appeared in my vision too," I interject, refusing to accept the fact that I might be delusional.

"In your vision?" Brody repeats, and I sigh.

"Yes. She said something like, 'You're welcome,' before I was slammed back into the present. That's when I started to glow," I grumble, waving my hands up and down the length of my body.

"That glow bit was fucking hot, I'm not going to lie," Raiden says with a contented sigh. It should surprise me, but in reality, it's just so freaking Raiden that it's impossible to shock me.

"What did it feel like?" Kryll asks as I spy Raiden adjusting his dick beneath his pants.

Opting to distract from his growing length, I focus on my dragon.

"It felt out of control," I state, and as usual, he doesn't push or nudge for me to continue, he simply gives me the wide berth I need to find my words. "It was controlling me, not the other way around. I wanted to kill those fuckers and teach them a lesson, but the light was hell-bent on using all of my energy to protect everyone."

"The dome it formed around us was impressive," Brody muses, and I shake my head.

"But if it wasn't there, one of us could have hit back at them," I state, completely aware that one of the people on the other side of that barrier was his father. We should probably have a conversation about that and what our response will be, but for now, we can focus on Vallie and her uncle. The rest will come later.

"I feel like I've read something about this before," he replies, tapping his finger mindlessly against his chin as he thinks. "I'm not sure."

"I thought you were a mage? Aren't you supposed to retain every scrap of information you've ever so much as glanced at so you can recall it in the most annoying circumstance possible?" Cassian grumbles, cocking a brow at his friend, who offers him a one-finger salute in response.

"You're damn right I'm a mage, but the shit I'm

talking about, it's not part of the formal curriculum. It's tingling at the edge of my brain, but I feel like it was a myth or something, so my mind didn't filter it in," he explains, offering me an apologetic look.

"Whatever it is, its sole focus seems to be on protection. I'm not a defensive person; I'm all about charging into the chaos," I state, releasing a frustrated huff that makes my chest deflate.

"Maybe it's a counter-balance to the chaos you usually seek. Maybe it's supposed to make you step back and think," Kryll offers, which does nothing to ease the annoyance rattling in my chest.

"There's stepping back to think, and there's stepping out of the picture entirely, and that's exactly what it felt like."

Footsteps echo in the distance, cutting off the rest of my grumbling as we all stiffen. The shrill sound of Vallie's voice makes my muscles bunch together, but I force them to ease as she draws closer.

"Ready?" Raiden asks as Brody starts to chant softly under his breath.

I take a deep breath, shaking out my bones as I lie down. "As I'll ever be."

"Quies. Lenio. Delinio. Resido. Quies. Lenio. Delinio. Resido. Quies. Lenio. Delinio. Resido. Quies. Lenio. Delinio. Resido. Quies. Lenio. Delinio. Resido. Quies. Lenio. Delinio. Resido." My eyes close as my words grow lower and lower. Once they take effect, I redirect my chanting. "Prensio. Captura. Tenere. Prensio. Captura. Tenere. Prensio. Captura. Tenere. Prensio. Captura. Tenere. Prensio. Captura. Tenere."

The telltale sound of the key entering the lock echoes around the room as my words die off. It takes all of my strength to pry my eyes open enough to check the room before a sense of satisfaction washes over me. It doesn't last long, not when the plan isn't entirely foolproof, but it's what Adrianna wanted, so it's what I will provide.

The shackles that lay against the wall now encapsulate each of our wrists as our bodies lay limp on the floor. Vallie steps into the room and the giggle of glee that vibrates off the walls is exactly what I was hoping for.

This dumb bitch is going to get what's coming, and I'm more than happy to be the one to give it to her if necessary.

"Uncle, I can't believe it," she sings with glee, clapping wildly as my heart rate slowly thumps in my ears.

"I told you, Vallie. Power is ours for the taking."

"I know, but my father said that too, and look what happened to him. He didn't make good on a single promise, unlike you," she squeals. "She's completely passed out and at my mercy. It's like the best birthday present I could ever receive, and it's six months away!"

My goodness, she's insufferable.

Just as my spell was designed to do, the grogginess begins to ease from my limbs as I groan. I mustn't be the only one coming to life from the heaviness of the magic because she sneers, but it's not aimed at me.

"Raiden!" she yells unnecessarily, and I manage to pry my eyes open again in time to watch her march in his direction. The vampire chained to the wall sneers up at her with pitch-black eyes, a venomous aura engulfing him.

"Fuck off," he grunts, shuffling to sit up and lean back against the wall.

"You don't get to speak to me like that. Not anymore. Tell him, Uncle," she preens, flicking her hair over her shoulder as I groan.

She really isn't dead, and that's fucking disappointing.

"Your uncle can fuck off too," Raiden snaps back, and Vallie inches forward, swiping the back of her hand across his face.

My gaze darts to Addi, but she remains flat out on the floor. I can't decide whether it's a good thing or not, but either way, Vallie isn't making this any easier for herself.

"That's Councilman Drummer to you."

"I didn't like the last Councilman Drummer. I can't see that changing with this one, but thanks," Raiden snorts in response, eyes narrowed on the pair.

I chance a look at Cassian and Kryll, who are now propped up against the wall again, hands in metal cuffs with their eyes fixated on our girl. Our unmoving girl.

I can sense the worry oozing from them, but I keep my mouth shut.

Drummer steps forward, baring his teeth as he crouches in front of Raiden. "My brother was a fool. He never could live up to me. Now, he definitely never will. I'll make sure to thank that bitch before I slaughter her," he bites, making Raiden tug at the cuffs holding him in place.

His stare spins my way for a split second, silently pleading with me to undo my magic, but it's too late now, and it's probably for the best. It makes this all look more real and appealing to them.

As if sensing my thoughts, Vallie laughs, tossing her head back as she holds on to her uncle's shoulder for support. "Don't talk about the little half-breed like that. You'll make my Raidy all mad," she says with a fake pout, wagging her finger in Raiden's face as she speaks.

Her taunting is unbearable. I couldn't tolerate it in the dining hall when Addi launched at her. Now, it's even worse.

Give them the upper hand. Give them the upper hand.

Addi's words repeat in my mind, holding me in place as I trust in her plan.

If our girl can hear the shit being said, she does nothing to react, which is better character than I expected because I was sure she would charge at her the second this dumb bitch opened her mouth.

"What do you want, Vallie?" Raiden asks, pushing up to his feet as the chains clang together. Vallie takes note of the metal in place, a smile spreading across her face.

"I want you, Raiden."

"Really? Right now?" Cassian grunts, earning a death stare from the wicked vampire herself, but her attention quickly snaps back to Raiden.

"Uncle, let me keep this one. The rest can perish," Vallie states, fluttering her eyelashes at the man as her grin spreads from ear to ear.

"Vallie, I—"

"I'd rather you kill me first and feed me to the fucking vermin that runs rabid in our kingdom than have to spend another fucking second in your presence," Raiden interjects, every word etched with truth as he looks at her with utter disdain.

Vallie rears back, a gasp on her lips as her hand lifts to her chest. The demure action quickly turns rotten as her hands ball into fists and her teeth extend into sharp points.

"Fuck you, Raiden. You never deserved me," she lurches toward him, nails ripping into his t-shirt as she pulls him closer.

She opens her mouth unbelievably wide, inching closer to his neck as I start to panic. I turn to Addi, hoping the magic has worn off, but she's out cold.

Fuck.

I yank at my chains, muttering the chant under my breath to undo what I did, getting the same sense of panic from Cassian and Kryll too. I mutter faster, the chant burning my tongue with every pass.

A flutter of a breeze is all the warning the room

gets before a bright light fills the space. It's blinding, mesmerizing, and fucking stunning. A scream rips from Vallie's chest as the projection of light narrows to Raiden and Addi launches herself through the air.

Barreling into Vallie, they fall into the far wall with a thud. Drummer lurches back, crouching as he shields himself from the blinding light. He's already stood on the other side of its shine; he knows the abilities that can accompany it.

Yanking at my chains again, the metal gives no freedom for me to move, turning my chants faster as stress starts to rise through my bones.

"Let them think they have the upper hand by giving them the upper hand. If my magic sees one of you in danger, it will bubble to the surface to protect you. That will catch them off guard and we can decimate them."

A plan. A solid-yet-uncertain plan, depending on how you look at it. And right now, it's not looking great.

"Come on, Brody," Cassian grunts, dealing with the same issue as me. I don't answer, though; I can't break my spell, otherwise, it will take even longer.

Movement out of the corner of my eye pulls my attention as my chants continue, and I turn just in time to see Addi gain the advantage, slamming Vallie against the wall with rage.

"Get this fucking mutt off me," Vallie yells,

hysteria echoing off the walls as she snaps her teeth threateningly at Addi.

My nostrils flare with anger as I remember the time Vallie sank her teeth into my woman. The rage it creates inside of me is like an inferno for my magic, and a moment later, the metal splits at my wrists and falls with a clatter to the floor.

Charging toward the pair of them, I forget about Drummer until it's too late. His arms hook around my legs, toppling me to the ground. I manage to catch myself with my hands, saving my face from disaster, but the second I take to compose myself is used against me.

A sharp pain explodes in my ribs, a hiss rasping from my lips as he shoves at my side, knocking me to the floor. I blink, my vision blurry as I stare up at the vampire pinning me in place.

He wrestles my arms beneath his legs, pressing down with a ferocity that can't be reciprocated. The burning at my side is hot yet cold, a dampness coating my skin, but I can't see what's happening. The world spins around me as I try to focus myself enough to think of a chant, *any* chant, but everything turns to jelly, including my mind.

The blow to my face that follows is the final disarming move needed to unravel me. In my haste to get to Addi, I left myself completely vulnerable, and now I'm helpless. The momentum snaps my head to the side, my vision worsening, but before I can take a breath, another blow follows, then another, and another.

Another sharp pain, another burning sensation laced with hot and cold chills, and still, I can't do anything. He relents, offering me a pointless reprieve as my watery vision settles on a familiar blonde braid. My pulse thunders in my ears as my mouth falls slack, the feel of another slice at my abdomen sealing my fate at the exact moment I watch Vallie fall to her knees. Her face is about as beaten as I expect mine to be, but Addi doesn't pin her to the floor like this. Instead, she wraps her legs around her neck, tightening them like a vice as she holds on tight to the chain bolt above her head.

A battle cry rings in my ears from her victorious lips as darkness shifts into my vision, tainting the corner of my eyes. She's going to bury this bitch, once and for all, while I edge closer to my last breath too. Seeing her shine like this will be worth it; I'll gladly give my life.

I should have fought harder; she deserved more from me, but I was helpless.

Contentment weighs over me as the world goes still. A numbness drapes across my skin, the pain etching through my limbs drifting to nothing as crimson droplets blur my vision. Screams and shouts turn to murmurs in my ears, nothing registering as I slip into the delirium that I can only describe as post-orgasm bliss. But without the pleasure. I'm floating, but there's no joy in anything I'm feeling. Definitely not post-orgasm bliss.

A bright light blurs the remainder of my vision, forcing my eyes closed. The moment they shut, a spark of color dances across the back of my eyelids. I watch, enthralled by its movements, each swoop across my lids becoming slower and smaller, and understanding dawns on me.

With every loop, my heart rate slows. With every twirl, my body falls weaker. With every shimmer, my own spark dies out.

Despite the pain, I know my consciousness is waning. I also know it's all okay.

To have been loved by her for five minutes is better than never to have been loved by her at all.

I'm certain a smile quirks the corner of my mouth, joy clinging to me as my breaths become even more labored.

The world shifts, though my eyes refuse to open. Darkness lures me in despite my curiosity about the outside world. The smell of sunshine, a scent I have only noticed around Addi, drifts around me like a beacon telling me it's time to go—to bathe in that scent for all of eternity.

I give in, exhaling slowly as my body becomes completely weightless. Then I wait... and wait... and still, the smell lingers in the air, but the promise of the afterlife remains just out of reach.

Trying to delve deeper into myself, I reach out for the tiny spark that barely flickers in my vision, but as I chase after it, it grows bigger. Only to fade again the moment I get close to it.

"Don't you dare fucking give up on me, Brody." Addi's words ring in my ears, luring me closer to the darkness as I chase after the spark, desperate to hear her voice again. I dive, deeper and deeper, until something presses against my face, prying my eyes open as I choke on a breath.

Bright eyes look down at me, the glimmer of blonde hair framing her face, but the blistering light that shimmers behind them makes it harder to see anything. But I don't have to see to know it's her.

My girl.

My Dagger.

"Is it working, Kryll? Tell me it's fucking working," she snaps, a ghost of a smile dancing over my lips as I bask in her anger. I still feel like I'm floating until the touch of her delicate fingers gripping my chin firmly. "Don't you grin like that. When you come around fully, I will rain Hell down on you for panicking me like that."

My lips spread wider, the dream I'm engulfed in lighting me from the inside out.

"We need to act now, Addi," Cassian grunts. Streaks of blood mark his face as he huffs, glancing down at me with a look of concern that's far too mixed with inconvenience for me to relish in his worry.

"Do it now, Kryll," Addi yells, and a moment later, the telltale sound of Kryll's dragon echoes in my ears. The ground shakes beneath me, the walls crumbling in dismay as fire issues forth from the dragon.

I don't feel the heat, not even a little, as a glowing dome shines around me.

A breath grows stronger in my chest, quickly followed by another and another, until the pain ricocheting through my body comes to life once again. I manage to roll over, a grunt falling from my lips as I stare in disbelief.

From the dome to my Dagger and back again, I repeat the sway of my gaze over and over before settling on my girl. She heaves a sigh of relief as the fire blooms on the other side of the shield and she drops to her knees beside me.

She catches a glimpse of me out of the corner of her eye, and her lips purse. Despite the fury I sense in her, she leans in close, stroking a hand down my cheek as she speaks. "You're in so much trouble, Brody. So fucking much."

"Trouble sounds better than death," I rasp, earning the smallest smile from her taut lips.

"You say that now," she muses, rising to her feet before she offers me her hand.

I frown as I take it, lurching to my feet as I try to catch up with what the fuck just happened. I was dead. I felt it. My body, my face... nothing is different. Only the remnants of crimson stains on my t-shirt confirm something was wrong.

"He stabbed you with poisoned blades," Raiden offers, pulling me from my thoughts as I blink at the stains, nodding as if that makes perfect sense.

"What else did I miss?" I ask, scrambling to understand a single thing, but I come up blank every time.

"Let's get out of here before the place burns down. Then, if you're lucky, she might offer you an explanation before she kills you herself." He smothers a hand over his mouth, trying and failing to hide his snicker as I shake my head in disbelief.

"She's not going to kill me," I grumble, swiping a hand down my face, only to smear more blood over my skin.

"Are you sure about that?" he retorts, pointing at the woman in question, and I gulp.

She looks mad. Real mad. But I already told her

I'll take her wrath over death. I'm right where I'm supposed to be, where I always will be. I'm just about to say it when the ground shudders and an explosion sends us flying through the air.

I hit something hard with a thud, the darkness creeping in faster this time as everything goes black, leaving only one thought on the edge of my mind.

It's definitely too soon for death jokes.

My lungs burn as I cough, the thick, smoky air swirling around me as I try to catch my breath. Panicked, I seek out the others. Kryll is standing by the rubble, hands planted on his hips. He stares down at the skeletal remains of Vallie and her annoying uncle while Raiden swipes at his ash-ladden clothes relentlessly.

Uncertainty wars inside me as I spy Cassian a few feet away, looking off into the tree line, a stark reminder that the dungeons are gone, along with a good quarter of the academy building. Something exploded with Kryll's fire. What it was, I'm not sure, but my protective light of magic managed to blast us to safety with the force of the explosion.

Where the fuck is Brody?

"Dagger." My nickname is barely more than a

husky whisper, hauling me to my feet as I spin in a circle, searching for the source. I sag with relief a moment later when I find my mage splayed out on the other side of the rubble. Soot coats his cheeks, brightening his eyes in the late-night air.

"Brody," I breathe, dropping to my knees with a grunt beside him as he pushes up to face me. I'm sure he thinks I'm joking, but he gave me the biggest scare of my life back there, and he's going to pay for that when I'm calmer.

"Did I miss much?" he asks, smiling up at me, and I shake my head in disbelief.

"You missed everything. You were too busy trying to die until my magic tugged me toward you. Thankfully, Kryll's blood did that thing it's good at, and you don't get to watch on from the afterlife," I state, giving him a pointed look, and he frowns.

"I don't know what you're—"

"I could feel you, your thoughts, your feelings... everything."

His eyes widen in surprise. "Oh."

"Yeah, *oh*. I don't want to hear that shit ever again. Do you hear me?"

"Yes, ma'am," he says with a sharp nod, and my gaze narrows.

"Don't ever call me ma'am again," I warn, and he grins.

"Whatever you say, Dagger."

My shoulders ease, some of my tension drifting away at the sound of my nickname from his lips. He really is okay. With a sigh, I cut the remaining distance between us, resting my head on his shoulder, and in the next breath, he's pulling me backward so we're lying amongst the rubble.

Dark clouds still swirl above us, a siren to the entire kingdom, I'm sure, as they billow higher and higher while we simply stare at the carnage.

"What happened back there, Brody?" I ask, reliving the moment in my head again. "One minute, I was strangling the hell out of that bitch, and the next, I'm being drawn toward you because her uncle was trying to turn you into a puddle of mage goo." My chest aches from the memory, my conscience refusing to remember anything deeper to keep my heart intact.

"I don't even know, Addi. He just grabbed my legs as I was rushing over to you, and I was powerless to stop him once he cut me the first time," he admits, eyes glazed as he looks off into the distance.

We really were close to losing him. Closer than I care to admit.

"I mean it, Brody. Don't ever do that again," I repeat, trying to ease the remaining tension, but it's impossible.

The plan was going perfectly, I had Vallie right

where I wanted her, but everything went to shit. For the most part. My head aches, but as I lie here, with Brody's arm as my cushion, I feel a sense of relief. They're gone. Vallie and her fucked up uncle are completely gone, and the remnants of them confirm they sure as hell aren't coming back.

Killing her felt entirely different from last time. It wasn't for me this time. Well, maybe slightly, but it was about protecting myself and the kingdom, too.

"What have you done?" The shocked voice comes from Bozzelli, but I don't lift my head to acknowledge her. Instead, I sigh, closing my eyes as I continue to relax.

"Your niece?"

"She's safe," she answers, clearing her throat nervously. I hear two sets of footsteps inch closer toward us, and a moment later, I find Beau peering down at us.

"I think it's safe to say there won't be any classes in the morning," he states, scrubbing at his chin as he assesses the mess, and I hum in agreement.

"That sounds like it might be a good idea," Brody replies, stroking soft circles on my arm in comfort, like I shouldn't be the one comforting him since he was almost freaking dead.

"Don't make me change my mind, Mr. Orenda. There are still members of The Council and foolish leaders of packs out there who are just as eager for your death as these two," Bozzelli retorts, and I sigh.

"Why are parents just awful?" I ask, mentally excluding my father, of course. But my mother, on the other hand...

"I don't know, but they're tomorrow's problem now," Cassian states, appearing at Beau's side as he offers me his hand. I place my palm against his, relishing in the warmth that spreads from him to me as he pulls me to my feet and into his arms.

"Hey, I nearly died, and I'm not ready to share yet," Brody grumbles, but Cassian only pulls me closer.

"You caused her more stress than necessary. If anything, you should be thankful we're even letting you be close to her," Raiden grunts in response, sauntering toward us with a tiredness that I sense deep in my bones too.

"Wow, this pissing contest is great and all, but the rest of us have shit to deal with now," Beau grumbles, stepping back with a few large strides.

"What shit?" Kryll asks, inching closer as he assesses his brother, who waves him off.

"You should all head back to my house. Flora and Arlo are waiting," he offers, but Kryll doesn't let it drop.

"What shit, Beau?"

"That's Professor Tora to you," Bozzelli interjects, but Kryll doesn't even bother to look her way. Instead, he stares his brother down, waiting for a response.

"The media are going to want to know about this, and the kingdom deserves to understand. It's now my job to paint you in the best light possible."

I wish I could say the morning light flutters through the window, dancing in the air with a summer's glow as the birds chirp in the distance, waking me from a deep slumber that rests my body from head to toe. I wish I could, but I can't, because this is not a fairy tale and I didn't sleep for shit.

Thankfully, the shallow breaths of my Kryptos kept me company as they slept while I tossed and turned relentlessly before I finally gave up.

Looking up at the sky, I try to guess the time by the location of the sun, but my brain is too tired to really care. I slipped out here hours ago, when I finally gave up on sleep, and I can't deny that Beau has a pretty house. The sun peeks above the tree line as the sound of the gentle stream nearby filters through my ears, a calming burble that tries to help me put things in perspective.

The academy is on the brink of failure and the kingdom is worse off than ever, leaving the ability to sleep far beyond what I can achieve. I can't stop thinking, I can't stop my mind from wandering down every possible avenue to bring peace to our people, but every road is blocked.

Despite my inner turmoil, which now seems to be my new state of mind, my magic has different ideas. Not my wolf, and not my new bright light, just my fae magic. My *royal* fae magic.

My bare feet are planted on the ground, my toes curling into the grass as I connect with my earth magic. It rejuvenates me slowly, filling the void my lack of sleep created as the gentle breeze swoops around my body, dancing along my air magic and zapping me back to life.

Despite how head tired I am, my magic is doing what I can't seem to achieve alone: bringing me back to life.

The fight isn't over. If anything, it's barely begun. Taking out Vallie and her uncle was nothing in the grand scheme of things, or so it feels like, so my magic is replenishing me, ready for the uphill battle that's ahead.

A shiver runs down my spine as my fire magic comes to life, and my eyes pop open. I hadn't even realized they were closed. Turning my hand so my palm is up, I smile when a flicker of heat dances along my fingertips before settling into a ball in my grasp.

It's funny how something so small can bring so much focus and strength to a moment. I'm sitting here, working my way along every road to certain death as I try to play out the future, while the embers in my palms remind me that things aren't always as they seem.

To the outside world, I'm a girl with pointed ears and a history of being a forsaken origin. I'm a lowly fae, just like the others. No real power, no superiority, no grace among the lands, but that's not what this is about. It's about purpose. It's about beliefs. It's about humanity.

Not just for the superior origins to rule down on others, but for everyone. From the assholes at the top of the food chain to the lowly fae at the bottom. If the academy has taught me anything, it's that I know how to fall, I know how to stand myself back up, and I know how to dust myself off.

If I want a different outcome, then I have to fucking find one myself.

It's not going to just fall in my lap; I have to choose it, I have to want it, I have to fight for it.

Tomorrow isn't promised, only today is guaranteed, and what I choose to do with it is all that counts.

What do I want to count? What matters the most?

My eyes fall closed as I take a deep breath. If all of this was to end tomorrow, what would I want? Not for the kingdom, not for anyone else, just for me. What would matter then?

A flash of my father and Nora comes to mind, my heart guiding me back to my family, just as it always has. Only this time, they're not alone. Brody, Cassian, Kryll, and Raiden stand beside them, with Flora and Arlo hovering in the background.

That's my family, both blood and chosen. I didn't find them, they found me, in the mess that embroils the academy and kingdom, they found me. I can't take any responsibility for it, not when I've used all of my might to push them all away as far as possible. If it was my doing, I would be sitting here alone with no one to call my friend or my love.

My chin dips to my chest as I take in another deep breath. I try to see what else I would want today to hold, but I draw a blank. Selfishness isn't something I've ever had the privilege of. If it's not my family, my devotion has always then fallen to the kingdom, just as my father taught me.

I can't see selfishly when there are so many things that matter more to me.

"It's insane how beautiful you look. Even when you're deep in thought. Your eyebrows furrow so tight I'm certain you're going to kill someone, yet really, this is the softest side of you."

My eyes open as I turn to find Kryll hovering by the back door. His words warm my soul as I offer him a slight smile.

"It feels like I'm always plotting someone's death," I murmur, amusement curling my lip as he approaches.

"As long as it's not mine, I'm all in," he replies, offering his hand out for me to take.

I consider pulling him down beside me, but think better of it when my wolf senses pick up on more voices coming from inside the house.

"Do I want to go back in there?" I ask, nodding toward the door as I stand, and he grins.

"If you want peace and quiet, no. If you want to hear what Beau has to say, then probably. It would be a definite yes if you knew everyone else needs you to guide them."

I roll my eyes at him. "No one needs me to guide them, but I'm intrigued with what Beau has to say," I answer, and he stops me in my tracks as I attempt to move toward the door. Only when my gaze is fixed on him does he speak.

"I feel dumb. I'm such a man." He rolls his eyes. "That was definitely my dragon's thoughts coming through," he grumbles, rubbing at the back of his neck nervously with his free hand. "What I should say to you, what I should have said forever ago, is that we only function with you. This only works because of you. Our only chance of surviving this carnage is *you*. I'm sorry for thinking you would just magically know what I was thinking." I blink at him, a few times for good measure, as I struggle to find the words to respond. He must sense my struggle because he swiftly pulls me into his side, guiding me toward the house. "You're even prettier when you're stunned," he muses before brushing his lips against my temple.

The second we step inside, the noise turns up to new levels. Making my way into the kitchen, I find everyone standing around the dining table like there aren't any chairs for them to take a seat. Arlo has his arm slung protectively around Flora's shoulders as they both stare expectantly at Beau, the man seemingly causing an uproar as Raiden and Cassian both yell over each other and the professor in a bid to be heard. Brody stands at the other end of the table, hands planted on his hips as he stares at the mess unraveling in front of him, as if he's trying to find a solution to the madness. His head dips after a beat, making it clear he doesn't know what to do with them.

Sighing, I move out from under Kryll's arm and slide between Raiden and Beau. "That's enough," I yell, my voice carrying through the room as everyone falls silent. Wow. I wasn't actually expecting that to work. "I don't know what you're all yelling about, but it's done with. Someone speak calmly and make sense so I can understand whatever is causing this mayhem," I add, pressing my back against Raiden's chest as I turn expectantly to Beau.

Something tells me it's going to be him that has answers for me, while Raiden is going to need the distraction of my body against his to quiet him down enough for me to hear. I'm not ashamed to use my body as a weapon in this fashion, especially not when his hands find their way to my waist. His fingers flex on my hips, making me shift farther back against him as Beau sighs.

"I tried to breeze over whatever I could, but it seems like they already had information," he states, pushing a hand through his hair, and I frown.

"Who?"

"The media."

Fuck.

"Of course they do," I grumble, my lips pursing with agitation. "What do they know?" I ask, just before a newspaper is pressed against my chest. I look up at the hand flattening it against me to find Cassian's narrowed eyes and taut jaw.

"They know that the kingdom is in uproar and everything is a mess," he grunts, taking a step back when I reach for the papers, my eyes quickly scanning over the front page of the Harrows News.

Fuck. Fuck. Fuck.

"They know everything," I rasp, turning the page to see the story continue. They know of Kenner's leverage with The Council, even though he's never been a member, they know about the fated mates, they know I'm a wolf; they know every last detail, right down to Vallie's death, resurrection, and redeath.

My chest clenches, my heart thundering in my ears as I place the paper on the dining table.

What the fuck am I supposed to do with that?

"At least there aren't any secrets," Flora murmurs, and my gaze cuts to hers. I stare into her eyes, deep into her irises, watching as she swallows nervously. At first I worry it's guilt, like she might be the source of it all, but that's not it. I can sense it around her eyes and in her heart. She's a bystander in this for the most part, and she has a point.

"You're right," I breathe, nodding as she offers me a weak smile. "The issues with The Council have gone on for so long because they've maintained a level of secrecy that isn't fair to the kingdom. The people deserve to know this."

"They don't deserve to know everything about you, Addi. That's not their right," Cassian grunts, nostrils flaring as he glares at me, and I shrug.

"If I had been Princess Adrianna all of these years, they would have known anyway. But I was hidden, kept a secret, to protect myself, yes, but it hasn't worked in the kingdom's favor or my own. Them knowing all of this is better than trying to face anyone outside of this room without them knowing."

"Spoken like a true leader," Beau murmurs, making my eyes widen as I face him. He takes a moment to stare at me, like he's trying to convey something, but I have no idea what. Likely aware that his efforts are futile, he sighs, and I feel the weight of the words before he even speaks them. "Bozzelli has lifted the lockdown on the academy. Students who wish to return home may do so."

What the fuck does he mean the students are free to leave? Is this a joke?

"There's no way anyone has left." It's a statement, not a question, but the way Beau looks at me, I know there's an answer coming anyway. One I'm not going to like.

"Unfortunately, that's not the case."

I gape at him in horror before passing my gaze over everyone else in the room. Nobody else looks as shocked as I do. "People are running at the first hurdle," I blurt, tucking a loose tendril of hair behind my ear as I step out of Raiden's grasp. I need to think, and I can't have him touching me while I try to accomplish that.

"Some do, it's how we weed them out," Beau states, and I scoff at him.

"Maybe you should have started with that exercise when we all arrived here instead of putting people through trials. Loyalty outweighs strength, and if they were never loyal to the kingdom then they shouldn't have been here to begin with," I snap, my voice rising with every word.

Calm and collected, Addi. Calm and fucking collected.

This is some grade A bullshit. I can't even process where to begin. "How many?" I ask, bracing myself as I turn my attention back to Beau.

"More than half of the student body." My jaw all but hits the floor. Why were they even here to begin with? "Really, it's closer to three quarters," he adds, and a snort of laughter parts my lips.

It's ridiculous, yet hilarious.

"What do we do now?" I ask, forcing myself to cling to the things I can't control when there's still so much mess for us to cover.

Beau looks from his brother to me, back and forth again three times, before he finally settles on me. "You should stand up and lead."

I frown at him, shaking my head from side to side in confusion. "I can't just do that, and you can't just go around saying that either," I grumble, feeling the adrenaline quicken in my veins.

"Why not?" Brody asks, speaking up for the first time since I stepped inside. My gaze collides with his as he stands his ground, baiting me as I try to find a solid response, but my thoughts are interrupted by the short and snappy tone chiming from someone's cell phone.

Everyone stuffs their hands in their pockets, checking their devices. Everyone but me since mine is still at Raiden's; a fact I need to rectify, but the look on Cassian's face as he glares down at his cell phone pushes the thought to the back of my mind.

He curses under his breath, dragging a hand down his face as he looks everywhere around the room but at me.

"What's going on?" I ask, cutting the distance between us, but he turns away from me before I can gain his full attention.

"Kenner," he mutters under his breath as I reach for his arm, but his body turns still as I try to spin him back to me.

"What about him?" I push, clearly understanding there's more to the situation, and he shrugs. "Cassian," I insist, circling around to stop him in his tracks before he tries to put more distance between us.

His eyes collide with mine, a troubled expression washing over his features before he quickly shuts it down. "Fine," he grunts, stuffing his hand in his pocket and retrieving his cell phone again. He turns the screen my way and my stomach tightens in knots.

.   .   .

I SKIM over the message twice before returning my stare to his. "What does it mean?" I ask, and Cassian simply shrugs in response. "Tell me what it means. Now," I snap, aware I'm being just as demanding as his father. The only difference being that I'm doing it because I care and he's trying to put distance between us.

Fuck that.

"Cass," Brody says calmly, trying to aid and defuse the situation all at once. An attempt I'm sure is going to fail, but to my surprise, my growly wolf locks eyes with me.

"It means he's panicking. It means everything he wants he can't have anymore, and it's time to take it all out on his favorite punching bag."

My heart sinks as the pain twists in the man before me. The look on his face seems like one he's all too familiar with wearing, but that was before me. Before we all chose this.

Now, he's not only one of my Kryptos, one of my

men, or even my wolf; he's one of my fated mates. All because of the decisions they made. Their persistence brought us here. Now they can face the consequences of that.

"Then we all go together," I say firmly, but it doesn't seem to stick with him because he's shaking his head before I even finish speaking. The consideration of ignoring him altogether flutters through my mind, but it's clear from the look on Cassian's face that it's completely off the table as an option.

"No."

One word. So final. So fucking Cassian.

He turns away, hands balled into fists at his sides as he starts toward the door, but I race to catch up, using my wolf speed to reach the doorway before he can.

Planting my hand on his chest, I wait until his eyes are on mine before I speak. "Yes."

He shakes his head again, irritation flooding my bones as I glare at him, but he continues unfazed. "No, I should do this alone."

Like hell he's going to do this alone. Never, ever. I refuse.

I sigh, outwardly admitting defeat as I lean into him. The tension bunching his muscles together eases as he thinks victory is heading his way, but I swiftly slip my hand in his pants pocket, grab his cell phone, and dart across the room.

"What are you doing?" he bites out, his frustration barely contained, earning a glare off Kryll, who I rush toward.

"I'm doing you a favor," I state back, but all he does is give me a pointed look like all I'm actually doing is inconveniencing him.

"You can keep the cell phone. I don't care," he states, his shoulders slumping as he waves me off and turns for the door.

"Oh, you can have it back. I'm done with it," I state, launching it through the air.

His eyes narrow to slits. "What did you do?"

It's my turn to shrug as I saunter past him, aware of the other steps following.

"I told Janie on you. Now, let's go. She'll be waiting."

"What are you doing here, Cass?"

I whirl around in the dirt to find Janie glaring at me. Her arms are folded over her chest, one foot outstretched in front of her as she waits.

Fuck.

Addi wasn't joking.

If I didn't love her so damn much I'd throttle her.

"Don't worry yourself," I murmur, scrubbing at my jaw as I turn away, but she rounds on me quicker than I anticipate.

"Thanks for meeting us here," Addi announces, her arrival no surprise after she dropped that bomb on me. I thought I would beat them here with enough time to seclude myself from them, but it seems I was wrong.

I don't want my father anywhere near her. She's

safer away from him, which means being as far away from me as possible. Besides, if my father is calling me here like this, then I know exactly what's going to happen and it's really not going to be all that pretty.

My father is the alpha for a reason. I might be strong and confident in every other aspect of my life, but with him? His words when I was a child have penetrated deeper than I can bring myself to admit.

Psychologically, he has the upper hand on me, and no matter how I try to look at it, it affects me physically too. He's stronger than me and he's calling me out in what I know will be a challenge. One that will end with my blood on his hands. Addi deserves better than to see that.

"What the fuck is going on in that asshole head of yours, Cass?" Janie's words cut through the air, tugging me from my thoughts as I sigh.

"I don't know what you're talking about," I reply, opting to avoid her stare as Addi, Kryll, Raiden, and Brody stand between us.

One thing is for sure, my girl sure knows what will work against me, even if it is to help me. Janie is a weak spot for me and Addi knows it. Previously, the girls on the compound have seen how Janie and I are and it's always been an issue. She's always been seen as a threat. Even though she's like the big sister I never had and also married to one of the coolest guys

I know. Jake has his hands full with her and I don't want anything to do with that.

That didn't matter to them though. A girl was a girl and jealousy was rife. Addi, however, embraces her more than I do. She wants a connection with Janie and she knows her presence here is good for me, even when I refuse to admit it to myself.

"I'm fine, Janie. I can handle this on my own. You guys don't need to be present." My words are weak and she knows it, but avoiding her gaze is impossible and she sees right through me the moment mine settles on hers.

"Now isn't the time to go on a solo rampage, Cass. You need to stick together," Janie states, her words firm but soothing as she moves to stand beside Addi.

We're in the middle of the woods, nothing is safe about this. If anything, I'm delaying the inevitable and making it worse.

"She's right, Cassian. We need to stick together. Now more than ever," Addi breathes, worry swimming in her eyes as she twists her hands together. It's clear she wants to move closer to me, but she's worried about spooking me even more than I already am.

Fuck. Why am I making it all worse instead of better? That's what I'm supposed to be doing.

"What, like you?" I grunt, my eye twitching as I

scream at myself internally. I'm trying to push her away, but my sharp tongue only makes her inch closer. I wave my hand for her to stay where she is, but she ignores me completely. She doesn't stop until we're standing toe to toe, and I can see it in her eyes.

She sees right through me and my bullshit. Every inch of it.

"Not like me. Nothing like me at all. I'm the worst, we all know that," she states, a sad smile stretching her lips as she places her hand on my arm. "But I'm learning, or I'm trying my best to." Her other hand lifts to my arm before her fingers stroke up to my neck. "Do you want to know what I figured out this morning?" It's on the tip of my tongue to say no and get the hell out of here, but she quirks her brow at me, like she's expecting that, and I find myself tipping my head in a nod, ever so slightly. It's enough for her to see, though. "I realized that none of this matters if we're not together."

Her words wash over me, churning in my mind on repeat as I digest them.

None of this matters if we're not together.

NONE of this matters if we're not together.

NONE of this matters if WE'RE not TOGETHER.

NONE OF THIS MATTERS IF WE'RE NOT TOGETHER.

Fuck.

I squeeze my eyes shut, the power behind the words vibrating through my mind as Addi's hold on my arms tighten like she knows I'm suffering at the hands of her truth.

"That's some realization, Alpha," I finally rasp after what feels like an eternity of drowning. Prying my eyes open, I spy a hint of worry still in her gaze, but there's a resilience and pride that stands firmer.

She believes in me, just like I believe in her, but I need to find a way to believe in myself.

"Where has this self doubt come from, Cassian? And why alone? I feel like I have an idea, but I need you to spell it out for me. It might help you too."

"Wow, she's a warrior *and* a soothing alpha," Janie says with amusement, making my jaw tic as I try not to smile. I'm so screwed with these two women and they know it. And now it's going to be clear that they can gang up on me to get me to do what they want, which is bullshit, even if it is for my own good.

Instead of responding to Janie, I chance a glance at my brothers, who all stand quietly amongst the trees, watching me fall apart and be pieced back together. A knowing look passes between the four of us, like they know what I'm feeling. Like they know the strength of our woman and what she does for us—to us—and they're letting me play catch up.

Settling my gaze back on my alpha, I take a deep breath and try to answer her because that's what she deserves—far more than the bullshit I try to tell myself.

"He's calling me here for a duel, Addi. He's calling me here to finally put an end to me, like I've been waiting for since as long as I can remember. I don't want you to see that. I couldn't bear witness to that if it was the other way around." My gut twists as emotion creeps up my spine.

She blinks at me, her lashes fanning across her cheeks a few times before she stands up on her tiptoes so we're eye to eye.

"He can call you for a duel, Cassian, but it will be over my dead body that he puts an end to you. I'm not watching you go anywhere. Not without me. We're united in darkness, we're intertwined in love, and we're undivided in strength. Don't let that man take that away from us. We deserve this, we deserve each other, and it doesn't end simply because someone other than us deemed it so."

My jaw falls slack as I stare at her, unable to comprehend the wisdom and power in her words that hold me captive. It's like she knows what I need to hear, even when I don't have a clue myself.

"She's right, Cass," Brody states, slowly approaching with the others until we're practically huddled under a tree. "There's no I in this team. It's us against the world, deranged family members included," he adds, and I snicker despite myself.

Janie catches the movement and takes that as her hint to join us. Addi releases me, pulling Janie into her side so the pair of them can stare me down together.

"You're so screwed, Cass," Janie whispers, watery eyes shimmering at me as she wraps her arm tightly around my woman.

"Yeah, you could say that," I rasp with a nod, which makes her grin.

"I thought I could smell half-breed blood on my grounds."

My heart stills at the sound of my father's voice, and I curse at myself for letting him turn up on us like this instead arriving prepared like I should have. There's no time to dwell on the fact now, though. It's true what Addi said. We're united, we're inter-twined, we're undivided. Always.

"Father," I state, my voice void of the emotions I was carrying mere moments ago. I turn to face him, spying the flutter of wolves among the trees as he summons an audience, but he's not looking at me, he's looking at Addi.

"I declare a duel," he announces, and she frowns. He must sense her confusion because he carries on before she can speak. "Don't worry, I'm not dueling with you, Pet. I'm dueling with him," he reiterates, pointing a finger my way while keeping his eyes locked on hers, and his next words explain why. "We'll duel to the death. The winner gets you *and* your powers."

As if my father hasn't put me through enough, he's determined to break me *before* he tries to put me down. A feral shiver burns up my spine at his words, the disgust bringing a coppery taste to my tongue as I sink my teeth into my cheeks.

Win her? Win her powers? Over my dead body because it certainly won't happen any other way. I will never understand the confidence this man possesses. The ability to think so little of others while thinking so mightily of himself.

Those aren't the tendencies of a wolf. If anything, it sounds like I'm describing a vampire, but even that doesn't seem worthy enough of the egotistical bastard that he is.

"I won't duel for that," I spit out, my lip curling with anger as my hands ball into fists. He sparked a reaction out of me, just like he wanted, but fuck the consequences. She's mine to protect, especially from him.

"Now, now, Cassian. You know that's not how this works. I'm the alpha of this compound, duels are as I see fit," my father taunts as more wolves sweep through the forest, descending on us as they await the long-overdue duel between father and son.

"When are you going to understand that I washed my hands of this compound long ago. You banished me, remember?"

"Yet you still come back," he sneers, stepping toward me with a challenge crinkling his eyes. The dark rings that circle them confirm his lack of sleep. I wish I could blame this delusional state on that fact, but it's not true. He's been this deranged for as long as I can remember.

Edging toward him, I make sure I stand perfectly in front of Addi so he can't look at her. "I come back for the people I care about. I come back because I always wanted this to be my home, I just never wanted you to be my father."

The words leave my lips and a weight lifts from my shoulders. It has such an impact on me that it leaves me lightheaded. I've carried the weight of that fact for so long, I don't recall life without it. Now, as I stand here with my woman, my brothers, and my sister behind me, everything makes sense.

This man is my tormentor. He was never truly my father, or my alpha, he was my pain and suffering. Without Janie, I would have never known kindness. Without my brothers, I would have never known loyalty. Without Addi, I would have never known love.

Kindness. Loyalty. Love.

Three powerful words that can't be used to actually describe my blood connected family.

Twisted. Sinister. Treacherous.

I would use those for him instead.

A flicker of my mother dances at the edge of my vision, but I tamp it down. He took her away from me as well.

Everything I am is a byproduct of wanting to be nothing like this man. I should thank him, really, for teaching me how not to act, but he doesn't deserve my thanks, not even as a thought.

"You are the most ungrateful heir of this compound that has ever existed. I gave everything for you to follow in my footsteps and you tossed it all away. You could have been forged in greatness, but instead, you're tainted by weakness," he snarls, his face reddening with every word. He takes slow measured steps around the clearing between us, leaving me to follow after him, anticipating his first move.

"Your footsteps were never worth walking in.

Your legacy was nothing worth chasing." The barbed words part my lips, freeing me more and more with every one.

He can taunt me all he likes, but he's never truly seen the pent up anger and rage he's infused in me.

"My legacy isn't over. I'm yet to rein, and I'm going to make sure you're obliterated in the afterlife, forced to watch down on me as I claim everything that was yours."

"That sounds like you're trying to take *my* legacy, old man, and there's no chance in hell," I roar back, watching as rage consumes his body. He launches at me in the next breath, shifting midair into the wolf I've always feared, but I'm done being scared now.

I have something to fight for, someone who offers a possibility of tomorrow, and a legacy I want for my own.

Every part of me wants to run to her, claim her lips one last time, but that would only draw the attention back to her, putting her at risk, and she's already the highlight of this shitshow. Instead, I hit the ground running, leaping through the air as my father's paws hit the dirt. The breeze dances over my body as I shift, my wolf consuming me as I land with a thud, turning to stare him down with murderous intent.

Declining a challenge in honor of Addi is out of the question now, but I'll fight to the death for her.

He charges at me once again, the thunder of his paws hitting the ground echoing in my ears as I snap my teeth and barrel toward him. He doesn't falter, never fearful of my presence, which only serves to outline me as the underdog.

Perfect.

I've spent my whole life with him underestimating me, which will only make taking him down that much sweeter.

He pushes off the ground a second before I can consider it, giving him the advantage, but instead of leaping into the air as I intended, I drop low, right to the ground as he flies over my head. The moment his back legs pass me, I'm up, spinning toward him with bared teeth.

As he hits the ground, I push toward him faster, sinking my canines into his back leg, earning a howl of pain. My triumph is short lived when he kicks at me. My hold relents and I skid across the forest floor, grinding to a halt in front of a row of wolves.

I anticipate one of them stepping in, pinning me in place for my father to devour me, but to my surprise, they take a step back, giving me space to gather myself before he pounces.

Scrambling to my feet, I don't even get my head

up before I'm knocked to the ground again, the deep brown fur of my father's coat flashing before my eyes as I hit my head. A small yelp parts my lips, but I refuse to give in. Clawing and kicking, I blindly make contact with his side, pushing him off me enough to catch my footing and rise to my feet once again.

He doesn't waste a second turning back to me, standing with his head held high so he can look down his nose at me, even in his wolf form. Just as I expect him to charge toward me, he tilts his head, looking off to the side, and despite my efforts, I can't help but turn to see what has his attention. I snarl with rage when I see it's Addi.

She's standing shoulder to shoulder, wedged between Kryll and Raiden while Brody holds the spot right behind her protectively. Janie is mixed among the fray too, but she's in her wolf form, standing even more protective than my brothers.

A swell of love blossoms, but it quickly disappears as my father slams into me, knocking the wind out of me and taking me to the dirt once again. He tries to narrow in on my throat as he pins me to the earth, snapping and snarling as saliva drips from his feral teeth.

I push back, but he still manages to worm his way closer, inch by inch, until I extend my claws the best I can and stab them into his side. I blindly aim for the weak spot, right beneath his front legs, and he howls into the night.

Instead of weakening him as I hoped, I make him more crazed. A sight I didn't think could be possible. His teeth graze just beneath my jaw, threatening to pierce my throat and bleed me out, but the sight of Addi over his shoulder fuels me with a strength I can only harness from her.

With every ounce of force I can muster, I push at him, adrenaline coursing through my veins as my pulse thunders in my ears, and he's helpless to resist the strength behind my hit, slamming into the closest tree with a thud.

Shaking my head, I try to rid myself of the feeling of his teeth at my throat before I take off toward him. He's injured, a slight whimper on his lips, and I know I have the opportunity I need to take him down once and for all, but just as I leap through the air, ready to take what is mine, another wolf charges at me.

Knocked off course, I hit the dirt hard, and it takes me a whole second to realize who has come to my father's aid. The familiar black and white fur can only belong to one person.

Dalton.

Motherfucker.

He has me pinned, my body aching from the

impact, but I still fight. Pushing, kicking, clawing. Whatever it takes, it can't end like this. As if sensing my internal pleas Dalton snaps my neck to the side, rendering me helpless before sinking his teeth into my throat.

A howl burns from my lungs as the world spins, but I refuse to succumb to the darkness that beckons me as the piercing sound of Addi calling out my name cuts through the air.

I have to get back to her. I have to be strong enough. Not just for her, not just for the kingdom, but for the little boy inside of me who deserves to know what life is truly like without an overbearing father weighing down on him.

My howl turns into a cry of rage as I use every ounce of strength I have left to send him flying through the air. I don't hear him land, I don't feel the ground shake, and I don't bother to look for him. He broke the treaty, the rules of a duel.

No one should interfere.

Yet here we are.

It doesn't matter, though. I'll rise above it.

Acutely alert, I search for my father, desperate to put an end to the misery, but when I find him, he's not alone. My pulse thunders in my ears, muting the noise around me, but the growl that vibrates from him grows weaker as another wolf heaves off him.

Panic sets into my bones at the sight of the white

wolf, but a quick shift to my left and I see my girl. It's not her. The wolf looks so familiar, though. Sensing my approach, the white wolf in question turns, tilting their head back to look over their shoulder and it all makes sense.

Addi's mother.

She slinks back a step, then another, and another, her head dipped as she retreats, offering my father to me on a platter. I falter, unsure if I should continue now that she's helped, but Dalton reacted first. I think.

Peering around at the gathered wolves, I pause, waiting to see if anyone else is willing to interject, but even as I begin to approach my father, no one steps in. Blood stains his fur, pooling at his side as he pants in short, sharp breaths.

He's dying.

He just needs a little help toppling over the edge.

His glazed eyes find mine before he shifts, the remnants of a broken man lying in his wake. "C-Cass-Cassian," he croaks, feebly lifting his hands to his throat in a failed attempt to stop the bleeding. "Help. Me," he chokes, wild eyes searching mine, and I frown.

He can't be serious, can he?

This man has done nothing but break me. Repeatedly. I was convinced I would never heal, that it was never even remotely a possibility, but the woman standing across the way, she's proved it all wrong.

Glancing over my shoulder at her, I see the worry in her eyes, the pain in her rigid frame, and my heart aches, not just for me, but for her. Helping him would only serve as an opportunity for him to continue his torment, not just on me, but her too.

My body relaxes, the thrumming through my veins dulling in comparison to the desire I have to bring this to its end. I feel nauseous as I shift, my human form carrying the same struggles, cuts, and bruises as my wolf, yet I manage to remain standing over my father.

"You don't deserve my help," I rasp, dropping to my knees as his eyes grow wide with panic. "You don't deserve anything. Not from me, not from any wolf here, not even from Dalton. Your time is over. I hope you enjoy spending eternity in the afterlife, watching me correct all the wrongs you made."

Taking a deep breath, I focus on my wolf and shift my hand. Claws protrude from my flesh, making me hiss, but I want to see him through my eyes as he takes his last breath. His lips part, ready to make one final plea, but I'm done listening. I've been done for a long time.

Before a single syllable can be spoken, I slash my claws across his throat, draining the remainder of his blood in one swift move. Garbled chokes echo around me until his body goes limp.

The forest remains silent, drenched in blood and stained with the challenge that will forever be remembered tonight. Rising to my feet, the pain at my neck growing unbearable, I search the eyes watching me until I find exactly who I'm looking for.

Dalton.

Crazed eyes glare back at me from where he lies nestled beneath the weight of another wolf. Not just any wolf. Those piercing green eyes looking at me with a sense of care that can't be named. The level of care he promised to always offer the day Janie took me into her fold.

Jake.

I nod, silently communicating my thanks, and he takes the hint, releasing the fucker from his grasp. Dalton bucks quickly, pounding across the dirt without thought, and I brace for impact, ready to tear him to shreds too. But the wait lasts longer than expected when he detours at the last second, leaping just out of reach and colliding straight into the kneeling white wolf.

No action is quick enough to stop the inevitable. Time slows as Dalton's rage splatters the ground in thick crimson.

One beat of a heart. That's all it takes to kill another.

One beat of a heart, and then it's all gone.

One beat of a heart, and the afterlife gains another citizen.

One beat of a heart, and all the unspoken words cease to exist.

One beat of a heart, and Addi's mother joins my father.

I choke on a gasp as I watch Cassian fall to his knees. The world shifts in slow motion, playing out like a movie scene. I can't breathe. My feet are carrying me before I even realize it as I drop to the dirt beside my wolf.

Pressing my palm against the wound at his neck, I scream out for Brody to help, but he's already at my side, planting his hand over mine as he chants under his breath.

It does nothing.

Nothing.

Chaos continues to erupt around us, but my sole focus is on Cassian.

He just killed his father, and now he's not healing.

I frown, looking at Brody for an answer as his gaze narrows in thought. Retracting his touch on

Cassian, he reaches for my hand, placing it back over the wound once more.

"The only thing that can heal a wound received during a duel is the person the duel was for," Brody breathes, and realization washes over me. My hold is firmer, my need to heal him raw. This was a duel, just like the rest, but because it was his father, I hadn't acknowledged it in the same way.

My eyes fall to Cassian's face. "Come on, Cassian," I breathe, reliving the entire scene in my mind as I will his wound to heal.

The second Kenner launched himself at Cassian, I tried to interject, but Janie had held firm that I couldn't. Nestled between Kryll and Raiden, I stood my ground, hating every second of the distance between us, until an idea had come to mind.

Before I could think better of it or be talked off the ledge, I lifted the mental blockers in my mind and gushed toward Cassian.

I felt everything he felt.

I ached over everything that pained him.

I choked when he garbled as Dalton sliced through his flesh with his bare teeth.

It was too much, threatening to bring me to my knees more than once. But as much as it hurt, I couldn't stop. I wouldn't. He couldn't experience this without someone to understand. If standing beside him in his most suffering moment is all I can offer him, I will do so gladly because he deserves someone to pain themselves for him.

He's been through enough. The overwhelming emotions that catapulted themselves at me didn't make sense, but to him they would, and that made me ache even more.

Brody gently squeezes my fingers, bringing me back to the present as the sound of wolves howling fills the air. I meet Brody's gaze and he offers me a small nod, silently conveying for me to look, and I slowly turn to look at where my hand is still pressed against Cassian's throat.

His head is slumped, his chin resting against his chest like it's too heavy for him to lift his head, so I do it for him. He may not be ready to face the world, and I'll have to apologize for it later, but I need to see him.

"Cassian," I breathe, cupping his chin as I tilt his head back. His fiery eyes find mine and guilt washes over him.

"I'm sorry about your mom," his words are so soft they could have been stolen by the wind, but I can feel them through our connection too, solidifying how fated we are.

Blinking at him, I shake my head. "That's not your fault." Prying my eyes from his, I spy Janie's wolf standing protectively over my mother's lifeless body while a jet black wolf with piercing green eyes pins another in place.

I knew it was my mother immediately. The moment she launched through the air, a striking resemblance to my own wolf, I knew. My heart had leapt in my chest as she rushed into the fray when Cassian was attacked by the wolf I now know is Dalton, but it was short lived before the latter got his revenge.

Looking at my mother now sends a numbness over me. I don't know how to feel, so my mind chooses to feel nothing. There will forever be words unspoken between us, no finality worth documenting, and that's what weighs heaviest on my heart.

Otherwise, how am I supposed to mourn someone twice? She hasn't been a part of my life for so long, it leaves me confused. Clinging to the numbness, I turn back to Cassian at the same time Janie's voice snaps through the air.

"You're the alpha now, Cass."

The man in question freezes beside me, shaking his head as he takes my hand and rises to his feet, taking me with him.

"No."

"Cass—" Janie appears at my side, eyebrows drawn tight as he shakes his head.

"I said no. He can have it," he grunts, pointing

toward Dalton, which earns a scoff from the woman standing shoulder to shoulder with me.

It's like there's a sense of solidarity between us, especially when we do this, but panic creeps up my throat. Cassian as their alpha? That's not for me to state.

"Nobody here wants that man to be our alpha, Cassian," Janie insists, not even bothering to look in Dalton's direction. It's clear Cassian doesn't believe her, so she takes a step back, gaining support from the wolves that have lurked in the shadows the entire time. One by one, they step forward, silently confirming Janie's words. "That man doesn't deserve the power that comes with being our alpha and you know it. This is *your* time, *your* compound, *your* pack. *Take it.*"

Cassian shakes his head, blood staining his clothes as he tries to take a step back, but he's quickly blocked off by the wolves circling around him. If I didn't have the context for this moment, I would think he was in danger, but the air is filled with silent pleas and unanswered promises of a better future.

"Over. My. Dead. Body." The words are called out on a snarl, garnering everyone's attention and swinging the focus to Dalton, who is still pinned beneath the black wolf. His gaze is locked on Cassian's, the darkened edges of his pupils replicating the sinister promise, just like Kenner's always did.

"With pleasure," Janie snarls, knocking me back into waiting arms as she charges toward the man in question.

I barely have time to register that it's Raiden who prevents me from falling over before she's pummeling the man with her bare fists while the wolf holding him in place doesn't move.

"Fuck. Janie!" Cassian yells, trying to interject, but he doesn't manage a single step with the wolves surrounding us holding him captive.

I gape, wide eyed, completely out of place as the pounding of flesh on flesh echoes through the night air. Janie finally stands after what feels like an eternity, blood coating her knuckles and splattering across her t-shirt to match. The second she's out of the way, the black wolf finishes off the job, ripping and tearing at Dalton's flesh with his teeth until there's little to recognize the man by.

A satisfactory smile spreads wickedly over Janie's face as she turns to look at Cassian. "What? Don't give me that look. He said over my dead body and I was happy to oblige." Her smile grows from ear to ear as she shrugs like the badass bitch she is.

"Janie," Cassian says with a sigh, swiping a hand down his face as he looks at her helplessly.

Her shoulders slump as she takes a tentative step toward him. Like magic, the crowd of wolves create a path for her, solidifying what we all know.

They want Cassian as their alpha.

"It has to be you, Cass," she breathes when she's right in front of him, the truth empowering her words as he shakes his head, but his defiance is growing weaker. He knows it as much as she does, he's just not willing to admit it.

"I can't deal with this right now," he murmurs, groaning into his hands before his eyes find mine.

My body is moving of its own accord. My hands are at his neck, slipping through the hair at his nape as he instinctively rests his forehead on mine.

"It's okay." I don't entirely know *what* is okay, I just know he needs to hear it from me. I can feel it in my veins.

He sighs, his muscles easing a fraction as I inch closer, standing flush against him so we're chest to chest.

"We should go," Raiden states from behind me, reminding me we're not alone; far from it.

"He can't. Not yet," Janie answers, and I look deep into Cassian's eyes seeing the resolution clearly for the first time.

A soft smile curves my lips. "I swear, if you think I'm going to start calling you Alpha, you're in for a rude awakening," I muse, trying my best to lighten the situation, and he scoffs.

"You'll always be my alpha, Addi." His lips ghost over mine in the next breath, leaving me light on my feet as I sway in his grasp. "Are you sure about this?" he whispers against my lips, and I shrug.

"It's not for me to be sure of, Cassian. This is for you. If you want this, then take it. If you don't, then I'll stand shoulder to shoulder with you against everyone who tries to say otherwise. It's as simple as that."

"As simple as that," he repeats, eyes searching mine. For what? I'm not entirely sure, but he seems to find it a moment later.

"I want it. They deserve it."

I nod. "So do you."

His fingers squeeze at my waist, clinging to me for a moment longer before he steps back. "You should head back. I won't be far behind you."

I don't want to leave him, I don't want a moment apart, not after this, but there's a sense within me that vibrates from him, confirming that it's what he needs, and I meant it when I said this isn't about me. It's about him.

"My mother?"

"She'll be laid to rest as a respected member of the pack," he answers without missing a beat, and I smile, not really sure how to respond. He must sense the uncertainty warring inside of me because he places a soft kiss to the corner of my mouth before he steps back. "Go. The pack needs me, but the kingdom needs you more."

My heart aches, the worry only heightening as Brody transports us, the outline of the main academy building visible in the distance as the familiar water fountain appears at our sides.

"We shouldn't have left him," I admit the second I sit on the ledge of the fountain, and my face falls into my hands, dismay clinging to me.

"We did the right thing, Princess," Kryll states, crouching before me as he places a comforting hand on my knee. "It might not feel like it right now, but what we're feeling is our own selfish desire wanting us to be together, but he needs the freedom to claim his place."

My lips purse as I bite back a huff. He's right, and I hate it.

Cassian is now the Kenner Alpha, compound and all, and as much as it's clear that they need him, he needs them too. It's a sense of belonging he never had under his father's reign. He deserves a moment to bask in it and come to grips with what's needed from him without the rest of the kingdom's troubles overshadowing it.

"What do we do now then?" I grumble, earning a shrug from the dragon before me, so I turn my irritated glare toward Brody and Raiden. The former looks about as clueless as I feel, but the sudden tug of Raiden's eyebrows before he glances off into the distance has me lurching to my feet. "Raiden?"

He holds up a finger, silently conveying for me to be quiet, and I slam my lips shut, inching closer to him, only to see his frown growing deeper.

"Can you hear that?" he murmurs, closing his eyes to focus, and I do the same.

The first thing I can hear is the rapid beating of my heart, a sound I'm going to need to block out if I plan on hearing anything else, but it's hard. My adrenaline is relentless. Taking a deep breath, I try to center myself as I channel all of my energy into listening. For what? I'm not sure, and I'm almost certain there's nothing to note when a distant whisper echoes in my ears.

I tilt my head toward the direction it comes from, trying to pick up on what's actually going on, but just when I think I've got it, the sound changes.

"I can hear something, I just don't know what," I

admit, opening my eyes to find Kryll standing on the other side of Raiden in the same position. Brody shrugs, no wiser, until Raiden's eyes burst open and he tilts his head.

"It sounds like chanting, but not mages and their magic, more like..."

"Protests," Kryll adds, finishing Raiden's train of thought, and he nods eagerly.

"I don't think I've got the mental capacity to deal with protests after the events today has already given us. Honestly, the whole week has been a bag of dicks, and I don't feel like subjecting myself to anymore of it," Brody says with a sigh, letting his arms flop at his sides with a slap against his thighs. He tilts his face to the sky as a heavier sigh falls from his lips before he tilts his head and peers at me out of the corner of his eye. "You're not going to let us take a rain check on this, are you?" he grumbles, and I try to offer the best smile I've got, but it's not enough to boost his spirits. "Fine, whatever, but when something goes wrong, which it always does, then I want it to be known that I transported us to a quieter part of campus in hopes of avoiding any carnage."

"Stop whining and let's go," Raiden mumbles, reaching for my hand before he starts toward the sound.

Kryll and Brody are right there with us as he keeps a steady pace, opting against rushing into the madness with his vampire speed, and I'm silently grateful. Truthfully, my head told me to follow Brody's suggestion and hide from the noise, but my heart, and my damn gut, insisted. This is exactly what I get for wanting to protect the kingdom at all costs.

The sounds of protest register in my mind as we approach the academy building. It's almost impressive that from this side it doesn't look like we caused any damage here yesterday, but I'm sure the other side doesn't give off the same vibe.

Following the pathway, the chants grow to higher levels as a huge crowd of people come into view. They're standing shoulder to shoulder, signs in hand as they chant at the top of their lungs.

"Free our kingdom! Free our kingdom! Free our kingdom!"

I'm frozen in place, blinking at the bustle of people from all origins shouting in unison.

"What do we want?"

"Freedom."

"When do we want it?"

"Now!"

Kryll and Brody step in closer, attempting to create a protective circle around me while Raiden's hand tightens around mine.

"What's all this freedom about?" Raiden asks, but before I can even part my lips, someone ahead turns to face us. Their stare is narrowed until they take us in, and when their eyes latch on mine, they rush toward us.

"Free us from their torment. Save us!" she shouts, hands outstretched as she tries to reach me, but Kryll knocks her back a step. That doesn't seem to waver her attempts, though. "She's here, our savior is here." Her voice is shrill, cutting through the chants as eyes turn our way.

"Help us!"

"Help us, please."

"Save us from The Council."

I blink at the crowd moving toward us as Raiden curses under his breath.

"Fuck, we need to get her the fuck out of here. Now," he grunts, and Brody gives him a pointed look.

"What did I say about—"

"Now isn't the time for an I told you so, asshole," Kryll interjects, glaring at my mage with irritation before turning his intense stare toward Raiden. "Get her inside. We'll be right behind you."

My vampire doesn't need to be told twice. He's tugging me in the next breath, making me connect to my wolf speed as we weave our way through the crowd. He doesn't relent until the sound of the academy building door slams shut behind us.

"What's going on?" I ask, completely aware he

doesn't have the answer as we edge away from the door. I tug my hand from his, planting my hands on my hips as I think, when a voice answers me.

"The academy has been stormed. The people have had enough."

I turn in surprise to see Bozzelli standing with a small gathering of students that haven't left and a few professors too. Beau is among them, his eyes searching mine, but a moment later, Kryll fires into the building with Brody hot on his tail and the concern vanishes from his stare.

"What do they want? They were chanting about freedom," I state, trying to calm my breathing that refuses to come through any slower than short, sharp pants.

Bozzelli laces her fingers together, a tight smile on her lips. "An heir must be declared," she says, earning a gasp from the gathered students as my pulse thrums in my ears.

"By who?" I ask, disbelief etched into the two small words as I try to process the fact that everything's coming to an end already. The time has come, the journey is reaching its peak, and there's nothing we can do now but watch it unravel.

"By the people."

FORTY-SIX

ADRIANNA

The ballroom that changed my life looks nothing like it did that night. All of the glitz and glamor is gone. There are no tables, no center-pieces, no sophisticated touches or silk drapes. It's all gone. All that remains is a small platform.

I've seen Bozzelli stand up there before, giving one of her ridiculous speeches, but this time, my future hangs in the balance. Her lime-green pantsuit is perfectly pleated down the front, her blazer buttoned up, with just a peek of her white silk blouse underneath.

Her hair is twisted back into a demure chignon and her make up is minimal, allowing her outfit to steal all the attention. I watch her lips move as she speaks into the camera, addressing the kingdom as though they are in the room with us, but my pulse hasn't quieted. My gaze tracks her lips, trying to take in what she's saying over the internal noise.

She looks beyond professional, like the academy isn't crumbling around her, the kingdom along with it. We may have had our ups and downs, but watching her now, there are things I could learn from her. Especially if a miracle were to happen and I am given the opportunity to lead our kingdom to greatness.

I watch as she explains what is to come. The people want The Council gone, and she has the ability to offer that to them. I'm sure The Council still has plans in place, plans we must prepare for, but for now, my focus is on her lips as she lists off the remaining students on campus for the public to choose from.

Hearing my name on her lips sends a shiver down my spine. Even if I can only lip read it, it's enough.

I take a deep breath, willing my pulse to calm down so I can hear anything from her speech, but it's only when she's closing out her address to the nation that I can finally acknowledge any of it.

"It has been an honor to serve the Floodborn Kingdom in such a manner. I thank you dearly for allowing me such a profound opportunity, and I hope to serve you closure in these final moments. Ballots are opening across the kingdom and you have until sundown to add your contribution. Come morning, as the sun rises, its light will harken a new dawn, it will dismiss the final dusk under the control of The Council and begin a new era for us all as the heir will take their place on the throne."

She nods and a moment later, the camera is shut off. Her shoulders sag and she takes a moment to compose herself again before she turns her attention to the remaining students. I stand in the fray, Raiden to my left, Brody to my right, and Kryll behind me.

"Thank you for fighting for our kingdom. Thank you for offering yourselves selflessly for the greater good. It may not be the night to bask in glory since we're going to be holed up in here, but it's important we keep you protected during this time. Beds will be set up in the far corner of the room and dinner will be served as soon as possible. Get comfortable, rest, the kingdom will need you at your best come morning," Bozzelli directs, her words resonating deep in my veins as I nod in agreement, but she's already turned away, murmuring quietly with Beau as they dismiss us.

"Any luck with Cassian?" I ask, glancing at Brody, who has tried to reach out to him a few times, but he shakes his head.

"Not yet."

Fuck.

We can't leave to get him now either. I hate us

being separated like this. I just hope he's okay and The Council doesn't focus their attention toward the compound.

"Let's eat, keep ourselves alert, and I'm sure we'll hear from him soon," Kryll offers, wrapping an arm around my shoulders as he guides me to where a few dining tables have been set up.

The smell of food drifts in the air, beckoning us closer as I nod my agreement. "Fine, but the last time we chose to eat to stay alert, something went wrong," I mutter, dropping down into the seat with a heavy sigh as Brody wags his finger at me.

"See? I told you."

I roll my eyes at him, even though he's definitely not wrong, but Kryll is right. We may as well refuel and wait it out. There's nothing else we can do.

Muttering my thanks, I take the plate of food offered and dig in. Chicken, green beans, and mashed potatoes. It's not the last supper dreams are made of, but it could be worse. Once my plate is clean, I place my knife and fork on top as I lean back in my seat.

"Everything is a mess," Raiden states, his gaze catching mine from across the table, and I hum in agreement.

"It's always been a mess," Brody adds, earning a pointed look from everyone before he can give us his 'I told you so' spiel again, but to my surprise, it doesn't come. "The question is, what are we going to do about it?"

I sit tall in my seat, his words twisting a part of me as my mind starts to swirl. "That's exactly the question we should be asking," I confirm, earning a shit-eating grin from the mage, whose ego only swells.

"Don't encourage him," Raiden grumbles, and I shake my head.

"No, for real. No matter what happens tomorrow, our kingdom is going to need us in some way. As much as we've seen snippets of the media, we don't truly know what the public thinks of us, and the reality is, it doesn't matter. What matters is what the kingdom needs from us, and it's going to need something because you're right, it's a mess."

"You're so fucking hot when you've got that fire in your veins, Princess," Kryll states from beside me, and I snicker, trying my best to hide the effect his words have on me.

My nerves are calm, my heart isn't racing, and my soul is content.

Have I spent my whole life wanting to be the heir of the kingdom, live out the role I was born into and serve the people? Yes. Undoubtedly.

But the reality is, that might not be what the people want, and it's not the only thing I can offer.

I am willing to be whatever the kingdom needs of

me, even if that isn't the heir. Maybe that's what this journey has always been about, I just wasn't ready to truly see it yet.

Now that I'm here, I can see clearer than ever, and I know without a shadow of a doubt it all starts tomorrow.

Pride simmers through my bones as I bask in the revelations transpiring in my mind, interrupted only when a scream bursts in the distance. I still, peering at Kryll, Brody, and Raiden to see if they heard it too, but it's clear the entire hall did as Beau comes storming into the room.

"What's going on?" Kryll asks, rising to his feet as his brother races to get past him. He doesn't stop, but he does offer an answer.

"Vampires. The Council have released frenzied vampires upon the City of Harrows."

Rage boils through my veins as I stare after Beau. I'm on my feet without even realizing as his words wash over me.

Vampires.

Fucking vampires.

Not just normal vampires. No. The damn frenzied kind.

Beau's right, this is The Council's doing, but what twists my stomach the most is the fact that I know my mother is behind this. My father too? I'm not entirely sure, but one thing is for certain, I no longer wish to bask in the superiority that comes with being a Holloway.

It's a label that feels more like a curse than a blessing. I stepped through the doors of this academy on opening day thinking I was the shit simply because I was a vampire with a feared name. Now, it leaves me embarrassed more than anything else.

Everything I thought I ever knew means nothing. The only truth I've ever felt is in the grasps of my brothers and the presence of my Troublemaker.

Adrianna's chair scrapes across the floor as she rises from her seat, pulling me from my thoughts as Brody does the same. Kryll was already standing, but he's waiting for her next move before he makes his own.

She was our central point before The Council conjured their magic and fated us together for all of eternity, but now, it just shines even brighter.

Wherever she goes, we'll follow.

Her gaze darts from Beau's retreating form to the three of us around the table before she takes in the fact that none of the other students seem fazed by what's happening around them. A soft curse under her breath and a tight smile our way, and she's off.

We're a step behind her.

As our feet pound across the floor, I feel the tingles of the fated mates magic at my core. Even with Brody's guidance on how to try to keep it at bay, it still makes its presence known. My steps falter as I take a moment to think, and instead of doubling down on the threads of magic threatening to unleash and connect us all on a deeper level, I succumb to it.

My eyelids flicker as I sway on the spot.

I feel Adrianna first, her determination and strength flooding my thoughts, while Kryll vibrates through me with a darkness I can only relate to a dragon. He's dedicated to his woman, ready to attack or defend at any given moment, and it almost leaves me afraid that I don't love her enough.

Clearing my throat, I force my eyes open as I hurry to catch up, only to find Brody staring at me expectantly. Our connection is vibrant as he gives me a knowing look, confirming that he's letting the magic run through him freely too.

He falls into step with me without a word as we follow Adrianna and Kryll through the doors and down the corridor. If Beau knows we're following him, he doesn't acknowledge it. A knot twists in my stomach, a feral connection that I know only leads to one person.

Cassian.

Before I can think better of it, I tug as hard as I can, silently pleading for him to get his ass here, but there's no knowing if he senses me or not as we reel to a halt by the academy doors.

The screams are louder, the terror even more deafening as I peer through the stained glass the best I can to catch a glimpse of what is happening on the other side.

Even through the stained and mottled glass, blood splatter is visible as the carnage unravels.

"How many are there?" Kryll asks, looking to his brother, who shrugs in response.

"They're not birthday presents wrapped all pristine for me to count, Kryll. What do you want me to say? Thirty-six?"

Kryll shakes his head in irritation as he turns his back on his brother. "Fuck off, asshole. I'm trying to gauge what we're up against and you're being a dick. Next thing you'll want is for me to pat you on the back for counting them all yourself," he snaps back, but there's no time for this.

I can see it in Adrianna's eyes. She wants to get out there and help. She doesn't want to have to deal with this shit.

"Up against? You're up against nothing," Beau bites back, snapping everyone's attention to him.

"We're not doing this again, Tora," Adrianna grinds out, using his last name instead of his first. "You didn't stop us the last time we saw frenzied vampires on official academy time, and you won't stop us now," she adds before reaching for the door.

I sense his shift as he tries to stop her, but no one gets in the way of my woman and what she wants. I cut the distance in a single breath, shouldering him to the side as Adrianna continues, and the door swings open a moment later.

Just as she did that night in the middle of the City of Harrows, she charges at the enemy, ready to lay down her life in the line of duty for her kingdom. And just like last time, I'm right with her. Alongside Brody and Kryll. Aware of the missing puzzle piece, I tug on the connection I feel with Cassian again, hoping for the best before I enter the battle.

I lunge for the closest vampire, their beady eyes wild with need. They're so jacked up on the taste of blood, which drips down from their chin, that they don't even see me coming. His neck snaps like a twig in my hands and his limbs crumple to the ground a second later as a shimmering light dances in the night sky.

The first time I saw it, I was startled, distracted, and almost blinded, but now, I see its purpose and appreciate its glow. With my guard down, I also feel the connection with her magic as it projects into the night sky, coating one civilian after another.

I watch in awe as Adrianna stands center stage, light pouring off her like a fountain as it drapes over the innocent, allowing me to highlight the vampires in the darkness. Scrambling over lifeless bodies that we didn't get a chance to save, I track my next target.

The frenzied vampire is a woman with blood-stained hair and pitch-black eyes. Her back is hunched, her fingers curled at her sides as she desperately seeks her next prey. She reaches her hand into the light, eager to sink her teeth into her next piece of flesh, but instead, a blood-curdling scream parts her lips as she whips her arm back, sans any fingers attached to her hand.

She's too busy staring down at the burnt flesh to see me coming and I make quick work of dispatching her, watching her crumple at my feet. Satisfied, I peer into the darkness, ready to attack again, when a flash of fire burns in the distance. It takes a moment to spot where it's coming from, and I relax when I see it's Kryll decimating more of the frenzied fuckers on the other side of the light.

With the sound of Brody's chants echoing in my ears and my mates holding their own, I fall into a rhythm, slaying one vampire after another until no more remain.

A cocky grin tips the corner of my mouth as I wipe my hands. Adrianna must sense the same accomplishment because a moment later, the bright light dims and the civilians are no longer under her immediate protection.

Murmurs vibrate through the crowd, thanks and relief washing over them. Each one offers a glance of some kind in Adrianna's direction, but she doesn't seem to notice it as she squints at something in the distance.

"What's wrong?" I ask, sidling up to her side a moment later, and her frown only deepens.

"What's that?" She points in the distance, but all I can see is empty academy grounds. I shrug, certain she's seeing things, but then a roar from above makes me still. Kryll's wings swoop through the air as he circles the sky ahead before he heads back in our direction.

I feel it then, his emotions through our connection, and I curse. "You feel it too?" Adrianna asks, squeezing my arm in a mixture of comfort and concern, and I grunt.

"I have my walls down. He's alert, panicked, and—"

"Warning us," she finishes, eyes scanning the sky for Kryll's next move.

"Vampires. More vampires," Brody states, rushing to Adrianna's other side, and I curse. More? Of course there are more. That's all we need right now. "What do we do?" he asks, eyes fixed on Adrianna, but it's a pointless question when we all already know the answer.

Pressing my lips to her temple, I breathe her in for a split second before I face Brody. "We do what we always do: we fight."

Eager to get this over with sooner rather than later, I charge toward the stampede of vampires that rushes toward us. Light shines behind me, and I know Adrianna's magic is taking on a mind of its own again.

My eyes narrow as I charge toward the carnage, my vampire speed unmatched by those stumbling toward us. I take out the first six before they even realize I exist, while Kryll sets them alight from the back of the group.

Excitement buzzes through me, confirming that I'm slightly unhinged with every one of them that hits the ground. Instead of hiding from my delight, I relish in the feeling, taking out four from the next row before I'm stopped in my tracks.

"Really, Son? Do you want it to end like this?" My mother cocks a brow at me, her hair perfectly in place, her outfit as pristine as ever, as she wanders among the frenzied.

"Why are you here? Why are you doing this?" I snarl, fury boiling beneath the surface as I face the woman who has provided me with nothing but pain and anguish. Even that's a stretch. I've never been high on her list of priorities, not even when she was elected to be a professor at the academy. Now, I see that move for what it was; her weaseling her way into the folds of the new times. She thought she would be able to stay one step ahead of the academy if she was among it.

Now, she's the outsider she's always been, and I'm no longer at her side.

"Did you really think The Council would concede so easily? How foolish," she sneers, her eyes narrowing to slits as though she's inconvenienced with having to explain herself to me.

It's in that moment, in that single look, that I don't need an explanation from her. I don't need anything. I have everything I'll ever need already.

I could have nothing and it would still be more than what I need from her.

There isn't a nurturing bone in her body. Not one. She's all about herself. Always.

"You're the foolish one, Mother. For thinking you would still be relevant after all these years. You're no longer good for our kingdom, you're worthless to our people, and you don't deserve the power that's been so freely handed to you. Now, if you don't mind, I have an academy to protect," I state, taking a backward step as I offer her a small salute.

My dismissal does nothing but piss her off more and her hands ball into fists at her sides, but that's no longer my problem. Turning my back on her, I set my sights on the closest frenzied vampire, but before I can take a single step, fingers coil in my hair, wrenching my head back as whispers echo in my ear.

"You always were a worthless offspring. I sent you to the academy in hopes you would prove yourself to me, but I should have known you would fail. Worthless, unloved, and alone. That's what you always have been and what you always will be. Now, say goodbye to this little life you think you've created for yourself because I'm going to burn it all to the ground. Starting with you." Her threat coils around my body as her hands reach for my neck, ready to treat me exactly as I've been treating the frenzied.

My anger sees no limits as I reach for her wrists, but she's one step ahead, moving before I can. My throat clogs with the tightness of her grip, threatening to snap in the next moment, but before the world goes black at the snap of my neck, a growl rumbles through the air and her hold on me is gone.

I fall freely, my back colliding with the ground a moment later as my fingers curl into the strands of grass. It takes a minute for me to catch my breath, panting with every second as I confirm that I'm not fucking dead. At my mother's hands, no less.

Pushing up, I quickly topple back over when four paws and a set of snarling teeth leap over me, tackling my mother to the ground beside me. Twisting my head, I watch, completely enthralled as my mother is chewed up and spit out effortlessly.

Piercing hazel eyes meet mine in the darkness and the connection in my core flares to life.

Cassian.

Not just him, but all of the wolves.

I sit in awe, watching as countless frenzied vampires, along with their foolish leader, fall to the claws of the Kenner wolves and Kryll's flames, until a sense of calmness washes over the campus.

Rising from the ashes of night, with a wolf firmly at my side, I head for the glowing beacon, guiding me home.

I'm alert, I'm prepared, I'm determined. Because although the chaos may be gone, it's only temporary, and it's about time we brought it to an end for good.

"Get everybody inside. I don't think we need to anticipate another attack, but they're safer within those walls than out here," I command, nodding at Beau, who opens the doors without a single word.

It feels strange. I've got the weight of a battle resting on my shoulders, but no physical exhaustion. It's all mental. The protective light that blossoms through me is turning me from an act first, think later kind of girl, to a protective woman, and there's something poetic about it that warms my soul. Or maybe that's the magic.

Standing by the open doors, I wave everyone inside, gaining a whispered thank you from a few of the civilians as they pass. I simply give off a soft smile as my gaze darts through the night air in search of my men.

It's Brody I find first, sauntering toward me with an appreciative grin on his lips. He doesn't speak as he moves to stand beside me, his fingers ghosting along the back of mine, silently offering me his support as he urges everyone inside with me.

A flash of fur tears my gaze from the woman who's walking by, and I sag with relief when I see my vampire at his side, which can only mean one thing; it's Cassian. The tug inside of me confirms it. We were already fated together before any magic happened, so I'd be able to spot him anywhere, but Raiden would only walk so openly with one wolf. Two if you include me.

Cassian dips his head, remaining in his wolf form as he passes, while Raiden offers me a tight smile. He looks exhausted, haggard almost, as the corners of his eyes droop.

"Are you okay?" The concern is clear in my voice as I reach out a hand, and he sways just out of reach. His eyes glaze over as he tries to nod, but I see right through him. I can sense the bullshit about to spew from his lips, but so must Brody because in the next breath he's sidled up beside him.

"Don't worry, Dagger. I'll get him checked over. You wait for our dragon, yeah?" He winks before turning his eyes to Beau on the other side of the doors. "You keep an eye on her." He doesn't wait for a response, guiding Raiden inside as Beau simply shakes his head at him.

As the tail end of civilians gives way to a trail of wolves, it's clear Cassian didn't come alone. I'm not sure if this is his entire pack, but it seems like they go on for days, until a lone man brings up the back of the line.

Kryll.

Gone are his wings and dragon features, and in his place walks an exhausted man, whose face lights up when his gaze latches onto mine.

"Hey, Princess," he breathes, pulling me into his side and pressing a kiss to the side of my temple. I lean into him, stealing some of his strength as I sigh.

"Hey." I should offer him more, but that's all I've apparently got, not that he seems to mind as he quietly guides me inside, letting Beau lock the door after us.

My calmness doesn't last long as we follow everyone into the dining hall to find the other students growing agitated with the growing numbers now taking refuge in here.

"This is not our responsibility. These people need to return home, there's no space for them here!" a girl shouts, exasperation lacing her tone, and I'm not at all surprised to find that she's a vampire with a red cloak draped around her shoulders. She's wagging her fingers at everyone as she stands on the dining table, growing more frustrated as she goes unheard. But I heard her, and she's about to know it.

"Do we have a problem here?" I ask, slipping from beside Kryll as I step toward her. It takes her a split second to find me among the crowd, and her gaze only tightens as she takes me in.

"This is all your fault. Everyone needs to leave. You included," she bites, and I scoff, shaking my head at her in disbelief.

"Who are you?"

"Josie," she snaps, her eyes twitching with rage at the fact that I have no clue who she is, which only pleases me more.

"Why are you here, Josie?" I ask calmly, remembering my father's words instead of leading with the rage I want to.

"What?"

Great. This is going to take longer than anticipated. "Why. Are. You. Here. Josie?"

"You're not making sense," she retorts, waving her hands around as she garners a crowd, a trick it seems vampires are all too good at.

"Why are you at the academy, Josie?" I repeat, offering more specifics this time, and she huffs.

"To become the heir."

"And what is the role of the heir once appointed?" I ask, folding my arms over my chest as I take her in with a cock of my brow.

She falters, shrugging her shoulders as her sneer deepens. "It's the heir's job to rule the kingdom," she splutters, the exact answer I was expecting to pass her lips.

"And you don't think ruling the kingdom includes taking care of its people?"

"Yes, but—"

"Don't you think it is imperative to protect our kingdom? To stand against any threats and offer a calm and safe environment at every opportunity? That's what our people have been without for long enough. And now, after another attack from frenzied vampires, which are controlled by The Council, you want to send them out into the darkness where it isn't safe? Correct me if I'm wrong, but that's not what leadership looks like," I finish, giving her a pointed look before I turn away.

I can already tell she has no dignified answer for me, so I'm not waiting for one. I expect to walk into Kryll or one of my other Kryptos, but instead, I find a camera in my face instead.

"Could you repeat your thoughts for the public, Princess Adrianna?" The cameraman asks, and I stare at him with wide eyes. My surprise is clear, it clings to me from head to toe as I attempt to swallow past the lump forming in my throat.

"Thank you for the offer, but the importance of that conversation was heard by the person intended.

It doesn't need to be repeated for entertainment purposes," I decline politely while internally glaring at the asshole. I hadn't considered he would still be here after Bozzelli addressed the kingdom, and now I feel foolish for forgetting.

"Are you sure? Not even if it earns you more votes?" he pushes, making my eyebrows crinkle.

"This isn't a game. This is real life. We should be alert. I'm not about to throw some campaign out to the kingdom, luring citizens to believe in me when there are dangers and threats attempting to cause harm to them. That's my priority. Now, if you'll excuse me." I walk off before he can yell anything else at me, and I somehow manage to keep the tight smile intact as I find Kryll among the crowd.

"Have I mentioned how hot you are when you're all authoritative?" he asks, slinking an arm around my shoulder as I roll my eyes at him.

"Actually, I don't think you have," I retort, leaning into him as he points to where Brody is waving us over.

"Well, add it to the list," he breathes as we reach my mage.

"He's asking for you," he states, pointing over his shoulder, and my spine stiffens.

"Is Raiden okay?"

Brody bites back a smile as he points down the hallway. "We have everyone who needs treatment set up in Beau's office. Raiden, however, is in his mother's office. Go find out for yourself, or do you need me to show you?" he asks as a sensation tingles in my gut, and it makes a real smile touch the corner of my mouth.

"No need. I can sense him tugging at our connection."

The door to Holloway's office is open, revealing my vampire on the other side of the threshold. I pause where I am, leaning against the door frame as I take him in.

His fingers trail over the wooden desk planted in the center of the room with a wide window centered behind it. He rolls his lips in, exhaling heavily as a blank stare consumes his eyes.

I've never seen a contemplative look on his face before, and it's not one I'm all too happy he's wearing. A part of me wants to charge inside, demand to know what's wrong, and make it all better with a snap of my fingers, but the other part of me knows that's not what he needs.

He might need me, but it's clear from the expression on his face that he's processing more than I can imagine, and the least I can do is offer him the space to do so. With his focus set on the desk, I peer around the rest of the room, noting how bare it actually is. Besides the gray desk chair in front of the window, there's a brown leather sofa to the right and a gray cabinet set up in the far corner of the room. That's it.

Not a single photo, or ornament, or feminine touch graces the rest of the space, almost as if a woman has never stepped inside these walls before. It's strange. Every time I saw Holloway, she was dressed chic and elegant, and for some reason, I would expect that to translate into her surroundings too, but that's clearly not the case here.

"Do you ever wish you weren't a fae?" My gaze darts to him as his words pull me from my thoughts. My eyebrows gather as I step into the room, a soft smile trying to form on my lips as I tilt my head at him.

"No, never," I admit, approaching the desk with caution. He nods, dropping his stare back to the table as another sigh passes his lips. Intrigued with where that question came from, I slip around the desk, gently pushing for more. "Why?"

He taps his fingertips on the desk.

Once.

Twice.

Three times.

Before lifting his eyes to mine. "Because some-times I wish I wasn't a vampire." His Adam's apple bobs as he attempts to swallow down the emotion I know those words summoned. The sad smile curling the corner of his mouth looks far too pained, and before I can think better of it, I eliminate the remaining distance between us.

My arms tighten around his waist as I plant my face against his chest, breathing him in as he envelops me in his arms, rocking us from side to side.

Brody rocks his emotions and understands his feelings in a way only a mage can. Kryll grumbles that they exist sometimes, but he always seems unfazed for the most part. Cassian knows how to snarl and growl, but accepting the elements of his life that have caused him the most pain has been a real journey for him so far. It's a lesson he's learning with every step he takes.

Raiden, however, may be able to express his feelings and emotions when they come to me, even better than I do, but when it's about himself... this is the most I've ever heard, and it doesn't fully make sense.

I rub my lips together nervously, wanting to ask what's going on in his head without doing it at the worst possible time, but after an eternity passes, I realize there's never going to be one, and if I want to help, I'm going to need to guide him.

"What makes you say that, Raiden?" I ask, tilting my face so my chin rests against his chest as I strain to look up at him. His eyes find mine instantly, a ghost of a grin touching his full lips as he takes in our height difference before my question seems to register in his mind and he sighs. "You don't have to," I ramble, backtracking quicker than I thought possible, but he quickly tightens his hold on me.

"I'm okay, I'm just processing," he offers, a reassuring glint in his eyes as he takes a deep breath, and this time, the weight of the world doesn't echo in his exhale. "Cassian killed my mother." My eyes widen and my jaw falls slack as surprise floods my veins. I try to formulate words, but my brain fails me. "It's okay, I'm not looking for sympathy or anything. Not that I think it's necessary either, I'm just sorry because I know you've felt the same things I'm feeling today."

"Yeah," I breathe lamely, his words swirling in my mind. A part of me feels guilty for not hiding away to mourn my mother's death, but it lingers with me, and I'm sure it will be the same for him. "I'm sorry, Raiden."

"Don't apologize. She deserved it. I'm more annoyed that Cassian basically saved my life so now I'm screwed having to live with him holding that over my head forever," he says with a sigh and a dramatic eye roll, but my narrowed gaze must make it clear that further details are needed. "She was a breath away from snapping my neck. He saved me at the last minute." His words grow quieter, that truth behind them thickening the air as anger coils in my gut.

"I'm not sorry she's dead," I blurt, cringing at the bluntness before I quickly add, "I'm sorry she's left you feeling like this." He nods, lifting his hand to cup my cheek and stroke a thumb over my skin. "And just to clarify," I continue, looking up into his deep eyes. "I would love nothing more than to bring her back from the dead and kill her myself for even thinking about laying a hand on you."

It takes everything in me to bite back the raw snarl that threatens to take over me. I want him to know those words, but he doesn't need me redirecting my anger toward her at him instead.

"I can't decide if I like it more when you're jealous or protective. Both are pretty sexy," he muses, and it's my turn to roll my eyes at him, but when I settle my stare back on his face, a tightness grows across his features.

"I'm starting to hate everything about myself."

His words are a swift kick to the chest, stealing my breath as I shift my hands to grip his shoulders. I rise as high as I can go on my tiptoes, until we're almost eye to eye. "How can you hate the man that I love?" I rasp, the truth weaving its way through each word as I struggle to breathe.

"You love me?" His pupils are wide, his hands back at my waist as he pins me against him.

"Don't make me regret saying it," I grumble as he lifts me off my feet, spinning us around so much that a small giggle slips from my lips.

"But you did say it," he whispers, bringing us to a halt as he presses his lips softly against mine, and I hum.

"Yeah, because I feel it," I admit, a giddiness creeping over my skin, leaving goosebumps in their wake.

"What do you feel?" he pushes, lifting me once again, but this time, he places me on the desk, slipping between my thighs as he cups my face, giving me all of his attention as I struggle to find the words.

I consider rolling over the desk and hightailing it toward the door, but decide against it when I see the earnest look in his eyes. When was this man ever told he was loved? His mother could have said it moments before she tried to kill him, but realistically, after everything he's mentioned about being a vampire, it doesn't feel all that likely.

He didn't grow up in the environment I did. He had luxury, opulence, and materialistic things. But that's just what they were; *things*. I had my father, my sister, and our love. Those are the polar opposites of the same stick. Attempting to guess each other's lives is impossible, but I can see what he needs from me. I can feel it in my soul as our connection pulses with every heartbeat that rattles in my chest.

"I hated you from the beginning," I admit, and his cheeks hollow out as he exhales. "The words you would say, the beliefs you had, they were everything I stood against." I run my hands over his chest, hoping to show him that the connection between us now is different, but it's unfair to either of us to forget where it all began. "But before that," I start, and he frowns.

"There was no before that. I saw you that day in the forest and acted like a total ass," he grumbles, hating himself for it, and that alone alleviates the anger I remember swimming in at the time.

"There was. Maybe five seconds, but those five seconds. Damn, all I could think about was how someone shouldn't be that hot."

He rolls his eyes, his fingers flexing against my sides. "I have more than looks, you know."

"You do?" I tease, tilting my face as I widen my eyes, and a soft smile passes between us, lightening the mood. "I love that you own your faults. I love that you are so unapologetically you, with zero fucks to give about what anyone else says or thinks. I love that you understand what being a vampire is in our society. I love that you see me, not as a lowly fae, not even as Princess Adrianna Reagan. Me. Just me."

His mouth is on mine the second I take a breath,

melding our lips together as my fingers run through his hair, tugging him closer.

"I will love you for all of eternity," he croaks, his lips dragging across mine as he cups my breasts through the thin material of my t-shirt.

There's half a damn kingdom a few steps away, but I can't tear myself away long enough to remind him. His teeth rake over my throat, making my head fall back as I groan, when the sound of someone clearing their throat cuts through the heated room.

Snapping my gaze to the door, I find Flora, an amused smirk on her lips.

"Fuck off, Flora," Raiden grunts with no real snarl to his words, but I still whack his arm for good measure while Flora simply chuckles.

"It seems like you want me to leave so *you* can do the fucking, Raiden," she sings as my vampire's head drops in defeat.

"What do you want, Flora? We were in the middle of something," he retorts, his fingers digging into my flesh so hard I know there are bruises forming already.

"Yeah, that something is going to have to wait because Bozzelli's ready to make the announcement."

R aiden pulls me from the desk, carrying me toward the door as I try to straighten my clothes while Flora laughs at the state of us. My heart feels like it's about to burst out of my chest. It's beating so hard that when Raiden places my feet back on the floor, I sway, struggling to stand.

"Adrianna?" His eyes narrow on mine as I shake my head, and Flora laughs even louder.

"He thinks you're dickmatized by his weiner," she snickers, and I hide my face in his neck, holding back my own amusement, and it surprisingly helps to ground me.

"If she was dickmatized, she wouldn't be standing, Flora," he muses, and I lift my head just in time to see him wink at her. "I think our girl here is suddenly worried over what happens when we step in there," he explains, confirming my internal struggles in one sentence, and I groan.

Pushing off him, I stand tall, running my hands over my clothes, blindly pulling at an invisible thread until Flora grasps my hand. "You can stand here and fret all you like, or you can march your ass in there and be who you should have been this entire time." She cocks her hip, giving me a pointed stare.

"But what if that's not what comes next?" I murmur, internally beating myself up over the fact that I had come to an understanding in my head that being the heir didn't matter anymore.

Clearly, that was a lie.

It matters. I may have realized I don't need it, but I still want it.

"Are you guys coming or what?" Brody hollers from the end of the hallway, his eyebrows bunched together in confusion as he assesses us, and Raiden groans, linking his fingers with mine before he tugs me along.

"I could have been coming. I could have been having a great time, but you fuckers are intent on spoiling my fun," he grumbles, earning another burst of laughter from Flora.

The calmness they create lifts the weight off my shoulders just enough for me to reenter the dining hall. Bozzelli is up on the podium, smile in place and a camera set in front of her. A small gathering of students are at the front, with the survivors from outside filling the rest of the space around them, but it's the two men to the right of the podium, speaking with Beau, that have my attention.

My hand slips from Raiden's, and he doesn't try to stop me as I hurry through the sea of people. Cassian spots me first, his brows furrowing as he takes me in, but the tension shakes from his limbs as I reach his side. His arm is around my shoulders a moment after, tugging me into his side as he breathes me in.

"Alpha," he murmurs, nuzzling his nose at my neck, and I bite back a sigh, acutely aware that my soul really does feel much more content now that we're all together again.

"I heard I owe you a thank you for saving my vampire's life," I muse, grinning up at him as he looks over my shoulder.

"I didn't do anything," he retorts, waving me off, but I see the smirk on his lips as Raiden, Flora, and Brody join us. He's not going to let Raiden live it down. That's clear.

"Are we all okay?" I ask, needing to verbally check in even though I can already feel it in my gut.

"We're ready for the future to begin," Arlo states, sauntering toward us with an extra pep in his step. I look at Flora, wondering what's going on with him, but the look on her face is as surprised as mine.

I turn back to Arlo, intrigued enough to ask, but the sound of the tapping on the microphone cuts through the air, drawing everyone's attention to Bozzelli on the stage.

"That's my cue," Beau states, and Kryll catches his arm before he can leave.

"Do you know?"

Beau stares deep into his brother's eyes, not a single word passing between them before Kryll relents, releasing his arm, and he's gone.

What was that?

"Thank you so much to everyone who has kindly shown their patience as we make our way through these new and challenging times. I'm sure we can all agree that we're determined to create a better future for not just ourselves, but the generations to follow. That doesn't come with strength, we have to find that deep within ourselves, and it should be noted that it shines in each and every one of you right now. To our citizens who trusted in this unknowing process with us, and our students, willing to put their lives on the line to save our kingdom." Her eyes travel across the entire room, connecting with every single person. It's slightly amusing that her outfit has changed and she's now dressed in white. Some might consider it the tamest color she's ever worn, but the way it shines so bright leaves me questioning the fact. "In a few moments we are going to go live before the entire kingdom, courtesy of the media camera here, but I felt it was only right to take a moment and introduce the new heir to all of us here first."

Murmured agreements zip through the air as Cassian pulls me tighter against his side.

"Ready?" he asks, but I can't fathom a response, my sights set on Bozzelli as her bright red lips spread into a smile.

"It is with great honor and privilege that I announce the new heir of the Floodborn Kingdom, Miss Adrianna Reagan."

Cheers erupt from the civilians, the noise dulled by the thunder of my pulse ringing in my ears as hands pat at me from all angles. But I can't look away from Bozzelli, my body going into complete shock, leaving me frozen in place.

"Comments made from voters noted her heroic actions, her determination, her love for the kingdom, and her resilience to leave no one behind." Bozzelli finds me among the crowd, grinning from ear to ear as she waves me closer. "Please, give a round of applause for our new heir."

Lips press at my temple before I'm nudged forward, but I don't make it two steps before a roar of rage echoes from the other side of the ballroom.

"If you think The Council will be replaced by some adolescent embarrassment, then you're rudely mistaken."

Snapping my gaze toward the source, I blink as I take in Brody's father surrounded by two dozen soldiers. Before I can even compose a response, I'm swarmed. Layer after layer of citizens and students place themselves between Orenda and me, the barrier growing with every beat that passes until I don't have a clear view of the man in question.

Wolves.

Vampires.

Shifters.

Mages.

Fae.

Humans.

I don't recognize ninety percent of the people around me, but it can't be denied where their loyalty lies, and it makes my heart sore.

"May I?"

Brody appears on my right, reaching for my hand as he smiles softly. I try to return one of my own, but I'm so overwhelmed, I have no idea what face I'm pulling. He must take it as confirmation, though, because he's moving in the next moment.

"Father!" Brody hollers from the podium, leaving Bozzelli blinking at him in a picture of surprise and confusion. "Let me be the wise one to advise you that you are truly outnumbered. Not only within these walls, but throughout the entire kingdom. These are the consequences of playing God. It looks like your fate has now been decided."

Orenda's face appears among the crowd, but his attempts to step closer to his son fail with every try, making his cheeks burn red with anger. "Son, I—"

"The new leader of our kingdom requests the removal of this man. Lock that fucker in the dungeons. I'll deal with him later," Brody snarls, rage vibrating from him like I've never seen before. Clearing his throat, he waves a dismissive hand in his father's direction as mages restrain him and the soldiers, chanting their magic quietly as the rest of us look on in surprise. "Sorry about that, gang. Let's get back to the beauty that is our new heir, shall we?"

Bozzelli nudges him aside as he continues to wag his eyebrows at me, but when she clears her throat, she draws my attention to her. The look in her eyes startles me as pride fills the space between us. "It gives me great pleasure to say it, Adrianna. Bring the family home, it's time."

My fingers tingle, all the way to the tips. My heart is pumping blood so intensely through my body I can literally feel my veins thrumming, and for the first time ever, it has nothing to do with my magic.

Beau took over reaching out to the dragon kingdom while I was whisked off into Bozzelli's office. I haven't moved an inch since I came in here, but the same can't be said for the rest of the people here. I've never been dressed and preened before, but these women are professionals it seems.

Gone are the gray academy-issued clothes and cloak. In their place is a fitted gray combat outfit that hugs my body. There are discreet pockets every-where, fitted with daggers, and a pair of knee-high boots laced to the top, screaming bad bitch vibes.

My hair has been twisted and tugged in every

direction, weaved with braids in a half up, half down style, while my makeup is minimal, save for a dark brown lip and even darker streaks covering my cheeks and forehead. I don't know what I expected them to do when I came in here, but this wasn't it.

I would have guessed a ballgown dress over this, but as I stare at the length of myself in the mirror, I can't help but feel a sense of my father in my reflection. I recall a similar outfit from my younger years, only, he was always dressed in black with the odd touch of gold or silver here and there, but this feels more like me.

"Just open the door and let me see her, then I'll back off." The snap comes from the other side of the door and I know it's Raiden. I'm not sure who he's getting irate with, but a few moments later, the door opens and Bozzelli appears in the door frame.

"I feel like you need a crown for dealing with this man, never mind the damn kingdom," she grumbles, shaking her head as she steps inside. "Feast your eyes, then take your seat," she snaps, the humor gone when she turns back to Raiden, but he doesn't seem to notice. His gaze is set on me, raking up and down the length of me three times for good measure before he finally locks eyes with me.

"Fuck me sideways, Troublemaker. That's sinful. Wait until the others get a glimpse of this. Brody is going to stain his fucking pants again." Bozzelli grumbles under her breath, rambling about foolish vampires, but she doesn't immediately kick him out of the room. "Are you okay?" he asks, his voice taking a more serious tone, and I nod.

"Everything feels a little surreal, but I'm okay," I admit, and he eliminates the distance between us a moment later.

With my face nestled between his hands, he looks deep into my eyes as he speaks. "This is all a show, Adrianna, but you know that. I know this may not be your favorite part, but it's necessary for the grandeur of the moment. You've got this, you've got all of it. I know that. And you will too once it's all said and done. Alright?"

I nod, taking comfort from his words as he presses the smallest kiss to my lips before Bozzelli sighs heavily, reminding us of her presence.

"That's enough. Get out. We're already running behind," she snaps, and to my surprise, Raiden stomps out of the room without argument. "And you," she adds, whirling her attention to me. A softness exudes from her, lodging my next breath in my throat as I blink at her. "Thank you for not discarding me because of my terrible mistakes. Learning from you has given me a new perspective, and I can't wait for the academy to learn from you too."

I shake my head, a scoff bursting past my lips. "Learning? From me? I don't think so."

She gives me a knowing look before sauntering toward the door. "Come, it's time."

Muttering my thanks to the women packing away their belongings after working their magic on me, I rush to catch up to her. The second we reach the end of the hallway, she lifts her finger, silently ordering me to wait.

I watch from the limited view that I've got as the energy fills the ballroom, but I can't shake a strange sensation that weighs heavy on my chest.

There hasn't been a moment to think, to feel, to do anything other than prepare, but I can't be completely sure what I would have been preparing for anyway. I know my name is going to be called, and there's no going back from that. My life is about to change forever, and there's a part of it that doesn't feel right.

Maybe it's anti-climatic after everything I've been through.

Maybe Raiden was right, and it's this whole show that I don't care for.

Maybe it's the disbelief that I'm truly here.

I don't know, and there's no time to consider anything further before Bozzelli's voice raises.

"I give you, the new heir to the Floordborn Kingdom, Queen Adrianna Reagan."

Inhale.

Exhale.

Inhale.

Exhale.

Inhale.

Exhale.

Despite my lungs struggling to work under the pressure of the bright light now aimed my way, I get the overwhelming sense of awareness that a camera is aimed in my direction. Pushing it all back, I step into the ballroom and head for the podium where Bozzelli stands, a shimmering gold crown on a velvet cushion beside her.

It doesn't seem real. It doesn't feel real at all.

Panicked, I search for my mates among the madness, letting my heart guide me to where they are, and my breathing eases a fraction at the sight of them. I'm not the only one that's changed. Each of them are now dressed in similar attire except for Flora and Arlo, who are dressed to impress in ballroom attire. Where did someone even find a tuxedo and floor-length gown?

Raiden smiles at me, pride burning in his eyes, while Brody winks, wagging his eyebrows suggestively. Kryll rakes his teeth over his bottom lip as he takes me in, while Cassian's top lip curls, but it's not laced with anger, it's desire.

Clearing my throat, I do little to nudge the

swelling in my throat. I take to the steps leading up to the podium one at a time, trying to give myself a moment to gather myself, but it's futile. Especially when I see a familiar heart-shaped face and big eyes looking at me.

Nora.

She's sitting with my father on the other side of the podium, hand in hand as they beam at me with unshed tears in their eyes.

Delirious, I'm drawn away from them as Bozzelli grabs my arm and turns me toward the camera. Nothing is audible over my internal thoughts, the moment passing in a blur as the floor vibrates with stomping and hands clap wildly, but not a single other sound registers.

I feel like I'm suffocating until the weight of the crown settles on my head. The room spins at the victory I can smell in the air, but my stare is unfocused, the ability to digest any of this lost upon me until Bozzelli places her hand on my arm, a hint of concern in her eyes as she speaks.

"Queen Adrianna Reagan, please, a few words for your people," she encourages, jutting her chin as discreetly as possible for me to face the camera and be the wondrous leader they wish me to be.

I nod, then nod again, struggling to be present and alert until a warmth floods my veins. My gaze tugs to the table that holds my Kryptos to find a knowing look on each of my men. It's them. I don't know what they're doing, but whatever it is, it's working.

Clearing my throat, I stand tall, plastering a smile on my face. "Thank you so—"

The clink of metal rings in my ears, vibrating through the air as I spin to my left, my crown toppling to the floor as I watch in horror as Bozzelli's white suit turns red. Her eyes are wide with shock and disbelief as the garbled sound of steel running through flesh ricochets in my ears.

Her lifeless body slowly crumples to the floor, revealing her attacker in the next breath, and I freeze as my father yells at the top of his lungs.

"Clementine!"

"You," I breathe, staring at the woman in front of me before my gaze darts to Bozzelli once again. She just killed her. No care, no concern, no guilt. Just... dead.

The mysterious woman from the cell is as crazy as I recall.

"Me," she sings with a flourish, earning my attention again as I shake my head in disbelief.

"What is this?"

"Don't you want to know who I am first?" she retorts, planting her hands on her hips as she assesses me, and I shake my head.

"Introductions usually come *before* someone dies, not after. I'd rather understand what your plan entails, the smaller details make no difference," I retort, irritation coiling through my bones as I glare at her.

Gone is the delirious state I've been in, and in its place is the alertness I've been desperately searching for.

"I'm Clementine," she offers, ignoring me, and I sigh.

"I'm aware. My father said as much," I grumble, refusing to look his way in case it draws her attention toward him, but all it does is goad her.

"How would he know me? Don't you want to know?" she pushes, shaking out of her jet-black cloak and letting it pool at her feet to reveal a shimmering deep purple dress beneath.

"I'll find out once you've been dealt with."

She takes slow, measured steps around me, like I'm the prey and she's the predator. "Don't be sad about my presence, it's because of you I'm here, after all," she states, lacing her fingers together in front of her as if she's all sweet and innocent, when we both know she's not.

Not with a comment like that, not after the last time I saw her.

My brain whirls to life, raking through all of the things she said, until it settles on a thought, and my gut twists unbearably tight. "What does that mean?"

My pulse quickens, my mind already knowing the answer but refusing to acknowledge it.

"Addi! Addi!" My father's voice carries through the haze that twists Clementine and me together, and my gaze darts to his. "Addi, where is the amethyst? Your amethyst?" he clarifies, and I gulp.

"Gone. Shattered."

Clementine starts to clap, loud, thunderous claps that vibrate around the entire room before she leans in, hand covering her mouth as she whispers loudly. "Hint. Hint. You broke my prison."

Everything stops as she confirms my fear, and my hands ball into fists at my sides as I force my instinctive reaction to stay at bay. The entire kingdom is watching now and I can't react how they're used to The Council acting, even if I really want to.

"Who are you?" I ask, finally relenting as she bounces on the spot, tossing her blonde hair over her shoulder as she giggles.

"I am Princess Clementine Reagan, sister to the previous King, your father, August Reagan." She inches closer until we're chest to chest before she delivers her final blow. "And now that the crown is back on the table, in the grasps of a fae no less, it's mine for the taking."

AFTERWORD

Well, I don't know whose idea it was to end there,
but they need firing. ASAP.
I'm in love with these characters so much, and I'm
beyond excited for their story to overflow into a fifth
book! Man, it's a ride. I can't wait for you to embark
on this final journey with them, monster dicks
and all.
Truly, though, I am forever grateful that you are
here, devouring these words as desperately as I write
them. You complete me, you make me feel worthy,
and whenever the imposter syndrome gets too much,
I think of the kindness you have always shown me.
Thank you, from the bottom of my heart. Writing
this book was another rollercoaster for me, and I
wouldn't have it any other way if it produces such
magic.
Much love!

ACKNOWLEDGMENTS

Michael. At this stage, need I say more? It's hilarious how much I praise you in these damn books because I don't say it nearly enough to your face. You're a beautiful human being, inside and out, I'm going to love you until the day I die, and even then, you'll forever have my heart. - I should save that for a book, it sounds sick, but you deserve it!

My loves, my children, my heart. You've taught me what pride is, you fill me with it every day. One day, I hope to be as wonderful and magical as you are. I love you.

Nicole and Jeni, my gals. I fucking love you, like ALOT. ALOT. ALOT. I hope you never tire of me because you're stuck with me for lifies. Yes I made a word up. You're worth it.

Kirsty, my man, my fam. We love each other, even if we don't show it haha thank you for always being my rock, my sounding board, and my biggest protector.

You're a vibe, like autumnal vibe level. That's how superior you are!

My beta readers, I don't think anyone love/hates me as much as you guys, it means a lot, and I'm forever grateful for you being on this journey with me!

Lily and Sarah, the gals with the goods, making me look pretty with your hard work. Thank you! You make me look awesome!

ABOUT THE AUTHOR

KC Kean began her writing journey in 2020 amidst the pandemic and homeschooling... yay! After reading all of the steam, from fade to black, to steamy reads, MM, and reverse harem, she decided to immerse herself in her own worlds too.

When KC isn't hiding away in the writing cave, she is playing Dreamlight Valley, enjoying the limited UK sunshine with her husband, children, and furbabies, or collecting vinyls like it's a competition.

Come and join me over at my <u>Aceholes Reader Group</u>, follow my author's Facebook page, and enjoy Instagram with me on the links below.

ALSO BY KC KEAN

FEATHERSTONE ACADEMY

My Bloodline

Your Bloodline

Our Bloodline

Red

Freedom

Redemption

ALLSTARS SERIES

Toxic Creek

Tainted Creek

Twisted Creek

BETHANY & RYAN'S STORY

Burn to Ash

EMERSON U SERIES

Watch Me Fall

Watch Me Rise

Watch Me Reign

SAINTS ACADEMY

Reckless Souls

Damaged Souls

Vicious Souls

Fearless Souls

Heartless Souls

RUTHLESS BROTHERS MC

Ruthless Rage

Ruthless Rebel

Ruthless Riot

SILVERCREST ACADEMY

Falling Shadows

Destined Shadows

Cursed Shadows

Unchained Shadows

HEIR ACADEMY

Kingdom of Ruin

Reign of Blood

Hunt of Night

Fate of Eternity

Court of Truth - coming December 2024